ADVANCE PRAISE

Broken Eagle WITHDRAWN

A good man is hard to find, but the unputdownable – and deeply moral – *Broken Eagle* gives you two for the price of one: Jake, the finely drawn ex-Army lawyer and everyday hero; and Crouse, his creator, who clearly knows the world and ways of the law, the military and the South inside out – and who writes as assuredly and convincingly about women (hallelujah!) as about combat, aviation and courtrooms. In this tale's troubling and all-too-believable tangle of Washington politics, murderously venal business interests and scorched-earth tours of duty, you'll want both of these guys on your side.

Karen Shook
Books Editor, Times Higher Education, London

Broken Eagle is impressive on many levels. James Crouse brings you inside the mind of a trial attorney as he investigates and litigates a complex aviation case. Crouse's personal experience as a pilot and as an aviation law litigator combine to provide a vivid picture of the technical and legal issues involved as the hero of the story, Jake Baird battles to solve the mystery behind the crash of an experimental aircraft while also working against forces of the military-industrial complex who will do anything to stop him. This is a great book for anyone interested in a terrific thriller.

Lt. Colonel John "Jack" Veth (USAF, Ret.)
Vietnam veteran fighter pilot, SR-71(Blackbird)
Aircraft Commander, and aviation litigation attorney

Broken Eagle gets to the core of real issues in this fast-paced fictional setting. It is a believable story, well written and an easy read. In my aviation professional work, I spend most of my time reading technical manuals and reports and rarely have time to read for pleasure. But James Crouse did such an outstanding job bringing this story to the reader with his unique style and classic military flare that I postponed some appointments in order to read this book cover to cover. You will too…

Ben R. Coleman
NTSB/FAA accident investigation expert, Commercial pilot,
mechanic, parachute rigger, aviation safety industry advocate

James Crouse's gripping drama resonates with realistic details from his deep knowledge about the law, aviation and the military. It's a page turner in the mode of Scott Turow and John Grisham.

Sara Just
Executive Producer, PBS NewsHour and Senior Vice President WETA,
formerly ABC News Nightline producer for 17 years

Fighting the system is not for the faint-hearted. They will find it extremely difficult to recruit powerful support. Those who enjoy government largesse will not wish to lose it. Those in military service will be torn between the demands of justice and their oath of loyalty. Those who fight the system must be prepared to fight alone.

James Crouse has written a gripping book about such a hero. Crouse reminds us that below the smooth surface of supposedly exemplary societies there lurks another world; from its murky and evil depths few return victorious and none return undamaged. Read about this world in *Broken Eagle*. It may inspire you to assist those who find themselves in it.

Omar Malik
Accident Prevention Consultant, formerly Pilot RAF
and Captain, British Airways

In a riveting exposé using well-developed characters and a thrilling plot, Crouse draws from a thorough knowledge of both the law and aviation to expose the tempting flaws that can corrode character and morals when government and contractors have too much money and too little principles when developing new weapons systems. It's a great read.

William S Lawrence, Colonel USMC (Ret'd)
Aviator and Engineering Test Pilot;
Aircraft Accident Investigative Consultant

I could not put *Broken Eagle* down. I had to find out what was being covered up and why, who knew about the defects in the XV11 aircraft, and how Jake would live through all of the challenges he encountered. A great military-legal thriller!

Gary Little
former USMC Helicopter crew chief on MARINE ONE

It has been said that "billions of dollars, political clout, and outright lying cannot overcome the laws of aerodynamics." Author James T. Crouse proves that adage in his intriguing novel of deception and murder about a totally flawed aircraft, the XV-11 tilt rotor, that is pushed into production by a group of corrupt government, military and civilian contractors bent on serving their own narrow interests and financial gain at any cost.

This story unfortunately tells what too often happens in government-industry relationships, and Crouse's expertise in aircraft knowledge and the legal process provides a great authenticity to the dramatic, compelling tale. Crouse's hero, attorney Jake Baird, undertakes a harrowing journey to stop this evil intent and defend the nation's warriors from dying in a defective machine deployed way before it was ready. It's a great read!!

Tom McHale
Major Airline Captain (Retired) and
US Army Helicopter Pilot (Retired)

The military industrial complex is a force threatening our troops in this fast-paced, well-informed, and gripping thriller. Lawyer and U.S. Army reservist Jake Baird takes on those who pull out every stop to insure their pet aircraft continues in production, covering up the deaths of two Marines in flight-tests and worse. This is not atypical in the sordid world of competing for defense contracts.

Former helicopter pilot, James T. Crouse, writes about a world he knows well, and takes us on a tense read that will leave any citizen wondering about the intersection between military security and the lure of billions in taxpayer money. Crouse's thriller shows his blow-torch conscience when it comes to the national interest of the United States.

William E. Jackson, Jr.
Huffington Post contributor, former government and politics professor at
Davidson College, and former foreign and defense policy scholar
at the Brookings Institution

When Neil Armstrong famously broadcast from the moon, "The Eagle has landed," James Crouse makes us glad the "eagle" he was piloting was not the XV-11 "Sea Eagle" in this masterful work. Crouse takes the technical intricacies involved in the world of rotorcraft and fixed wing aerodynamics and simplifies them to give us a compelling story about what can go wrong in the world of military procurement of weapons systems. The reader leaves this entertaining journey through aircraft design and government conspiracy when they suddenly realize they also received an education in aerodynamics, piloting, aircraft systems and American law. Crouse uses his considerable military, aviation and legal experience to give us a compelling story that only he could write. His writing style and knowledge make this a delightful read for both the enthusiast and a newcomer to aviation, law and the military. The tale is so authentic that you will ask, "Was there a real Sea Eagle? "

Colin A. Sommer
*is a Professional Mechanical Engineer, Pilot and a
Rotorcraft & Fixed Wing Accident Investigator*

Broken Eagle leads the reader into a gathering vortex where a cutting-edge military aircraft with serious flaws, malevolent contractors and complicit government program administrators with deadly self-protective agendas, and the widow of a military test pilot seeking answers swirl around a military-reservist aviation plaintiffs' lawyer who comes to realize he is at its center. Pursued by those with a deadly agenda, aided by shadowy allies and protected by his own wits and experience, Jake Baird finds the case he wasn't sure he wanted leading him to answers for questions he he'd been afraid to ask.

Jim Crouse has the military aviation background and the aviation trial lawyer's experience to spin this story with gusto and credibility, which makes it very enjoyable - and just a little frightening - for the reader. Climb aboard, strap in and get ready for a memorable ride.

Gary W. Allen
*Editor, Lawyer-Pilots Bar Association Journal,
Former Director, Aviation & Admiralty Litigation, Torts Branch,
Civil Division, United States Dept of Justice*

Broken Eagle

This is a work of fiction. Names, characters, places and
incidents either are products of the author's imagination or are
used fictitiously. Any resemblance to actual events or
locales or persons, living or dead, is entirely coincidental.

CAROMOUNT ISLAND PUBLISHING

P.O. Box 33460, Raleigh, N.C. 27636

BROKEN EAGLE
Copyright © 2016

JAMES T. CROUSE

www.jamestcrouseauthor.com

ISBN 978-0-9974712-0-5

Printed in the United States of America

Cover design by Brett J. Miller
Interior design and layout by Brett J. Miller

First Edition
1 3 5 7 9 10 8 6 4 2

BROKEN EAGLE

A Thriller

James T. Crouse

To Janet

The Greatest Sister A
Brother Could Have

1

Raleigh, North Carolina

Monday, August 3, 2009

9:15 a.m.

"My husband died in a military aircraft crash, and I need to know why. There was no better pilot in the Marines."

"I'm so sorry for your loss, Mrs. Thorpe," Jake said to the sad-eyed, young brunette who sat on the other side of his desk. His words were genuine—he was now an Army Reserve aviator, but he had served actively for ten years. The loss of any military aviator was personal to Jake.

A familiar pit lodged in his stomach at the thought of taking on another military air crash case. The last two had hit his bottom line so badly that he'd had to take out a second mortgage on his home and cut back his secretary's hours. Jake knew from his own painful experience how near impossible it was to take on the military and its big government contractors and win.

"Madison Wright told me to contact you," Lisa Thorpe continued. "She came to our base to talk to the Officers' Wives Club about rights of military families in North Carolina. She said no one would be more committed than you, Mr. Baird."

"Oh yes, Madison. She's a very good lawyer herself," Jake said quickly. *Madison should know I can't afford any more of these cases,* he thought.

Jake's secretary poked her head in, smiling kindly at Lisa. "Coffee or tea for either of you?" A willowy, ladylike widow in her sixties, Florence Hilliard had begun work for Jake shortly after he opened his office two years ago. She was "damned and determined," she said, not to wither away after she buried her husband of forty-six years.

"No, but thank you," Lisa said, returning her smile.

"Thanks, anyway, Florence," Jake added.

Jake decided to go through the standard client questions while he figured out a way to let Lisa know he couldn't take her case. "Well, let's start with the basics first. I hope you haven't traveled too far," Jake said as he reached for a legal pad.

"Actually I don't live far—near Beaufort—just outside Cherry Point."

Cherry Point. Although not a Marine Corps aviator, Jake was aware of the importance of the busy Marine Corps Air Station just outside Havelock, North Carolina. Passing it on the way to the beach, he always looked for fighter planes roaring off its runways. "I see. Tell me, what happened?"

"Sam—my husband—and another pilot were in Maryland, at Patuxent River Naval Air Station." Jake nodded, and Lisa continued. "They were testing a new aircraft when it crashed. It was April twenty-second of this year, at around three in the afternoon," she said.

"Do you know—or maybe I should say—do you have any *ideas* about the cause of the crash? Has anyone in Sam's chain of command told you anything?" Jake asked, even though he knew the military rarely told families anything about the true causes of air crashes.

"I don't know what happened. I can't seem to get any information, and it's driving me crazy," she said, tightening her grip on the chair arm. "They seem super secretive about it, which isn't fair. It was *my* husband who died. I deserve to know why. Sam hated flying that plane, helicopter—whatever it was."

"Which aircraft was it?"

"The XV-11." Lisa's voice cracked slightly. "I just can't believe it was his fault. And we've got a son, a son who deserves to know that it wasn't his daddy's fault that he won't be there for him as he grows up. That's why I'm here."

"How old is your son?" Jake asked. He sometimes wondered why he had chosen a legal career that was centered on investigating and compensating for tragic, sudden deaths.

"He's five. He has his dad's name—Samuel." Lisa smiled. "He's quite a little man—very brave," she said, pulling out a picture of little Sam and his dad beside a Marine helicopter. The way the boy gazed up at his father reminded Jake of the way he had looked at his own.

"So you would like for me to find out what happened, but are you also looking for an attorney to file a lawsuit?"

"I don't need *an* attorney, Mr. Baird—I need you," she insisted, her quiet voice becoming firm. "I certainly would like for whoever is at fault to pay, but this is about more than money, more than about Sam and me and our future. We military families are prepared—well, as prepared as anyone can be—for a loss in war. But to lose a husband and a father in what's supposed to be a 'routine test flight' is worse. Much worse."

Jake exhaled as he fought the voice in his head. *Just tell her no, before you get in too deep.* "Is there something that you think someone did or failed to do—something specific—that you want me to look into?"

Lisa sat up. "I just know something went terribly wrong. The XV-11 is a dangerous aircraft, and it killed him. All of the spouses have heard the rumors, but nobody wants to talk about it. People said things, even before this crash, that made me feel like it wasn't safe. But now two men are dead." Looking right at Jake, she said, "That's why I need you—to find out why."

"I appreciate your confidence in me," Jake said, knowing that the time to say no was now or never. He took a deep breath and looked Lisa in the eye. "I'll look into it, but I don't know what I might find. Don't get your hopes up—these cases are very tough. I can't promise I'll take it all the way to filing a lawsuit, but I will start an investigation. Be sure to tell me everything you hear. Florence will get your contact information, and you'll have to sign a retainer to give me the authority to work for you," he said.

"Florence and I already took care of most of that," she said, smiling. "I'll make sure you know whatever I hear."

"Well, I don't have many clients who sign up before they meet me," Jake said.

"I was convinced after I talked to Ms. Wright. I just wanted to visit with you to get to know you a little bit." She stood up. "Now, I have to get back to Sam. He's at the museum with his grandmother. Now that his dad is gone, he gets really anxious when I'm not around," she said. Jake escorted her to his outer office.

Lisa extended her hand to shake his. "Thank you, Mr. Baird," she said, then headed down the stairs.

After the door shut, Jake exhaled and leaned back against it. Florence broke the silence, "Say what you will about our small practice, but there are no dull days around here!"

"You could have given me a heads-up on why she was here—you know, military air crash—remember?"

"Why Jake, it happened so fast, I just forgot to mention it."

"Nice try, Florence, especially after you already signed her up."

. . .

Because of his lifelong interest in anything that flies, Jake had followed the tortured history of the XV-11. He knew what it was supposed to be—a combination of the forward speed and payload capacity of an airplane with the vertical and horizontal versatility of a helicopter. It could get from ship to battlefield quickly. The idea had merit. But he knew the development process had taken an inordinately long time and wondered how the program had survived with all of its problems, especially in an age of budget cutbacks.

Jake ran a contingency-fee practice, where there was no retainer deposit, no hourly fee, and the lawyer fronted all of a case's expenses. By necessity, his first question was always the same: What was the likelihood of winning? If he didn't win, the expenses would not be reimbursed, he would make no money, and all of his time would be lost. Jake's practice was still just getting up and running, and he was years away from being successful enough that he didn't have to worry about finances. This case could further drain his already taxed resources and take time away from other cases that had better chances of paying off.

The first hurdle for Lisa Thorpe's case would be the time and expense of the investigation, heavy with fees for technical experts. Then, if he filed suit, the aircraft manufacturers' insurance companies would put armies of lawyers on the case, and Jake would be flooded with paper—motions, requests for documents, and questions known as interrogatories. The XV-11's contractors and the military would be quick not to let a widow and a small-time attorney embarrass them or threaten their multimillion-dollar program. They would play hardball.

On top of all of this were the rulings that had created tough restrictions on suing military contractors like the XV-11's manufacturers. A suit against the government itself was made impossible by a sixty-year-old US Supreme Court ruling. Finally, there was the *Machin* decision, which greatly limited access to the government's investigative files. A triple roadblock for Lisa Thorpe or any other litigant whose loved one had been harmed by a military product.

But a widow had asked for Jake's help, and there was the horrible possibility that other troops would be killed if he did nothing. How could he just ignore the fact that without his help, the government and its contracting friends would overpower this widow's efforts to find out the truth? Jake had been drawn to a trial lawyer's career because he wanted to help people who were being picked on by someone or something more powerful. Lisa's case was exactly the sort he found impossible to resist.

Jake googled *XV-11 crash April 22*. Nothing. He couldn't even find the news reports he had remembered reading at the time of the crash. He tried several different search terms and different sites—all yielded nothing. It was as if the crash had never happened.

Frustrated, Jake pulled up the number of Colonel Paul Field, USMC (Ret.) and pressed "Call." After his active-duty flying career, Paul had secured a civilian contractor position at one of the Air Force bases in Arizona. But Jake knew Paul stayed informed on Marine Corps aviation.

"Paul Field."

"Paul, Jake Baird here. Got a minute?"

"For you? Of course! What's up?"

"Well, I don't know for sure. I have an odd one here. Know anything about an XV-11 crash near Pax River in April?"

The phone went silent, and Jake thought he'd lost the connection. But then Paul shot back, "Uh, sorry, Jake. Gotta go. I'll call you later."

Jake held the phone to his ear for a few seconds, surprised. *What was that all about?* He considered calling back, but decided to wait. *Paul must have had another call.*

Jake tended to some other files that needed work, reviewed some research he had done earlier in the week and the draft correspondence Florence had put on his desk before he got in.

"It's that time, Mr. Baird," Florence said, sticking her head around the corner into his office around noon. "I've finalized all you left for me on Saturday, and it's in a stack on the corner of my desk whenever you get to it. Try not to make it any higher, OK?"

Florence was taking her one of her afternoons off to volunteer at the animal shelter. Working with Jake gave her the flexibility to do it.

"So long, Florence," Jake said, without looking up. When Jake got caught up in his work, he hardly noticed things around him. His meticulous attention to detail had grown out of maintaining and test-flying Army aircraft. If he missed something, it could kill him, or others.

Florence persisted. "Mr. Baird, don't stay too late today." Jake stopped working and looked at Florence. She continued, "You could use some rest. You had quite a load of depositions last week, and I can see you aren't at full speed yet, especially after whatever you and your basketball buddies did last night."

"You noticed the red eyes, huh? And the four cups of coffee probably gave me away, too, I'll bet." Jake said, grinning as he leaned back in his chair. "I really tried to leave the bar, but the guys just wouldn't let me." Florence's frown told him she wasn't buying it. "OK, Florence, I'll leave at a decent time. Message received."

After Florence left, Jake refocused on his work. Often in these quiet times his past replayed itself in his mind. He returned to the seemingly endless days of his youth, working with his father at the shoe shop and coming home to his mom's cooking. Throughout college, the Army, and law school, he had loved returning home to share his life and recharge his batteries. But that fairy-tale existence had been instantly wiped out when Jake had lost his parents to a drunk driver just after he finished law school.

Since that tragedy, Jake had struggled to find any semblance of his life's previous equilibrium. The chasm was always there, and it bothered him more than he liked to admit. He ached for someone to share his life as his parents once had, but no one could. Madison Wright provided—along with case referrals—companionship and love, which helped to ease the loneliness. And in some ways Florence filled the motherly void. No one, however, eased the loss of his father, a gentle soul whose values had made Jake into the man he had become.

. . .

As Jake reached to close the blinds and shut out the afternoon sun, his cell phone rang.

"Jake, it's Paul. Sorry for the abrupt end to our conversation, but I thought I'd better talk to you from somewhere else. It took me a while to find a pay phone."

"A pay phone?" Jake laughed, shaking his head in disbelief. "They still have those? What's up with the cloak-and-dagger stuff?"

"Look, they've done a good job of keeping this whole thing out of sight—the crash, the investigation, et cetera. You know this thing has had problems, and I imagine whatever happened in Maryland could kill the whole program. What little information that got out was rounded up and classified."

"Don't you know anyone who knows something about this?" Jake asked.

"Nobody's talking. Look, I'm sorry, but that's all I know. If I were you, I'd stay away from this one, Jake, but that's your call. Good luck."

"OK, sure. Thanks," He had never known Paul to get so rattled. This was getting stranger and stranger. This type of censorship was usually associated with true state secrets. But censorship on the XV-11, which involved no classified technology, made no sense. The tilt-rotor concept and its associated engineering were decades old. The trick was to get it to work—and so far no one had, at least without major problems.

Jake had been around the block enough to recognize that this information was being restricted by the Pentagon. This meant that requests to the government for information, such as Freedom of Information Act requests, would be denied. The same for litigation discovery and subpoenas. Without any information, Jake knew he couldn't help Lisa Thorpe.

Something must be very wrong with this aircraft. Was the government hiding the problems until they could find a way to fix or minimize them? Or worse, did they intend to permanently conceal them—a virtual guarantee that more service members would die in this kind of accident?

2

Raleigh, North Carolina

Monday, August 3, 2009

4:00 p.m.

Jake's attempts to focus on other cases didn't work. Thoughts about Lisa Thorpe and the XV-11 pinged around his head like BBs ricocheting in a shooting gallery.

He needed to clear his head. Exercise had a way of helping him get the cobwebs out, so he headed to the gym. His war-wounded knee kept him off the treadmill, but he could get some cardio on the stationary bike, and pumping iron would help him take out his frustrations.

After the gym, he got a dinner of his comfort food at the K & W Cafeteria: hamburger steak, collard greens, cornbread, mac and cheese. He finished just before six p.m. and decided to take a chance that a colleague who could help him sort through his thoughts on the Thorpe case might still be in his office.

Irwin Thompson, Jake often thought, must have been created by central casting to play the southern seersucker-suited lawyer, with a drawl that dripped refinement, bourbon, and a thorough knowledge of horseracing. Jake had first met Irwin when he taught a trial practice course at Jake's law school. Jake had been impressed not only by Irwin's subject knowledge, but also by his razor-sharp intellect, drenched in southern mannerisms that masked his steely toughness.

Jake pulled up Irwin's number.

"Irwin Thompson speaking."

"What are you doing answering your own phone, Mr. Thompson?" Jake teased.

"I take by this formal, military-infused voice that this is Colonel Baird, and sir, you should know that in civilized law offices, we let our help go at a respectable hour. I'll bet poor Mrs. Hilliard is still there, slaving away at the Baird Sweat Shop."

"Wrong, Counselor. Florence strolled out of the office hours ago. She is probably at home in her bubble bath by now."

"Have you no scruples, Counselor?" Irwin joked back. "To speak of Florence's private matters that way on a public communication device is reprehensible, sir! You obviously have forgotten your upbringing. Probably all that mess you did in the *Ahmy.*" Irwin said it in a way that refused to acknowledge the presence of the consonant *R*, similar to the way he left the *L* out of *golf.* "But what can I do for you, Counselor, on this hellaciously hot summer's afternoon?"

Jake laughed. There was nobody else like Irwin. "You can let me buy you a drink. I'll even take you to dinner, though I already ate."

"Now that's a great reason to answer the phone after hours! I can oblige you on the former, sir, but I am afraid I will have to pass on dinner. Mrs. Thompson needs me home so she can go cavorting with her fellow damsels of the boutique. Seems she doesn't trust our unsupervised hoodlums not to kill one another or practice their arson skills in the living room. So I must police the little monsters."

"Understood. How about The Oxford in about fifteen minutes?"

"Perfect! That should give us time for a couple of quick beverages. See you there."

Jake headed downtown.

. . .

"May we help you, sir?" asked the Oxford maitre d' as Jake tried to adjust his eyes to the dark, wood-paneled interior of the bar.

"Yes, I am meeting someone—there he is," Jake said, finally able to see Irwin waving to him from a table in the rear.

"Good evening, Counselor," Irwin bellowed as Jake approached. "Hope you don't mind that I started without you."

"Of course not," Jake said.

"Helps to know not only the owner, but the staff, don't you see?"

"Of course," Jake said, acknowledging Irwin's considerable interpersonal skills.

Irwin lifted his hand and pointed over Jake's head. "Clarence awaits your order."

A deep, booming voice startled Jake from behind. "Good evening, sir. I'm Clarence. How may I serve you this evening?"

Jake turned in his chair until he looked up at one of the tallest and darkest men he had ever seen. And thick. Jake was in his thirties and a six-foot-two Army veteran, but this guy made him feel small and weak.

"Sure. A Shotgun Betty, please."

"Right away, sir," Clarence responded, and headed toward the bar.

"Ah yes. A beer. How original, Counselor," Irwin sniped, leaning back in his chair, sipping his drink.

"Sorry, I don't have your social sophistication. I like to keep things simple."

"Understood, Counselor. Now, since I have domestic duties awaiting me, I need to ask why we are here imbibing? Not that I mind, of course."

"Right. I will get to the point," Jake said, as he leaned over the table toward Irwin. "A young widow came to see me today. She lost her husband in a military aircraft crash."

"Wait right there, Counselor," Irwin interjected. "Did you say *military* crash? My word, man, have you not learned your lesson on those types of cases?"

"Maybe you can help me remember."

"Why do you need reminding? You *swore* that you would not take another one, that you were over them for good, and that you had sunk too much money and time into them, with no reward for you or your clients. You need to stick by your prior decision."

"I do remember having said all that, Irwin," Jake admitted, "but this one is different."

"OK, Counselor. I am all ears," Irwin said, frowning. He took off his tortoiseshell-rimmed glasses, pulled his handkerchief from his coat pocket, and wiped his ruddy face. "Tell me why you're even remotely considering this."

"First, there is no information on this crash anywhere. I went to all the usual places and tried several different searches—nothing. For the first time I could find *nothing* about a domestic accident, even if it was a military crash."

"Might it be classified?" Irwin asked.

"No—well, that's part of it. It was a 'routine test flight,' at least according to the widow. The other difference is that this widow got my name from Madison."

Irwin burst out laughing. "That's one hell of a difference, Counselor. I don't even want to know how or why that happened, and I sure as hell am *not* going to offer any advice on how you get out of that one with the beautiful and frighteningly tenacious Ms. Wright."

"Thanks for the help, Irwin," Jake said. Irwin was right; Madison was a bulldog, but a damned sexy one.

"But back to the widow. What does she know? What could she know?" Irwin shook his head at Jake. "You know, Jake, for someone who has done what you have in the military, your naiveté is astounding. C'mon, now, Jake, wake up and smell the coffee."

"I hear you. But this one intrigues me. Besides, the widow is . . ."

Irwin's face tightened. "Convincing? What widow isn't, for God's sake? Especially a young military one, even more so if there are children. So you come in and save the day for them? It's time to get rid of that crusader mentality, Jake!"

"Look, I'll probably say no to her," Jake responded. "But if I decide to go forward—maybe just to investigate—I can count on you for some legal support, right?"

Irwin sighed. "You know I won't leave you out there hanging by yourself. But you really should turn this one down."

"You're a good man, Irwin. If I get to the point where I think this is doable, then we'll talk. Maybe I'll handle the depositions, discovery, and court appearances, and you can help with research and briefing—if, I repeat *if*, I go forward." Then, Jake added, "All for a piece of the fee, of course."

Irwin leaned back in his chair, exasperated. "There won't *be* any fee, Jake, because this will go *nowhere*. Against my better judgment, of course I will help. But I'm telling you, Jake, you're too concerned about the folks in uniform. It clouds your judgment." Irwin downed the last part of his drink and started to gather his things. "Now, I to my domestic duties and you to your bachelor's castle, damn you. I love those munchkins, but I would relish just a few hours in a quiet house with a good book."

"Come on, the single life is not all it's cracked up to be. But at least I'm not driving a minivan. Here, it's my treat." Jake threw some cash on the table as they got up.

"Well, thank you. Mighty nice," Irwin said.

They walked to the door, held open by the doorman, and out into the diminishing sunlight. Irwin asked, "By the way . . . what aircraft is the one in question?"

"The XV-11. The Sea Eagle."

"My God. That awful thing?" Irwin had never served in the military, but he had a curious mind and read everything, so he was well aware of the XV-11's history. "That's even more of a reason to run the other way."

. . .

After the short drive home, Jake arrived at the house he had bought two years ago so he could have a dog and privacy. He'd always had a dog as a kid. Escape from apartment life enabled him to both get a dog and get away from shared walls so he could play his sound system as loud as he wanted.

Max, his Giant Schnauzer, was already greeting him with a deep bark as Jake exited the car and walked to his screened porch. After giving Max a good workout in the backyard with a tennis ball and pouring out his kibble, Jake headed into the bedroom. He shimmied under the covers without making a mess of the bed—less to straighten at "oh-dark-thirty."

3

Ready to go to work the next morning, Jake locked up the house and walked into his detached garage. Once at his car, he spotted an envelope on the driver's seat of his open 1995 Mercedes convertible. At first, he thought it was something that had fallen out of his briefcase. But when he saw his name handwritten on the outside, he knew he'd never seen it before. His pulse quickened. *How the hell did this get here?* He looked around for any signs of a break-in.

Grabbing the envelope and ripping it open, he removed a small piece of paper.

Waffle House. Hillsborough Street. 10 a.m. Be there.

Jake now remembered that Max's barking last night had been different—more intense. Giant Schnauzers heard everything and barked a lot, so Jake normally thought nothing of it. But now he realized that Max obviously had heard something in the garage.

Someone had breached Jake's home security, and he was not happy. He'd get to the bottom of this. He got in the car and backed down the driveway. Before he got to the street, his cell phone rang. The caller ID said *Unknown.*

"Jake Baird."

"Did you get my note?" a gravelly voice asked.

"Who is this?"

"Did you get my note?" the caller demanded.

Jake's jaw tightened. He didn't like this game. "Yeah, I got it. What's this all about?"

"Lisa Thorpe. It's important. You need to be there."

"Lisa Thorpe? How do you . . ."

The caller interrupted. "I said it's important! Ten o'clock!" *Click.*

What the hell? This guy is probably a kook. But something about the man's voice did not sound kooky. And how did he know about Lisa Thorpe? Jake decided he had nothing to lose. What was a trip down to the Waffle House, anyway? If this man knew enough to know that Jake was representing Thorpe, then he would go.

Jake then realized the absurdity of his situation. *So it's come to this,* Jake groused. *Six years in the military, three years in law school, four years in practice, and here I am going to meet some mystery man at the freakin' Waffle House!*

He decided to call Florence, who was probably already at her desk.

"Hi, Florence. Good morning. I forgot an appointment. I have my cell if you need me," Jake said.

"What appointment? I don't have anything scheduled." Florence was protective of her boss's workload and his
schedule and guarded both with a ferocity that Jake appreciated as a midlife orphan. There was no way Jake was going to tell her that he was going to a meeting that had been scheduled via break-in to his garage.

"I know, Florence. My mistake," he apologized. "I'll do better next time." Jake hung up.

As Jake approached the Waffle House, he looked around for anything out of the ordinary, listened for any strange sounds, and prepared to react, scanning for exit routes.

He turned into the restaurant's front parking lot and was relieved to see that all looked normal. He drove in a slow, clockwise circle around the building and passed by the bushes along the railroad tracks in the back—nothing unusual. He continued around the side onto the gravel part of the lot, then began a slow turn into a parking space.

Thunk!

Jake's heart stopped. He slammed on the brakes. "What the—"

A man in a dingy coat and wrinkled hat jerked the passenger door handle, but it wouldn't open. "Unlock the door, Colonel!" the man shouted.

Jake complied, and the man yanked the door open and got inside. "There's no time. Get outta here," the stranger ordered as he jumped in the car.

Jake recognized the man's voice from the call. "Who the hell are you?" Jake demanded. He took in the man's rough, unshaven appearance. *How does he know my rank?* Even though his clothes were dirty and wrinkled, his voice conveyed authority.

"Move, goddammit! Head toward downtown!" the man said, swiveling his head around, checking the area.

"Not until you tell me what the—"

The mystery man pointed his finger in Jake's face. "Look, you stubborn bastard, if you don't get moving we'll be in deep shit! Drive, Colonel, now!" the man shouted.

The urgency in the man's voice was real. Jake obeyed and peeled out of the Waffle House parking lot onto the street, almost hitting an eastbound car.

"You tell me why you jumped into my car and who you are," Jake said, glaring at the guy as they streaked down Hillsborough. Jake guessed he was in his mid-fifties and noticed his chiseled face and thin build. He got the distinct impression this guy had been somebody once.

"It's all in here," the man said, lifting a large, three-inch-thick brown folder from inside his raincoat. "Well, most of it anyway. Read this, and I'll be back in touch." The stranger put the folder on the passenger side floor. "Now, pull over—right there," the man ordered, pointing to a convenience store on the right side of the street.

"Go around back by the car wash. Right there. OK, stop!" Just as quickly as he had gotten in, he was out. He lowered his head back down into the open passenger compartment. "Read it. You'll figure it out. I'll be in touch. You're in this now, Colonel, so watch your six!"

Jake had no question about what he meant: *Stay vigilant, especially behind you.*

Vigilent about what? Jake wondered, as he watched him head into a stand of trees. The man's voice didn't lie, and Jake decided he'd better move. As he started to drive off, his hands slipped on the steering wheel. He wiped his sweaty palms on his pants.

Jake hung a left on Faircloth, then another into the campus of a small college. Eager to look inside the folder to figure out what all this James Bond stuff was about, he parked near the library, grabbed the folder, and hurried inside.

To his relief he found the first-floor reading room empty. *Of course—summer*, he thought. He sat down at a long table and eased the dark red-brown folder from his lap as he looked around to make sure no one was in a position to see. For the first time he noticed the NAVAIR—Naval Air Systems Command—insignia on the front along with the word *NAVAIR* stenciled just below. He untied the brick-red string and pulled the contents slowly out onto the table.

"Holy shit," he whispered as he saw *TOP SECRET* stamped on the top of the first document. Clearly, he was looking at things he should never see. After glancing around to be sure no one was watching, he looked farther down the cover page. He found the subject: *XV-11: Timeline*. He looked around again, this time noticing the library's security cameras.

All of the documents were about the Sea Eagle, the same aircraft that Lisa Thorpe's husband had been operating when he died. Jake sifted through them—test results, accident summaries, interoffice memoranda, data printouts, and narratives of engineer studies. All the formal documents had notes and mark-ups. Even a quick scan showed that people inside the program were aware of the aircraft's technical flaws and safety issues and were covering them up.

The thoughts cascaded in. *Lisa Thorpe and the guy in the crappy trench coat are linked. But how? And what can I do with these classified documents, anyway? Isn't this a one-way ticket to Leavenworth?* Although Jake hadn't procured the folder himself, there was no denying that he was now in unauthorized possession of classified documents that were almost certainly stolen. No one would believe someone just gave them to him at a Waffle House. All he kept hearing was what the man had told him: "Read it. You'll figure it out. Watch your six."

His apprehension about having the documents collided with his anger about their contents. The file confirmed what the aircraft's critics had said all along: the XV-11 was a seriously flawed aircraft.

But Jake's immediate concern was that the Pentagon and its intelligence

BROKEN EAGLE: A THRILLER

buddies at the National Security Agency would be after him in an instant if they knew he had this damaging evidence. If this went public, it could strike a fatal blow to the Sea Eagle program and its proponents.

The college library now seemed like it was too close to his rendezvous point with the stranger, so Jake pushed the papers back inside the folder and headed out of the reading room toward the exit. Carefully pressing the folder against his hip so *NAVAIR* and its seal wouldn't show, he walked past the receptionist station, avoiding eye contact with the young woman behind the console.

Jake pulled out of the college and, without thinking, headed toward Hillsborough, the shortest route to his office. As he passed the Waffle House, he spotted two sedans and men in dark suits with sunglasses, searching the area all around the restaurant. A couple of the men had bulges underneath their jackets: weapons. One of them was on a cell phone, hand on hip, looking frustrated, as though he had been tricked. Jake had no doubt they were after the mystery man he had just met.

I'm so stupid, driving past the restaurant! He couldn't be sure these people hadn't gotten a description of his car from someone inside. He executed a left turn down a side street and drove away as normally as he could, controlling his anxiety, checking his rear view mirror.

Jake could only hope that the dark suits were not aware of the handoff and were looking only for the other guy—but he couldn't be certain. In case they were looking for his car or him, Jake decided the best thing for him to do was get out of town for a couple of days, to a place where he couldn't be found. He needed some time to study the documents and do some hard thinking.

4

It was already one of those scorching, oppressive days that sets the North Carolina sandhills on fire. The humidity of the still, dead air made it difficult to breathe and the sun turned the tarmac into a skillet. At 1100 hours, United States Marine Corps Majors Bill Harris and Gary Bennett walked through the ungodly heat to their aircraft for another operational test mission. Their sage-gray Nomex flight suits, designed to keep flames out, were doing a good job of absorbing the heat and keeping it in, fully roasting them. Under the flight suit, the bulky survival vest, and the body suit of fire-resistant underwear, there was no way to stay cool.

"You know, sometimes I think the old man really believes what he's saying," Gary said.

"What do you mean?" Bill asked as they trudged past the line of the venerable H-46s, the twin-rotor aircraft that had for years been the mainstay of Marine Corps rotary-wing aviation. Serving long past their original retirement dates, they sat there peacefully, blades drooping, looking tired and worn out, but with an air of willingness to launch again if needed.

"All that stuff about us being the luckiest aviators in the world . . . at the forefront of a new technology, the machine that will save Marines' lives, change the battlefield, you know," Gary said, wiping the sweat off his face.

"Major Bennett," Bill replied, "your civilian-oriented head is so far up your ass you haven't noticed those things happen to be true. We're *real* lucky to have been selected for this operational testing unit, and it sure will be good for our careers. Just consider it getting your ticket punched—one more rung on the big military ladder."

"Jeez! You sound like the old man," Gary responded. "Must be that lifer orientation you have. And lucky me, I'm stuck with you!"

"You just can't handle the fact that I have knowledge superior to yours, you ROTC puke. Hell, it's a miracle that you made major the same year I did. Who do you know?" Bill shot back.

"It was pure ability. But I know . . . we poor ROTC officers should be grateful to wear the same uniform as you academy types. Thanks for letting us play on your team. By the way, how's the commandant these days?" It was a running joke that the military academy grads had instant access to their service branch chiefs at any time through a little two-way radio hidden inside their monstrous academy rings.

"He's fine," Bill said. "In fact, he just called to see how I was doing and to ask if any noncareer types were bugging me. Don't worry. I didn't give you up, bucko. But if you keep whining," Bill added, smiling, "I'll be forced to report you. Then God help you. You'll probably be working at a supply warehouse at some shithole base in Mississippi."

"As opposed to this garden of Eden?" Gary joked.

They arrived at their aircraft, a hideous gray beast, with its short, fat fuselage squatting on the three nubs of tricycle landing gear, huge engine nacelles pointing skyward at the end of its stubby "wings," and its truncated, thick, black rotor blades, three to a side, capping each nacelle horizontally, like a helicopter's main rotor blades.

This was the XV-11 "Sea Eagle." It didn't look a thing like the real bird, Gary thought, picturing the beautiful creature of sky and sea. Nothing about the graceful raptor was represented in what Gary saw in front of him: a metal monster that looked like some out-of-control junior high science project. "This thing gives a good bird a bad name" was Gary's saying. *Nothing* was this ugly.

"You know, if I die in one of these goddamn things, be sure to tell the commandant that I knew it was a piece of shit and I hung in there just to save him the embarrassment of quitting the program and telling the world why," Gary said.

"He will be truly grateful for that—he might even give your family two flags," Bill said.

Gary smiled. He liked the banter, and he liked Bill—"Mister Mean Marine." Bill's gallows humor and military repartee helped Gary handle his apprehension, but there was no denying he was worried about this aircraft. A crash had already cost the lives of two pilots from this squadron. One of them had been in Gary's initial entry flight school class. Each had left behind a wife, and one had a five-year-old boy.

Gary was suspicious that the current XV-11 crews had never received a detailed accident briefing on the prior crash. He also found it odd that there had been no post-crash safety-of-flight messages or changes to the Naval Air Training Operating Procedures Standardization (NATOPS) manual. Either they didn't know what had happened, or they knew and weren't telling—probably because they didn't have a fix. Either way, it was bad for the crews.

Rumors about control problems causing the crash bothered him, since he had himself experienced intermittent control problems on several XV-11 flights during comparatively benign maneuvers. He wondered what would happen with aggressive maneuvers or in combat, when crews would really be challenging the aircraft, "yanking and banking" to avoid enemy gunfire—all with a full load of twenty-four troops and gear. What about the inevitable aerodynamic performance degradation at higher altitudes? Would the beast just fall out of the sky?

On the flights where he had experienced control problems, Bill had said he hadn't noticed anything. Gary believed Bill, but Gary also knew that it was in Bill's best interest *not* to notice anything—complaints were not well tolerated in the military, and certainly not in *this* aircraft program. Aviators who had expressed concerns in this program were quickly moved out via orders from the highest levels. Someone was watching.

But would this silence mean that somebody else would die before the aircraft's flaws were fixed? Would that somebody be him?

"So, how are the studies going there, Mr. Student?" Bill asked as he buckled in and prepared for the pre-start checklist.

"Could be moving a little faster, but it's OK. Six more months," Gary replied.

"Hell, that'll fly by, and you'll have that MBA and be outta here, diving headlong into the big bucks."

"I wish. Let's just hope the job market is good when I cut the cord," Gary added.

"OK, you all ready? We might as well get this show on the road," Bill said, stopping the chatter.

"Yeah, go ahead."

Bill placed the checklist binder in his lap, and began reading.

"OK, seats?"

"Adjusted."

"Seat belts and shoulder harnesses?"

"Adjusted and locked."

"Flight controls?"

"Adjusted. No binding."

They continued the checklist, but just before "engines start," Bill stopped, lowered the checklist to his lap, and turned to Gary. "Seriously, man, you think it's gonna be tough out there?"

"We'll find out. I'll probably go into the Reserves, you know. I don't want to make a total cold leap into the civilian world. I like flying. Hell, I even like being around assholes."

"Thanks, butt-face. Here I am trying to show my caring side and you slam me."

"What makes you think I was talking about you?" Gary shot back.

"OK, starting engines—battery on . . ." Bill resumed the checklist.

The difference between them was that Bill, outwardly at least, believed in the program. Bill actually thought that anytime a new weapon system was tested people would probably die; it was just part of the price to be paid for advancement. In the end, the Marine Corps, the military, and the country would be better and more secure.

Gary understood the nature of Bill's "bottom line" approach, but couldn't help but wonder why, in this day of computer analyses of everything, they were still in the put-the-guy-in-the-cockpit-and-wring-out-the-problems mode of flight testing. Couldn't they figure out more of this stuff on the computer *before* pilots strapped themselves in?

Gary had heard that if the aircraft didn't become operational soon, the program could be canceled, and that would mean losses of anticipated jobs in all fifty states where the contractors had wisely placed manufacturing or supply operations. The Marines would suffer because the '46s were ancient, and there was no other replacement on the drawing boards. But Gary thought the real drivers of the program were the members of Congress whose districts stood to lose the most, along with the manufacturers' executives and stockholders. There was also the potential for various civilian versions of the craft. The possibilities were limitless.

As they neared the end of the checklist, the pit in Gary's stomach grew. The end of the checklist meant "start engines" was approaching, and then flight. At least they had a simple daytime—as opposed to nighttime—protocol.

As Bill called out, "Number one engine, start," Gary consciously tightened his shoulder harness and seat belt. As the turbine engine began its accelerating whine and the big blades started their rotation, he stared through the overhead cockpit window at them, and found himself asking them to behave. As he heard, "Engine number two, start," he looked at the other blades out his window and inaudibly demanded that the aircraft not kill him today. Once at flight idle, Gary transferred the aircraft controls to Bill. "You have the controls," Gary said into the microphone.

"I have the controls," Bill responded. He reached up for the throttles and brought the aircraft to full power.

As Bill began to apply power and the aircraft got light on its gear, Gary said one more short, silent prayer. The monster became airborne, and they were off.

5

Jake was becoming more concerned that the men in suits at the Waffle House already could be tracing his license plate. Sweat suddenly broke out on Jake's brow. It wasn't unusual for a man to be sweaty in August in Raleigh, but the air conditioning in his car was on full blast.

Maybe he was being overly cautious. Maybe those guys had come after the rendezvous and they had no idea he was involved. Still, Jake decided that returning to the office wasn't the best idea. Fearing that his cell phone might not be safe, he was cryptic when he called Florence.

"Law Offices of Jake Baird," Florence answered.

"Look, Florence, we haven't had lunch together in a while, so I thought this would be a great day for it. How about meeting me at my favorite restaurant—say around one?" That would give him time to run by his house and grab some things for a spontaneous "vacation."

"Does that mean you're going to pay this time? What a rare and unexpected treat," she kidded. "You mean—"

"That's right," Jake interrupted, "I'm sure you remember. I'll see you there at one." He hung up. He knew she would figure it out and be there precisely at one p.m. She was never late.

Jake also feared that the men in suits might have found out where he lived. So he checked the area around his house carefully as he approached, then went inside and stuffed some clothes into a suitcase. While he packed, Jake wondered where he might go. Then it came to him. In one of his first cases after going out on his own two years ago, Jake had represented a farmer and his wife who'd had lost their thirty-year-old son in a regional jet crash. He visited their farm often and remembered there was a small motel about five miles from there, in the middle of nowhere. Not even Florence would think of that as his hideout.

Just before heading to his car, he grabbed his military .45 Colt automatic out of the gun safe, chambered a magazine, and grabbed two extra magazines. Although Jake had not grown up with guns and was not a hunter, after the military he'd bought three handguns—the .45, a 9mm and a .357—and a Defender twelve-gauge shotgun. Jake usually traveled with one of his handguns on a highway alone, especially at night. He already knew how it felt to shoot somebody and didn't want to do it again, but he didn't like being defenseless, either.

Jake said good-bye to Max, realizing he needed to remember to ask Florence to take care of him. Now if he could only decide what to tell Florence as easily as he'd decided where he would be spending the next few days.

Once in the restaurant, Jake asked the hostess for a booth in the back.

After a few minutes, he saw Florence enter and stood up to wave to her. Florence spotted him, broke off her conversation with the young hostess, and headed back to his table.

Once seated, she let it fly—with a bit of vinegar. "OK, Mr. Stealth Lawyer, what went on this morning? We agreed that you would keep me informed of what you're up to, remember? That was the deal."

"Sorry," he said.

"I am very capable of handling anything and everything that you or anyone else throws my way, including last minute schedule changes. I am sure you noticed that I was not born yesterday."

A waitress appeared and took their orders. As soon as she was gone, Jake responded to Florence's demand. "Well, I'm glad you can handle anything, Florence, because I've got a strange one for you," he began. "This morning, a guy left a note inside my car at my house, then called my cell and asked me to meet him at the Waffle House on Hillsborough. When I got there, he gave me a folder full of classified documents. I have no idea who he is, how he got the documents, or even how he found me. I am guessing he's ex-military, especially since he passed the documents to me face-to-face, rather than just leaving them in my car—that's the government's way of ensuring a secure handoff. I know he's in trouble—I saw men searching the spot where I picked him up. I don't know if he stole the documents or what."

"Do you still have them?"

"Maybe," Jake responded, giving Florence a look that told her he did. "Anyway, since I met with the guy, and they're after him, they'll soon be after me—if they aren't already. I need to get away for a couple of days so I can sort out the information he gave me—without the guys chasing him breathing down my neck."

"If you do have these documents, would it help if you just give them back and explain what happened?"

"Giving them back is out of the question. Too late. I've seen them, so I have personal knowledge of classified information I was not authorized to see—or possess," Jake explained.

"What's in the documents?"

Jake recoiled at the directness of her question. "Florence, I don't think I should tell you. Besides, I don't know what I am going to do with them, so why involve you?"

"The only way I can help you is if I know what is going on," Florence argued, adjusting her scarf around her neck.

"Look, the more you know, the more dangerous it will be for you. You can't lie to these people—they'll know that you know," Jake warned.

Florence tried again. "I already know enough to be in trouble, but not enough to help. Let me help you, Jake," she urged.

Jake hesitated. "The XV-11. The Sea Eagle," Jake finally said.

"The one Lisa Thorpe's husband was flying?"

"That's the one," Jake responded.

"What's so secret about that?" Florence asked.

"It doesn't work, Florence, and it probably never will. And it's dangerous. These documents lay it all out—what was wrong, who knew, and what they were—or actually weren't—going to do about it. Obviously, there's a connection to the Thorpe case, but using them in the case is a whole other issue."

"I am sure you'll find a way they can help."

"I can't put top-secret documents into evidence. And what else could I do with them? Hold a press conference and demand the XV-11 program be halted?" Jake asked. "Besides, it's a military air crash case, remember? I swore I wouldn't take on another one."

"I understand you had bad luck in the past. But you know the military. You know the law. And you know how to investigate. If it's wrong, you'll stand up and do what is right."

"Maybe. But there's another problem: Madison sent Lisa Thorpe to me. So I have to figure out how to address that one, too."

"I'll let you handle Madison. She's almost as stubborn as I am." Florence smiled.

"I may need you to help me coordinate some things, but beyond what I ask you to do, you have to stay out of this."

"I've been covering lawyers' butts for over thirty years. I can certainly cover for two days—longer if necessary," Florence said.

Jake smiled at her scrappy attitude. "Let's figure out a way to communicate while I'm gone. Keep things as normal as possible. Just be careful on the phone to anyone. No names, places, et cetera."

Jake reached for his wallet to pay the check.

As they headed to the entrance, Jake stopped. "One more thing. Can you please look after Max for me?"

"Already in the plans, sir," Florence answered, giving Jake a mock salute. She had taken care of Max before and had her own security code and key to Jake's house.

Jake stood where he could not be seen, but where he could watch Florence walk all the way to her car. She got in and drove off. Nothing unusual.

He waited a few minutes and headed to his car. Before he hit I-40 West, he had one more stop to make.

. . .

"Hello, Jake," the receptionist said as Jake crossed the marble foyer floor at Alexander, Johnson & Wright, LLP.

"Hi, Sandy. I didn't call ahead, but I need to see Madison for a few moments if she's free."

"Let me see if I can find her," she said, picking up the handset. "Would you like something while you're waiting? Coffee, water?"

"No thanks. I'm fine."

"Hi, Beth. There's a good-looking man out here to see Ms. Wright once she gets off her call . . . OK, I'll let him know." She said, smiling and turning to Jake. "She's finishing up a call and she'll be right with you."

Jake saw Madison coming down the hall. Her perfectly styled blond hair and great figure didn't scream "lawyer," but since the day she was born, she had been groomed for the law by her father, a named senior partner in her firm. Jake watched a big smile cover her face as soon as she saw him. She gave him a big hug. "Well this is quite a surprise! What's the occasion?"

"Can we go somewhere to talk?"

Madison led him toward an unoccupied conference room, just off the foyer. "Is anything wrong, Jake? You never come here unannounced."

"Well . . ." He hesitated. "Lisa Thorpe came to see me—the Marine Corps wife you met at Cherry Point? She just lost her husband in the crash of an XV-11 Sea Eagle."

"Yes. She called me a couple of days ago, and I gave her your contact information. I know these cases are tough, but I thought you could at least talk to her. Hope that was OK. I was going to tell you about it, but I've been slammed here."

"Don't worry, it's fine. I just need to go out of town for a couple of days to do some research, and I won't be able to use my cell phone."

Madison tilted her head, intrigued. "That's not your standard MO when you take on a case. Anything you want to tell me?"

"Not yet."

"OK. When do you leave?"

"Well, right now, as a matter of fact."

Madison's eyebrows shot up and she groaned. "Now? Jake, you know we have dinner plans with Mom and Dad tonight."

"Afraid so, Maddy. If I could put it off, I would. But I really need to leave."

She slumped in the chair and said nothing, but her body language spoke volumes. This was another time he couldn't do what she wanted him to do.

"This is all very strange and mysterious, babe. But let me know what you can, when you can."

"Of course. I'd better head out," he said, standing and giving Maddy a hug. She led him to the elevators, and they said good-bye.

6

Jake's conscience weighed heavy on him as he headed into the foothills of the Smokies. The illegal possession of classified military documents smacked directly against his patriotism, but at the same time, he questioned the patriotism of those who knew the aircraft's problems yet pushed for full-scale production.

Jake had grown up in a small North Carolina town. There, if you weren't a lawyer, doctor, or highly successful businessman, then you basically didn't exist. The exclusion extended to the children of those who did not work in suits and ties.

In spite of Jake's talent and accomplishments, he was not selected for the high school newspaper staff, was not named captain of any sports teams, and got little notice in the town's newspaper for any of his athletic or academic successes. Determined to escape this caste system, Jake, at the tender age of sixteen, had asked his parents to send him away to finish high school. His parents found a small, Methodist military preparatory school in northern Virginia that offered him a scholarship. One fall night, after his dad closed his shoe shop, they drove six hours in the dark to the small town where the boarding school was located. The next day, after being fitted for uniforms, picking up books, meeting his roommate, and a quick tour of the campus, Jake bade his parents good-bye.

The sudden separation from his parents took some getting used to. The harsh military environment caused a lonely ache in Jake's chest, felt most acutely in the morning, before the activities of the day distracted him. He missed his friends and his home life, but eventually he became acclimated to the rhythms of the place and hit his stride. He posted record-high grades in three different subjects, became the first two-year officer in the history of the school, an all-league basketball standout, and valedictorian.

The colleges came calling, including West Point. He earned a congressional appointment, which he turned down to accept an Army ROTC scholarship at a brainy, small, liberal arts college in his home state. He wanted his college years to be true college years, not spent in a military institution like his prep school.

In college, he became sports editor of the paper and commandant of the ROTC program. He played intramural sports, but he didn't try out for the varsity teams for fear it would take too much time from his studies. Graduate school was in his plans, but only after he'd fulfilled his six-year commitment to the Army.

Jake was the first person in his family to get a four-year college degree, let alone a graduate degree, so to ensure academic success he followed a path free of distractions. This included romantic relationships. He was popular with women because of his all-American good looks, but Jake always kept it light and noncommittal.

In his Army career, he became a "shooting star," meaning that he was headed for general officer rank. After a year as an infantry platoon leader at Fort Hood, Texas, he went to flight school, where he finished first in his class. He thought about going into engineering test flight, but instead decided to attend Aircraft Maintenance Officer's Course and test pilot school. This route would keep him in a troop unit with other soldiers, rather than in a test facility. As a certified helicopter maintenance test pilot, he was selected to join a newly formed "black unit," which had been developed to conduct and assist in conducting clandestine operations throughout the world.

The memory of some of those missions horrified him even now; what specialized weapons did to human flesh was indelible. He couldn't forget what an improvised explosive device did to his own troops. He tried to keep those memories locked away—but they found ways to come out. To avoid triggering the flashbacks, Jake stayed away from war movies and was careful about what he watched on television.

The Army brass recognized his skill and bravery in the air and on the ground and encouraged him to pursue a military career. But six years of service were more than enough for Jake. Being on the cutting edge of battle in remote locations, knowing what would happen if he was captured, and working day and night to keep aircraft and systems operational had taken their toll. He was exhausted physically, mentally, and spiritually. So he exchanged his active commission for a reserve one, left the service, and entered law school.

During and ever since law school, he'd flown in the Army Reserves, where he found people who shared similar backgrounds. He worked hard to provide caring leadership and insisted that subordinates and superiors follow the same principles. Reserve duty provided a respite from law school and law practice. It seemed many law students were there just to get a high-paying job and weren't concerned about legal principle or ethical practice, but those were the main reasons Jake had chosen the legal profession. In practice, he found many attorneys shallow, self-interested, and generally unpleasant. He had a few lawyer friends like Irwin, but he preferred his Army Reserve buddies.

· · ·

As Jake drove westward, he pondered several initial questions about the XV-11. What were the design engineering flaws that produced the operational problems? Who knew about these problems—industry, military, and legislators, or all three—and didn't fix them? How far up did this go in the government and in the companies that stood to profit? Jake figured the mystery man who gave him the documents knew at least some of this, but he had no idea how to get in touch with him. He didn't even know his name.

"Well, since he gave me a NAVAIR folder I guess he's Navy, so why not call him John Paul Jones?" Jake said out loud, remembering the famous Revolutionary War naval captain.

Then there was the fact that Madison had referred this client to him—he didn't want the decision over whether to take the Thorpe case to be another source of friction between them. Worse, what if he took it and lost? She would be supportive as usual, but he wasn't concerned about how the loss would affect her. For their relationship, he was more concerned about what it would do to him.

. . .

Near Sparta, North Carolina
Tuesday, August 4, 2009
5:45 p.m.

Jake was only about ten miles south of the mountain motel when his cell phone rang. "Meet me at the gas station eight miles south of your current location. I'll be there at 1800." It was that same gravelly voice, and this wasn't a request.

"OK," Jake responded, and the phone went dead. Jake was amazed that this guy knew where he was headed, but sickened when he realized that if the mystery man could track him, so could the men who were chasing him.

A few minutes later, Jake saw the country store and gas station "Jones" had identified. Jake pulled off the road and to the side of the building and got out to stretch his legs. Right at six p.m., he saw an SUV coming up the road, slowing down. As it drew closer, he could make out Jones's profile.

Mr. Jones approached Jake's car. "I think I have a good idea why you chose this place, but I don't know if it's a good idea for you to be here," he said, then leaned closer and whispered, "If I know about those people, then the bad guys could figure it out, too. Your presence could put the Johnsons in danger."

"I understand," Jake said. "Wait—they don't know about me yet, do they?"

"Probably not yet, Colonel. Anyway, we need a safer way to communicate. Here's a secure phone," he said handing Jake a regular-looking cell phone. "I was going to give this to you in Raleigh, but they got too close, too quick. So I had to track you down. Anyway, your phone number is 222-410-4877, mine is 222-410-4875. Remember both numbers. Don't write them down. These phones are secure only to each other. You can't call anyone else and be secure. If you do, they'll find you—got that?"

"Yes," Jake said as he committed the numbers to memory. "Look, I need to know who you are and why you are doing this."

Jones ignored the questions.

"For now, just study the material I gave you," he replied.

"I'll read it and get back to you, then we'll talk about what comes next," Jake replied, keeping his doubts about going forward to himself. "But I need to get some things straight between you and me—including how you know where I am."

"Fair enough. We'll do that once you have studied the materials. Let me know when you're done." Mr. Jones said, starting back to his vehicle. "I installed a tracking device on the rear end of your car's passenger door in Raleigh. Now, I've got to get out of here—and away from you."

"Wait!" Jake exclaimed, moving toward the SUV. "I need another phone."

Jones wheeled toward Jake, a scornful look on his face. "Why?" he demanded.

"My secretary. She'll need a phone." He didn't add, *If I continue with this.*

"I would ask why you let her get involved, but I don't have time to listen," he said as he headed back to his SUV. "Here!" He tossed another phone to Jake. "The number will be one number higher than yours." Once again he drew closer. "When you speak to Florence about using this phone, Colonel, remind her to be careful. I don't want her hide on my conscience."

"Look," Jake began, surprised Jones knew her name. "There is no way to keep her out—and I might need her."

"Your call, Colonel, but be smart—for everyone's sake. People are counting on you," he said as he closed the door of his SUV.

What people—Lisa Thorpe? There were so many other things Jake wanted to know, but Jones was gone before he could ask.

• • •

Shortly, the motel came into view. It looked safe—inconspicuous, set back off the road, and with multiple exit routes.

He pulled to the front, parked, and entered the office, passing underneath the neon "Vacancy" sign. The door hinges creaked, stirring the man behind the desk, who stood up to greet Jake.

"Hey, how ya doin', mister?"

"Just fine," Jake said. "Need a room for one night. Something around back, away from the road."

The man laughed. "I could give you a cot beside the road and you would be fine, 'cause we ain't got much traffic here at night. Not much in the day-time, either. Just the early mornin's."

The man pulled a key off a hook on the board behind him. It was classic: a plastic diamond-shaped fob with a big number 12 and the hotel's address and seal that said "Guaranteed Postage Anywhere." *Haven't seen one of these in years,* Jake thought.

"Fifty dollars, please. Cash if ya got it," the man said. Jake gave the man two twenties and a ten and headed for the door.

"I'm Eddie, by the way," the man said as Jake left the lobby. "Be here till midnight, too, if you need anythin'."

Around back, Jake saw room 12 was in the middle—not too conspicuous. He grabbed his bag, the briefcase with his laptop, and stuffed his pistol into the canvas bag containing the documents. *I'm sure this high-tech establishment will have high-speed internet,* he thought sarcastically.

The room had the latest 1960s decor—pea-green walls, gold bedspreads and green-and-yellow shag carpet—and came with a heavy musty odor. He cracked the sliding picture window, pulled the curtains closed, and turned the air conditioning on high. Maybe it would help.

He needed to shower after his long day. He found a tiny bar of soap, threadbare towels, and plenty of hot water. He stayed in longer than usual, the hot water relaxing his tense body. He attempted to dry off with the paper-thin towel and got into fresh clothes.

Settling down at the small table in his room, he lifted up the satchel and pulled out the documents. It was as he'd feared from his initial review: the XV-11 was a nightmare with one major problem after another. Difficult to maintain, aerodynamically unstable, poor shipboard performance, powerful concentrated downwash, failure of lightweight composite aircraft parts in combat maneuvering, and twenty common hydraulic lines—so a bullet in one could cause simultaneous failure of several different hydraulic systems.

Then he found the two most damning reports. First was the study that showed that the XV-11 could not autorotate, a life-saving maneuver in any rotary-wing aircraft. The procedure had saved his life one afternoon in Afghanistan, when an enemy gunner fired rounds that went through one engine, which disintegrated and threw its guts into the remaining good engine, destroying it. Flying low with no power and with barely enough time to initiate emergency procedures, he slammed the collective down to enter into autorotation, which enabled the rotors to continue to turn by windmilling as the aircraft descended through the air. This procedure conserved precious rotor rpm, which he then used to decelerate his forward speed and cushion his descent in order to land safely, saving his life and those of his passengers. After three days of evasion, he led everyone to a pick-up point where all were extracted—their lives saved by autorotation.

Now in front of him was written acknowledgement by someone named Oliver that the XV-11 could not autorotate in the helicopter mode. In fact, the XV-11 hadn't even been subjected to a test involving a sudden loss of engine power. In the one low-power test that was done, engine power was slowly reduced so that the crew was able to enter into a stable autorotation. But even in benign flight configuration, the aircraft descended at the rate of 4000 feet per minute—a fatal velocity when the aircraft met the ground.

Instead of properly classifying the autorotation problem as critical, the document said that the lack of autorotative capability was a minor issue since "autorotation is not necessary due to low probability of a dual engine failure." *The bastards,* Jake thought as he read the bullshit being handed to NAVAIR. *I can give these idiots a dozen causes of dual engine failure: contaminated fuel, ballistic damage from bad guys shooting at the aircraft, and fuel exhaustion, just to name three.*

The Naval Air Systems Command personnel—led by Marine Lieutenant Colonel Raymond Beech—had accepted the nonsense without criticism. In fact, Beech even authored a briefing memo that explained how the absence of autorotative capability was "not a major shortcoming." Jake saw no evidence that NAVAIR, which was responsible for conceiving, planning, developing, testing, and procuring all Navy and Marine aircraft, had raised a single question or challenge. *This Marine Corps officer is shafting the Marine crews and troops that will be on this aircraft,* Jake thought. *Why? For what? Did these guys have no oversight?*

Jake reached for his bag and retrieved the next folder, labeled *VRS.*

Vortex Ring State had been explained to him in test pilot school as a flight condition that causes fluctuations in the rotor system without any input from the cockpit flight controls. It occurs primarily at slow speed and in descending flight conditions when the airflow is interrupted by combat maneuvering or turbulence. The document said, "This problem is especially pronounced in shipboard operations where the wind conditions are constantly changing, especially when the ship is underway."

Holy shit! This aircraft will not only be highly dangerous in combat, but also on ships!

In conventional helicopters, the recommended corrective action for such rotor excursions was to reduce the severity of the maneuver and simply fly out of it. But similar action would not be so easy in the XV-11: the side-to-side location of the rotors could cause rolling movements that would quickly overwhelm the pilot's control. In the XV-11, asymmetric VRS could well cause a corresponding "death roll."

Then there was this statement in another shocking memo from Beech: "Entry into Vortex Ring State is precluded by an onboard warning system." *Maybe so, if you're not flying around dodging surface-to-air missiles, ground-fire missiles, and enemy aircraft while trying to find your LZ and complete your mission— maybe that would work,* Jake thought. But Jake knew that in combat situations, pilots wouldn't be paying attention to any stupid light telling them they were exceeding the capabilities of the aircraft. They would be too busy "yankin' and bankin'" and trying to save their hides.

There was no way this thing would work as a combat aircraft with all these problems. Someone had to stop this program. Maybe there was something Jake could do. Maybe.

7

Jake leaned back in his chair and rubbed his face with his hands. He pulled out a legal pad and began to draft a summary of what he'd read to get a clearer picture of what it all meant. His efforts were interrupted by the ringing of his secure phone.

"Hello."

"I'm just outside your location. I'll knock in twenty seconds," the gravelly voice said.

Jake heard light taps on the door. Mr. Jones's six-foot frame stood in the door, cleaned up from the last time Jake saw him. In a short-sleeved knit shirt this fellow looked fit, no excess weight, and carried himself like a soldier. *Hard and tough.*

"Aren't you going to invite me in, Colonel?" he asked.

"Sure. Sorry," Jake said, as he motioned him into the room, quickly closing the door behind him. "It's just that I . . ."

"Didn't expect to see me . . . I know. You're going to have to learn that old saw about expecting the unexpected," Jones said, moving to a chair and removing his baseball hat, revealing a full head of salt-and-pepper hair, closely cut. "Have you read the material?"

"Yes, just about finished."

"Did you ever think you would see your uniformed cohorts sell their souls so completely? Not to mention the contractors with those TV ads about how much they love the soldiers? Pisses you off, doesn't it, Colonel?"

"That's an understatement," Jake said. "I would like to meet up with Lieutenant Colonel Beech and his friends in a dark alley . . . and that Oliver asshole too. But speaking of those guys, I still don't even know who *you* are—and why you're doing this. How did you get these documents out of the Pentagon, anyway? Let's start with those questions."

"Let's just say I'm a friend to the troops and an enemy of shitty weapons programs. Who I am isn't important—what we need to do is important. Right now you don't need the details of how I got the documents."

"That's not good enough. But I'll ask another question: how did you know about Lisa Thorpe's visit to my office?" Jake waited for the answer.

Jones sat down, throwing his hat on the bed. "OK. I am a retired naval officer who spent a lot of time at and around NAVAIR. I am in this because I know about the history of this aircraft—not all the details, but enough to know the thing should have been scrapped and the whole process started over. And as for Lisa, I know her husband's father and I encouraged Sam to go to flight school. I have been after Lisa to talk to an attorney since this thing went down. When she told me she was going to see you, I checked you out. She was very impressed with you—so was I."

"OK. I'll take that for now." Jake decided not to pursue how the documents got out of the Pentagon.

"Now, what are you going to do with this info?" he asked.

"I am working on it, but I gotta tell you, a lawsuit may not be doable even with all of this damaging information. This file shows the aircraft's flaws, but it also shows the government knew and approved it anyway, which would be fatal in a suit against a contractor because approval by the government of a contractor's plans—even when flawed—means that the contractor could share the government's immunity. Then there's the issue of using classified information without winding up in jail," Jake said.

"Look, Colonel, we took lots of risks to gather that information. The goal here is to help Lisa Thorpe, but ultimately to prevent more deaths. You can't say no. We have to get this into the public arena, and soon."

"Yes, I *can* say no," Jake said, rationally. "It's my ass and my practice, and I'm not going to waste either on a lawsuit that is doomed to fail. Plus, if you wanted it made public, you could have just gone to the press."

"No way. The press isn't smart enough to know what to do with it, and if they did, it would be just written off as another instance of the liberal media trying to kill a weapons program. But Lisa gives it context, and you give it a credible mouthpiece."

"And a bull's-eye," Jake pointed out. But Jones had some valid points. "Well, at least now it kind of makes sense."

Jones kept pressing. "Just figure out how to play your end of it and I'll play mine. We can't waste any time—lives are at stake. I'll keep the bad guys off of you until you get it done." He walked to the door. "I gotta head out. I don't want the people chasing me to get too close—especially not with you here. Rise to the challenge, Colonel."

"I'll do my best—no promises. Right now I need someone who really knows about this stuff, a subject matter expert that I could call to testify. Do you know of anyone like that?"

"There is one guy who could take you to school on this. I got to know him when I was at NAVAIR. I've stayed in touch with him ever since he left the program. But I've tried to keep him out of this."

"Who is he?"

"His name . . . well, his new name is Sommer Collins. He used to be Dr. Stanislas Kolinsky. The people where he's located think he's a retired school-teacher who does some moonlighting at Virginia Tech teaching basic algebra. That's just his cover—he could teach quantum physics to quantum physics professors. But he was the original creator of what should have been the XV-11. He's a certifiable genius. He worked on both the tilt-wing and the tilt-rotor, and decided the tilt-wing was better. His version of a tilt aircraft would have worked. But they said it was too expensive, plus he refused to decentralize manufacture. Too hard to monitor quality. He didn't want to see his program so badly mishandled, so one day he just didn't come into work."

Jake frowned. "Just didn't show up? No explanation, no story?"

"Nothing. They freaked. They tried to find him, but couldn't." He paused. "It is not every day the chief rotorcraft design engineer at the Department of Defense doesn't show up for work. But he took his life savings and disappeared."

"How did they explain his disappearance?"

"They said he lost his mind after his wife's sudden death—also a lie—and that he went hiking and fell off a cliff. They even produced a body and gave it a funeral. With no children and all his siblings dead, it was easy for them to pull off."

"Fell off a cliff? Really?" Jake responded.

"Believe it or not. But the ones who know the real story are still looking for him—and not so they can offer him his old job back. Now that the XV-11's faults are in danger of being made public, they've ramped up their efforts to find him. They want to make sure he doesn't show up in a big I-told-you-so news conference."

"How has he evaded them?"

"He's smarter than they are. Plus he had a little surgery to change his appearance."

"OK, where is he?"

"He lives a quiet life on a lake in Virginia, near Blacksburg. Here is his address," Jones said, jotting down Collins's info on a piece of paper. "No one knows where he is but me, and now you. I'll need to coordinate this. I'll give you the green light once I talk to him. But don't delay. Get up there tomorrow if I can work it out. I can only talk to him via regular phone. It's risky, but probably necessary."

"If they're tracking you here, maybe I should leave too."

Jones turned. "No need. You don't want to raise suspicion by checking out early. That guy up front looks like he'd spill his guts for a shiny new quarter."

"Ha, you're probably right about that," Jake acknowledged. Guys who work the night shift at a barren roadside motel probably don't rake in the big bucks.

"We know that they know about me, but the longer they don't know about you, the better our chances for success." A cold tremor shot down Jake's back. What the man was really saying was that they would know about Jake sooner or later.

After Jones left, Jake got back to work. He thought about what Collins had given up. To those who had it, principle was a powerful, but sometimes costly, behavioral force. Yet Kolinsky's sacrifices hadn't stopped the program or saved a life. So far, it was all for nothing. Then it hit Jake: *This could turn out the same for me too. Everything I've worked for, down the tubes for nothing.*

Jake got to a point where he had trouble keeping his eyes open. He closed the files and put them back into his briefcase. He crawled over to the bed and set the alarm on his phone. After unchambering a round, reinserting the magazine, and safetying the weapon, he put it on the pillow beside him and turned out the light.

. . .

As Jones drove away in the mountain darkness, he picked up his secure phone and dialed his contact at Quantico, retired Sergeant Major Ron Hadley.

"Yes?" the voice answered.

"Just left our boy. He's headed up north to see the doctor tomorrow."

"Is he on board?"

"I think he's close. I am hoping the visit tomorrow convinces him. If not, I'll have to find another way to do it. "

"We don't have much time. We gotta make our move."

"Understood. I'll keep you posted."

"Roger. Out."

8

"Attention!" the Marine at the door shouted. The NAVAIR commander, Admiral Wilson Lawrence, strode briskly into the briefing room at the Marine Corps' area of the Pentagon. The room was filled with Marine Corps officers and enlisted men in their tan shirts and olive drab slacks, adorned with ribbons and badges that, to the initiated, revealed the bearer's military career. Four naval officers were also in attendance, wearing their summer whites.

Admiral Lawrence, six foot four, well built and ramrod straight, was resplendent in his white dress uniform with shoulder boards. He had collected many ribbons and medals over the years, but he was beyond the point of needing to wear any of them on his chest. Instead, the only badge he wore was his Naval Aviator Wings.

"As you were," he commanded in his baritone voice, followed by a Marine barking: "Take your seats."

"Good morning," he said. The Marine Corps seal adorned the podium. Even though the XV-11 program was ultimately the responsibility of the NAVAIR, the Navy had kept all nonessential personnel out of the meeting. The XV-11 was the Marines' aircraft, and this briefing was their show.

"Thank you for all of your hard work on this vital program and for letting this old salt enter Marine Corps territory." He smiled as the audience laughed, then paused and looked at the entire audience—seemingly at each person individually. "I have to travel up to the Hill next week to provide testimony on the XV-11 to the Senate Armed Services Committee. I go directly from here around the corner to brief Secretary of the Navy Parris. So this briefing is very important. Colonel Hartman, you may proceed."

"Thank you, Admiral," Colonel Hartman said as he rose to his feet, then slowly moved toward the podium. Colonel Charles Hartman, the XV-11 program manager, was a distinguished Marine war veteran. A stocky, tough man, he had been cited for bravery at the end of the Vietnam War when the unit he commanded as a new second lieutenant fought off an overwhelming force of North Vietnamese regulars. His refusal to lose, which he had instilled in his Marines, saved the day and produced a victory, but nearly cost him his life. He spent six months at Bethesda Naval Hospital recovering from his wounds. Those injuries still plagued him, and he'd never fully recovered from a round that had pierced his throat. To this day he spoke with a raspy voice. A bad heart didn't help matters.

Hartman took a moment to gain his breath as he gripped the podium. Speaking in a soft, scratchy voice, he said, "As you know, sir, I have been spending more time back at Bethesda Naval Hospital recently than I would like. In my absence, Assistant Program Manager Lieutenant Colonel Beech has prepared the briefing this morning, and with your permission, sir, he'll begin."

"That's fine," the admiral responded.

"Thank you, sir. Lieutenant Colonel Beech, you may begin," Hartman said.

"Yes, sir," Beech replied, approaching the podium while Colonel Hartman returned slowly to his seat. Beech was wearing Marine khakis, with all of his ribbons, his blond hair slicked down. At thirty-four, Beech had no combat experience, aviation or otherwise, and had worked his way up through the acquisition side of things, in large part due to his aeronautical engineering and management degrees earned courtesy of the United States government. He viewed the XV-11 program as his ticket to promotion. Rumors were that he was on his way up, and no one wanted to get in his way.

Beech tried to use his considerable smarts and aeronautical expertise to persuade Colonel Hartman of his viewpoints on how various aspects of the program should be handled. But Hartman viewed Beech with skepticism. The only thing the two men shared was a desire to see the XV-11 program succeed, but for different reasons: one wanted it for the Marines, the other for his career.

Once at the podium, Beech said, "Admiral Lawrence, it's an honor to brief you on this essential program for Marine Corps aviation and for our nation's defense." He sounded like a pitchman from one of those late-night TV infomercials. "The program is in excellent shape. We are presently—"

"If the program is in such good shape, Lieutenant Colonel Beech," the admiral interrupted, "why are our civilian friends on the Hill so eager to get me up there so they can chew on me for a while?" Some nervous laughter rippled through parts of the room. Lawrence was a quick study who hated kiss-asses. He wanted the facts and knew how to get them.

"Sir, they are misinformed. They and their allies in the media are overstating a couple of the most recent setbacks. They have agendas, sir. For instance—"

"Two points, Lieutenant Colonel Beech, if I may," the admiral interrupted again. "Some of those 'critics' on the Hill are fine patriotic men, many of whom were soldiers, sailors, and Marines. Perhaps their *agenda* is to ensure that our Marines are safe, not only from enemy fire, but also from underperforming equipment."

"Understood, sir," Beech replied.

"Second, I have my own concerns. I don't consider any program that loses two of its finest test pilots in an operational test flight to be in great shape. Now, as long as we understand each other, you may proceed," the admiral replied, glaring at Lieutenant Colonel Beech.

"Thank you, sir." Beech cleared his throat and his face began turning pink. "Although somewhat delayed by the unfortunate mishap—"

"If by 'mishap' you mean the crash that killed Major Thorpe and Captain Hudson," Admiral Lawrence fired at Beech through clenched teeth, "that was a *tragedy*, Lieutenant Colonel Beech, not a mishap."

"Yes, sir. I was just using the official Safety Board term, sir." He didn't lose any time getting back on message. "Since that time, we have made great progress and are within a few months of being back on schedule. Further, the future—"

"Have the aerodynamic problems with VRS been fixed?" the admiral demanded.

"Excuse me, sir?" Beech responded. He had heard the admiral, but was jolted by the directness of his question and surprised by his specific knowledge.

"Have the aerodynamic problems been fixed, Lieutenant Colonel Beech?" the admiral repeated.

"Sir, that matter has received the highest priority, and I can—"

"Lieutenant Colonel Beech, please do an old sailor a favor and give him a simple answer that he can understand. Have the aerodynamic problems been fixed—yes or no?"

"Yes, sir," Lieutenant Colonel Beech responded, raising more than a couple of eyebrows, especially those of Colonel Hartman. Hartman had not heard this before today.

"Good. Thank you. Then I'll let the secretary and Congress know," Admiral Lawrence responded, his words telling Beech that this response was seared into his memory. "Please continue."

Beech went on, but many had stopped paying attention. Most had heard rumors about the aircraft's aerodynamic problems and were surprised to hear that they had been resolved. There had been stories of theoretical fixes, but no actual modifications to the aircraft or its flight envelope had been made.

Finally, after seemingly endless fluff-filled minutes, the briefing ended. "Thank you, Lieutenant Colonel Beech," Admiral Lawrence said, standing. He left with his small contingent. As a courtesy, Colonel Hartman followed him out.

When they were several feet down the hall and around the corner, Admiral Lawrence stopped, turned, and waited for Colonel Hartman to catch up. When Hartman got close, Lawrence spoke to Colonel Hartman so only he could hear.

"Charlie, that guy is a great pitch man, and that is what concerns me. I know if your health had allowed you to do it you would have been fully informed about the program. But now I have to ask you to get me some good, candid intel before I go up to the Hill. Dig deep and find out what's really going on. Can you do that for me?"

"Sure, Admiral. Let me see what I can find out."

"Thanks, Charlie. I appreciate it. I can be candid with Secretary Parris about my concerns, but I can't go up on the Hill without the facts, good or bad. Plus, people on the operational side of the Corps have floated a plan for squadron deployment and I have to have accurate information about the aircraft ASAP to weigh in on the viability of deployment." Placing his arm around Hartman's shoulder, Lawrence said, "Most importantly, Charlie, take care of your health. If you need some time, take it. The Corps needs you, the country needs you, and I need you, but only if you're well. That comes first."

"Thank you for your kind words, Admiral," Hartman responded, his soft voice cracking. "I'll make sure my health doesn't get in the way."

With that, the two shook hands and went their separate ways.

Lieutenant Colonel Beech was still in the briefing room, engaging in small talk as his enlisted men cleaned up. As soon as he could, Beech quietly said to his assistant, Sergeant MacRitchie, "Get Alex Oliver on the phone and tell him it's time for an updated briefing. Tell him I need for him to meet me at our usual Georgetown place at 1900 hours this evening."

"Yes, sir," Sergeant MacRitchie responded.

Moments later, Beech was almost at his office when Sergeant Mac-Ritchie approached him. "Sir, I talked to Mr. Oliver. He'll see you there at 1900 hrs."

"Great. Thanks, Sergeant. As you know, much about this program is classified. So remember to tell no one anything about what you see or hear. Is that understood, Sergeant?" Beech demanded.

"Roger, sir. I understand," replied MacRitchie.

. . .

Back in his office at NAVAIR, Colonel Hartman already knew whom he would tap for information. He called to his secretary, "Marjorie, see if you can find our friend Sergeant Major Hadley down at Quantico. Tell him his old commander needs to have dinner with him tonight. See if you can persuade him."

"I don't think it will take much persuasion, Colonel," Marjorie responded. "Official or unofficial?"

"With old friends it's always unofficial. Just tell him I'll want to have some of that good seafood at the Marlin in Occoquan. Say eight p.m. Traffic should be gone by then," he said.

A few minutes later, Marjorie called on the intercom, "You're good for eight, Colonel. I made the reservations. He's on line one."

"Thanks, Marjorie. Reservations at the Marlin? What's this world coming to? And please will you call Betty and tell her I won't be home for dinner?" Colonel Hartman asked.

"That's a suicide mission, Colonel, but I'll do it because you asked so nicely," she said.

"Ah, if you weren't a civilian I'd have you decorated."

Hartman picked up the phone. "Sergeant Major, you there?"

"Yes, sir! Standing at attention!" Hadley responded.

"Looking forward to dinner and glad you can make it on short notice. Listen, this will be just you and me—no spouses tonight, OK?"

"Certainly, sir. You doin' OK? You sound a bit tired," Hadley said.

"I'm fine. Just having a bad day is all."

"Anything in particular you wish to talk about?"

"Let's just say we need to talk about fish-eating birds that haven't hatched. See you at eight."

"Yes, sir," he responded.

Hartman and Hadley had entered the Marine flight program at the same time and served together on numerous flight and ground assignments, including Vietnam. Hadley was now a high ranking civilian in the Marine Corps Aviation Directorate at Marine Corps Air Station Quantico, and Hartman knew that in thirty years in Marine Corps aviation, Hadley had developed lots of contacts and knew how to use them.

As Hartman turned back to his desk, he felt the pain come back in his chest. He opened his desk drawer quickly to remove a medicine bottle, and swallowed a nitroglycerin tablet. He wouldn't let it hold him back. Not, at least, until he got the Sea Eagle back on track.

"Colonel," Marjorie said from his office door. "Mrs. Hartman would like a word with you. She's on two."

"Uh-oh—guess you didn't get it done."

"I just told her you were going carousing with Hadley—that was all it took," Marjorie joked.

"I might have to pull your clearance. You aren't handling government secrets too well." He turned to pick up the phone.

"Hi, honey. What can I do for you?"

"Charles, you just be sure to take it easy. You know what the doctor said."

"Don't worry, honey. I remember and I'll be careful. It's just dinner with an old friend."

"No business?"

"Well, maybe a little. I should be home by ten thirty."

"OK. Be safe. I love you."

"Me too, honey. I love you, too."

Hartman wasn't going out with a bad program on his record. He would make sure this thing was right—or die trying.

9

The Georgetown bar was full of young and wannabe-young private sector and government executives, all smiling, talking, and trying to impress. Alex Oliver, a forty-five-year-old veteran bureaucrat who was the civilian assistant program manager in the Department of the Navy's Aircraft Acquisitions Office, sat in a corner booth by himself. He was still in his suit and tie, eyeing the door so he could spot Lieutenant Colonel Beech when he came through the door. Oliver was older than the majority of the crowd, and his dated suit and thinning black hair made him stand out even more.

Finally, Oliver saw Beech enter the bar and waved to get his attention. *He looks so out of place in his white-sidewall haircut,* Oliver thought.

Eventually, Beech maneuvered through the crowd to the booth where Oliver was sitting.

"Good to see you, Lieutenant Colonel Beech," Oliver said as Beech sat down. "Got us a couple of Buds coming."

"Good to see you, too. Thanks for coming," Beech responded.

"OK. You go first. What's the big deal?" Oliver asked.

"Admiral Lawrence is what. He was very curious at today's briefing about the XV-11. It was like someone tipped him off. But I assured him that the VRS problems with the aircraft had been fixed."

"That wasn't very bright, Lieutenant Colonel Beech. You should know as well as I do that that thing is still screwed up. Couldn't you have finessed it a bit?" Oliver asked.

"Finesse Lawrence? Are you nuts? Tell you what—I'll let you try it next time." He looked around the room, and then, almost in a whisper, said, "Frankly, I didn't think he would challenge me so much today, or we would have had this conversation before the briefing. We have to come up with a plan to allay Lawrence's concerns. He's going on the Hill next week to testify about the XV-11. I need your help in getting a follow-up to him that sounds like either I had mistaken info or that we are, in fact, making progress. So, what can you tell me?"

Oliver started to answer, but was interrupted by a cute brunette waitress arriving with two beers. Her short black skirt distracted them momentarily from the stark reality of their discussion.

Oliver returned to the topic. "My engineers have gone into turtle mode. They aren't talking much about anything—even to me. I have some real friggin' concerns that maybe the damn thing isn't fixable. We'll have to learn to live with a less-than-perfect machine."

"Christ, don't even think that, let alone say it. If we don't produce what we've promised, we'll all be toast."

"Look Beech, I have been at this aircraft design game longer than you, and since the beginning of this project, I've had serious concerns about this thing working out as a tactical combat aircraft." Oliver took a deep breath and slowly exhaled. "I have worked my ass off to keep this program going, but the basic design is screwed up. Has been from the beginning. Their little tilt-rotor demonstrator couldn't be transformed into a do-everything combat vehicle. We all know the Marines kept loading it up and the Apex and Vertical people kept trying to adjust, but it just got worse and worse. The engineers gave up trying to fix something that wasn't friggin' fixable, but the higher-ups kept saying what 'great progress' we were making. I tried to raise the issues at first, but no one wanted to listen. So, in order to keep my job, I went along with what the big boys were putting out, just as you and our friend Mr. Webb at Apex did." Gritting his teeth, he said, "I have been covering shit up since day one. If they didn't care, why should I?"

"OK, OK . . . sorry, man," Beech said, realizing he had struck a nerve.

"No, it isn't OK," Oliver fired back. "You'll get reassigned to the fleet somewhere or moved along to another job in the Corps. Mr. Webb will find some other position at Apex or elsewhere, but with major weapons programs being shitcanned daily by the friggin' liberals, I'll be lucky to have a job—if I'm not indicted."

"Whoa there! What is this 'indicted' stuff?" Beech asked. "I know this is getting hairy, but what the hell are you talking about?"

"There's this other problem," Oliver said, lowering his volume. "Lawrence is the least of our worries."

Beech looked confused. "What other problem? What's worse than the situation with Lawrence?"

"You said it's like someone tipped him off? Well, I think I know how that might have occurred."

"OK, how?" Beech asked.

"There's been a security breach." Oliver opened the discussion with the passive institutional language that he had learned in the past six years. It was impersonal—and protected him from the bureaucratically fatal *I* word.

Beech shifted in his seat. *Security* and *breach* were two words that should never be used in the same sentence.

Oliver leaned across the table and whispered the bad news. "My get-out-of-jail file is missing. I'm sure you know the one I'm talking about. It had everything that showed how the program developed, what went right, what went wrong, and what we did to move the program along."

"How did this happen?" Beech demanded, raising his voice. "How could you be so careless?" People at nearby tables turned to stare at Beech as his outburst briefly drowned out the bar noise. Realizing this, he sought to control his volume. "You told me that information would be safe there."

"It should have been safe there," Oliver protested. "It was never out of my possession. It was either in my hands or in my locked desk drawer at all times. Besides, you know stuff like that can't be removed from the Pentagon, especially with *TOP SECRET* written all over it."

Beech leaned over the table. "OK, let's say you're right, but who even knew the file existed, except you and me?"

"I don't know," Oliver said. "The list of people who have access to my office is extremely small and none of them have a key to my desk."

Beech took time to reflect. His fury with Oliver had shut down his normal ability to think quickly. "I told you that keeping the file was risky. You and your cover-your-ass mentality. The chance you would ever need it to save yourself was really remote. Neither your ass nor mine is covered if this gets out. Heads will roll everywhere."

"Look, we both knew what was coming back from the flight test people could kill the program and our jobs with it," Oliver shot back. "I was making a record to keep all of us protected. We—you, me, and Webb—all agreed to modify the data so the program could continue. All we did was tell them what they wanted to hear. Besides, they always fix the problems eventually— we were just buying some time. The really bad stuff was either massaged or removed. Managers see to that. In this case, me," he explained.

Beech just stared at Oliver.

"I know, you thought you and Hartman run the program. You don't. The managers do. We're below the big execs and above the engineers. We push things through. We have continuity; you military guys come and go. We know how to get the money and how to work the system. And we know where all the congressional skeletons are buried. Without us, you'd still be flying biplanes."

"Well," sighed Beech, "I guess we're in damage-control mode now. You have to get the file back or find who took it before all hell breaks loose."

"Already in the works. I've got friends retired from the NSA who owe me some favors and they've hired some folks to help them," Oliver said. "It isn't cheap, and I've had to move some funding around to cover the costs. They've found a way to use some NSA resources and equipment without anybody asking questions. They've bought my story that it's 'highly classified' and agreed to keep a lid on their work. The good news is they already have a lead."

"Really, who?"

"Stanford Kemp."

"*Captain* Stanford Kemp?" Beech had heard the legendary stories about Kemp once he started working at NAVAIR. From what he knew, Kemp was highly respected. "Why him?"

"Before I was promoted to this job, I was at NAVAIR. Retired Captain Stanford Kemp was there functioning in a special ombudsman-type position. I say retired, but they actually somehow unretired him to bring him back in to straighten out some big-time procurement screw-ups." Oliver paused to take another sip from his beer, finally undoing his tie and wiping his mouth with his hand. "The stories about his integrity and honor are legendary. He is a real, no-shit, gold-plated Navy legend."

"Kemp doesn't sound like someone who's going to steal classified documents. Why do they think it's him?"

"First, he goes after programs or policies that he thinks won't help the Navy, and he doesn't lose." Oliver said. "Second, my people started shadowing him and they have seen him with what they think is the missing file but haven't gotten close enough to confirm it. We also picked up some intel from friends we have at Quantico who've identified his contact there, a retired Marine Sergeant Major."

"But Kemp hasn't been around this program—and I don't know of any retired Sergeant Majors from Quantico being involved."

"You know the XV-11 has its enemies, and some of those enemies must know Kemp," Oliver replied. "Kemp has relationships that he could call upon to learn what they know, or to do some inside work for him—like the guy at Quantico. But he's gotten older and a bit careless, and that's how we spotted him with the file."

"How long before your friends get him?" Webb responded.

"Not that easy, I'm afraid," Oliver cautioned.

"What do you mean?" Beech asked, eyebrows raised. "Even if he is a legend, he's an old legend, and they're ex-NSA! What's the problem?"

"Kemp has extensive experience in black ops. He was a naval liaison with the boys at Langley," Oliver responded. "He helped write the SEALs' SOP and worked on the NSA's clandestine operations procedures—the very book they're using to try to catch him. Nobody on this whole friggin' earth knows better how to play the game."

Beech leaned back. "Assuming Kemp took it, you can bet he shared it with someone, maybe made copies."

"Maybe, maybe not. Let's just say that what I am working on will fix the entire problem. Meanwhile, be very cautious how you present information on this project in case someone already knows what's in that file," Oliver warned. "Word is that people are asking questions, like your Colonel Hartman."

"Hartman? That sick old man has no idea what is going on," Beech scoffed. "What makes you think Hartman knows something?" Beech asked.

"You don't want to know. Just know that I'm working on it from my end, but you better take care of things on your side."

"Kemp needs to be stopped before he executes whatever his plan is," Beech warned.

"Obviously," Oliver responded.

"What can I do?"

"Cover yourself."

"I don't know how I can cover myself except to go back and destroy everything with my name on it, but that doesn't seem smart. Besides, the people above me would notice," Beech said.

"Maybe, maybe not. But you know the big boys and girls never get hit," Oliver said. "Look, you are in this just as friggin' deep as me. Nobody will believe you didn't know. You will be sacrificed. Trust me," Oliver advised.

Beech shook his head. "Maybe we'll dodge a bullet."

"Maybe," Oliver said. "OK. Let's head out. I'll keep you posted."

"Thanks for totally fucking up my day."

Beech found his car and sat down in the driver's seat, sweating. His once bright future was now in serious peril. Eventually, he started the car and headed toward the parking garage exit. Suddenly nauseous, he slammed on the brakes and opened the car door. The beers came gushing out. He collapsed back against the driver's seat. "Jesus!" He shut the door and drove off.

. . .

After leaving the bar, Oliver positioned himself in a corner, removed his secure phone from his pocket and placed a call to his contact, ex-NSA agent Donald Chaney. "Where are we?" he asked.

"We're ready," replied Chaney, who was now in Virginia after chasing Kemp around the North Carolina mountains. "My people are in position and should have phase one taken care of tonight. Just need your OK."

"You got it. Call me after it's done," Oliver said.

"That'll work. Anything else?"

"Yeah. We gotta step everything up. Folks are getting nervous, and that isn't good. We might need to move quickly on phase two."

"Understood," Chaney said.

Oliver closed his phone, straightened his tie, and continued toward his office at the Pentagon. *Marine? Beech looked like a scared child. Likes the glory but can't handle the crap. He could crack.* This was another situation that might need to be addressed eventually.

10

Occoquan, Virginia
Wednesday, August 5, 2009
7:55 p.m.

Colonel Hartman pulled off the interstate onto Cove Road and followed its curves toward the village of Occoquan. More condos were going up in what used to be a quiet fishing village on Occoquan Creek. *If they keep this up*, he thought, *there won't be any beauty left anywhere in northern Virginia.*

He arrived at the Marlin, a small, one-story, cinder-block restaurant that stubbornly remained unglamorous, despite the influx of "gourmet" eateries. The parking lot was almost empty, so Hartman easily spotted Sergeant Major Hadley's World War II jeep—or in military nomenclature, "truck, quarter ton." Virtually unchanged from its original issue appearance, Hadley had kept it in pristine condition by unfailingly following the military maintenance manual. The only top he ever considered was the USMC canvas in all its olive drab glory.

Colonel Hartman parked his car next to the jeep, and, noticing the clouds gathering, grabbed his umbrella. Once inside the open dining hall, he saw Hadley waving to him from a corner booth. *The man never changed.* Short crop of black hair on the top of his head, sharp features, and leathered skin from too much time in the sun. He was the poster image of a Marine—even in civvies. Hadley had had a distinguished career, but was forced to retire when a back injury sustained early in the Iraq war put him on disability. He maintained his military bearing in his civilian post in the Marines' Aviation Test Directorate at Quantico.

As Hartman approached the booth, Hadley stood up, Marine Corps erect, and sharply stuck out his hand. "Colonel Hartman, sir, good to see you," he said.

"Same to you, Sergeant Major Hadley," Hartman said, returning the firm handshake. "Please, sit down. Thanks for coming." Sergeant Major Hadley sat down as the Colonel sat.

"You know what I'm having," Hartman said, pushing the menu away.

"Yes, sir. Soft-shells."

"You got it, Sergeant Major. Maryland doesn't have a thing over this place."

At that moment, the waitress appeared with two waters. She was a throwback right out of the 1950s: white uniform, small apron with pockets for pens, pad, napkins, and silverware, her graying hair pulled back into a bun.

"Hi fellas. I'm Rosie. What can I get you?"

"I'll have the soft-shells and some iced tea," the Colonel responded.

"I'll have the flounder, baked, and a Pepsi," Hadley answered.

"Thank you, gentlemen. I'll be right back with your drinks." She took the menus and walked away.

Colonel Hartman chuckled. "You know, there was a time when we would have ordered a pitcher, a couple of shots, and none of this baked stuff."

"Roger that, sir, but age does creep up. I can't get away with anything anymore," Hadley said.

"Our wives used to question us about booze and women. Now it's food and exercise."

Hadley let a slow smile come across his face. "Good thing we're in aviation and not ground-pounders. We couldn't take it." Actually, Hadley probably still could take it, but the Colonel's sluggish movements and softening voice made it clear Hartman couldn't.

"Amen," Colonel Hartman said. He leaned over the table toward Hadley as his expression changed into one of pure business. "Ron, I'll get right to it. I'm concerned about the XV-11, and I need to know what's really going on. I think I'm getting a whitewashed version from Lieutenant Colonel Beech. You're down here at the test directorate and I figure you can call in a few favors and get me the real skinny, if you don't already know. Two pilots are dead and I'm still not sure why. Admiral Lawrence is going to the Hill next week and I want to make sure he's got the right information. And rumor is that the operations side of the house is proposing deployment."

"Yes, sir. Understood." Hadley carefully honed his response. "You should be concerned, sir. The scuttlebutt here at the Test Directorate is that it isn't close to what it should be. The aviators on staff here are hearing bad things from the test pilots at Cherry Point and at Pax River."

"What are they saying, Ron?

"A couple of things, sir. They say it's unreliable. They don't know what will break next. And they're scared to fly it like a combat aircraft because of what happened in April at Pax River."

"You mean VRS?"

"Yes, sir."

"Lieutenant Colonel Beech briefed us that the VRS issue has been fixed."

Hadley shook his head. "Bullshit, sir. He's either misinformed or just plain lying. The only fix even on the table is a proposed change to the flight manual, which tells the pilots not to fly it in a way that will get them into VRS. But in combat, that's not gonna work."

"Right—fly it like a bus and let the enemy kill you, or fly it like a combat aircraft and let it kill you," Hartman said.

"Something like that, sir," Hadley nodded.

"So on VRS, no engineering work has been done—no airframe or rotor system modifications, is that right?"

"Roger that, sir."

"Are any Engineering Change Proposals being discussed?"

"Not that I know of, sir," Hadley said.

"Do you know of anything that documents this situation, Ron?" the colonel asked.

Hadley hesitated. The fact was that he did know. He had gotten a few test results from someone at the Test Directorate who owed him a favor, and by working with Kemp, he knew what was in the file Kemp had given to Jake.

"There might be some flight test reports and field engineering reports,"

Hadley offered, "but they keep that stuff very secure. They don't let it get too far from their hands."

"See what you can do, Ron. I could use that material, or at least enough info to know where I can get it," Hartman said. "When you get what you can, call me, and we'll have dinner again to discuss what you've learned. No emails, nothing over the phone, OK?"

"Roger that, sir."

"Now, to change the subject," Hartman said, leaning back, "I want to know when you're going to get rid of that antique in the parking lot."

"Never, sir," Hadley replied, smiling.

"They're unstable as hell. At least install a roll bar. You know they've made some rather major improvements to auto safety since 1941."

"That's not how it was issued, sir," Hadley said.

"You're a stubborn son of a bitch, Sergeant Major."

"Roger that, sir. That's what my wife tells me," Hadley said, flashing the Colonel a knowing grin.

As they relaxed over dinner, neither noticed the man drinking coffee in a booth on the other side of the restaurant. Skilled at blending in to his surroundings, he sat where he could see the two men in the restaurant and one of his cohorts across the street in the woods. With his left side against the wall, his earpiece wasn't noticeable. It was coupled to the microphone under his coat collar, which was used to radio men across the street, one in the woods and another in a sedan parked on a dirt road nearby.

"OK. Food's here. Go!" Agent Nolan, the man in the booth, whispered into his microphone. Agent Leith, in coveralls, raced from the woods, across the parking lot, and dove under Hadley's jeep. He crawled to the front axle and, from his pocket, removed two wrenches and a pair of needle-nose pliers. He reached into the jeep's steering hardware and loosened the tie rod attaching point on one side of the front end by removing the cotter key and the castellated nut. He then turned to work on the other side, but after he got the cotter key out, he had trouble removing the nut.

After a few minutes, Nolan radioed, "Progress?"

"One side is done but I'm having trouble with the other," Leith responded.

"You got one more minute. Hurry."

The nut wouldn't budge. The space on that side of the front end was especially tight. Leith gave it one more twist and felt it loosen, but he couldn't get a good grip with his wrench. He started another turn and—

"Time!" Nolan whispered.

"I've almost got it—"

"Now!" Nolan ordered, almost speaking too loudly. Leith crawled out from under the jeep, looked around, and dashed back across the street into the woods. The first part of their plan was in place.

After a few moments, Nolan again whispered into his microphone, "All ready?"

"Yeah, he's back," Agent Freid responded from inside the car, as Leith removed his coveralls and jumped into the sedan.

"OK, stand by," Nolan said from the restaurant.

Colonel Hartman and Sergeant Major Hadley finished their meals. "When does the admiral go on the Hill?" Hadley asked.

"In about a week, next Wednesday."

"OK, not much time. I'll get right on it," Hadley said.

"Thanks, Ron. We need to do all we can to make sure this thing is right."

Hadley leaned close to Hartman. "It's going to be OK, sir. Trust me, it's going to be OK," he said.

"I know, Ron, I know you will—"

"No, sir!" Hadley's forceful interruption startled Hartman. Now with Hartman's full, focused attention, Hadley was emphatic. "Trust me, sir, *I know* it's going to be OK. That's all I . . . that's all you need to hear, sir."

It was clear to the colonel that Hadley was delivering a message, and he wanted to ask Hadley how he could be so sure. But Hartman left it alone.

"OK, Ron, message received," Hartman said.

"It's for the Corps, sir. It's got to be handled," Hadley said.

Rosie returned and asked, "Anything else for you gentlemen? More tea? Coffee?"

"No, thanks. We two old men need to get home, right Sergeant Major?"

"That's absolutely correct, sir," Hadley laughed.

"OK, well, here's the check. You can just pay up front on the way out. Thanks for coming in, fellas."

"We'll see you next time," Colonel Hartman responded.

As they approached the front door, Colonel Hartman extended his hand and grabbed Hadley's shoulder. "You're a damn fine Marine, Sergeant Major Hadley, and a fine man."

"Thank you, sir. The feeling is mutual," Hadley said, shaking the Colonel's hand and gripping his forearm.

At the cashier's station, Hadley looked outside and noticed it was starting to rain. "Get your car for you, sir?"

"No, no, but thanks," Hartman said. "I'll be fine."

As they left the restaurant, the two saluted, the rain intensifying as they hurried to their cars.

Hadley watched the colonel's sedan pull away. He then pulled out a secure phone and placed a call. "We're going to have to accelerate. The admiral is going on the Hill in a week."

"Yeah, I know. Looks like I'll have to press my friend to get moving," Kemp said. Then he asked, "Did you say anything to your dinner companion?"

"No. I just gave him assurances. Maybe we can give him some of what he needs and still keep him out of this. This is *our* mission," Hadley insisted. "We'll continue what we started and I'll keep working with my contacts down here."

"We'll get it done."

"Roger. Out," Hadley said, turning off his secure phone and putting it into his briefcase.

. . .

Nolan radioed the men across the street. "Target's in his vehicle. I can't tell what he's doing. The other one has departed the area. Hold tight until I tell you target is on the road."

"Roger," Freid responded.

Sergeant Major Hadley started his vehicle and pulled out of the lot onto the two-lane road, its blacktop now covered with rain.

"Target is on the road. GO!" came the command from Nolan as he walked to his car. The driver in the dark sedan in the woods put the vehicle in gear and sped toward the Cove Road intersection where it slowed down to wait for Hadley. When Hadley's jeep passed, the sedan pulled out onto the road behind him. Leith and Freid didn't say a word to each other—they knew what to do.

"Got him," Freid radioed back to Nolan.

"Roger, I'm headed the other way. Let me know," Nolan said as he exited the restaurant parking lot.

The rain pounded on the windshield of Hadley's jeep as he drove down the winding road. He noticed some headlights in his rearview mirror, but thought nothing of it. The plastic rear window in the jeep's military-issue cover was hard enough to see through in dry weather; in rainy weather it was impossible. He could not tell what type of vehicle was following him, but he could tell that it had closed in and was now on his tail.

"Why don't you pass?" Hadley asked out loud. He considered pulling off, but he was eager to get home. He sped up to get some distance between him and the vehicle behind him, but the vehicle stayed on his tail.

As Hadley's jeep entered a sharp curve, the sedan suddenly slammed into the rear of the jeep, pushing it toward the outside of the curve. "What the hell?" Hadley yelled as he tried to keep the jeep on the road. Despite his efforts, he was being forced off the road toward a steep drop-off. Hadley had no choice but to correct hard left and try to stay out of the ditch. But with the steering controls loosened, maintaining control was impossible. The jeep immediately rolled violently to the right several times, finally stopping upside down, collapsing its top and pinning Hadley underneath.

The sedan did a U-turn and sped away from the scene. The men inside weren't sure, but the speed and the four rotations of the jeep told them that in all likelihood they had accomplished their task. Freid spoke into his mouthpiece, "It's done."

"Are you sure?" came Nolan's response.

"No, but highly probable. Four hard rollovers," Freid responded. "He won't be asking any more questions."

"Understood. I'll report in and find out if we're ready to move on the other one," Nolan said.

"I understand. We'll head in that direction and stand by," came the reply.

"Roger. I'll check in now and let you know tomorrow," Nolan said, speeding away from the interstate and the wreck. He wanted to put some distance between him and the scene of the event, and then he'd relay the status to Chaney. Chaney would pass the news to Oliver that his instructions had been carried out.

. . .

Gasoline mixed with the rainwater on the ground as Sergeant Major Hadley struggled for breath underneath the jeep. He tried to crawl out, but there was no way—he was pinned solidly underneath it. The pain in his chest was unbearable. He was fighting to stay conscious. The warm, salty taste of blood filled his mouth, then he began coughing it up. He knew what this meant—serious internal injuries.

After all the combat missions, he couldn't believe it was going to end this way. He reached for his briefcase to try to get one of his cell phones, but it was too far away. As the rain fell even harder, he looked out from under the jeep and saw the shoes of someone coming to help him. Just before he slipped into unconsciousness, he heard the man say "Hang on, buddy, I've called for help. Hang on, I'll . . ." Those were the last words Sergeant Major Ronald Hadley would hear.

11

The alarm on Jake's phone woke him out of a deep sleep. "That was a short night," he muttered. He put on his jeans and a knit shirt, slipped on his topsiders, packed up his gear and the documents, then cracked the door and looked out at the parking lot. It was six fifteen and all seemed normal.

He put his weapon in the small of his back, scanning the area around the motel as he left the room. He threw his stuff in the front seat and thought about just leaving the key in the room and heading out, but he really needed a cup of coffee. It had been a while since Jake had slept on a mattress that uncomfortable.

As he opened the office door, he was greeted by Eddie.

"Short night!" Eddie said.

"My exact words," Jake said, handing over the key.

"Hope everythin' was OK for ya! Some coffee before ya take off?" Eddie asked, pointing to an old Mr. Coffee machine on a table. "Made it myself fresh 'bout fifteen minutes ago. Ain't no Starbucks, but I haven't killed no-body yet," he chuckled.

"Thanks, smells good," Jake said. As he poured his coffee, Jake was star-tled by the sounds of vehicles pulling in front of the motel, tires squealing, followed by several car doors slamming shut in rapid succession. Jake's heart raced as he saw two men get out of a black sedan and three out of the black

SUV. All of them had crewcuts, two of them in dark suits. The three wearing solid black fatigues carried submachine guns.

The men in suits started walking into the motel while the others stayed by their SUV, looking around, checking out the area. Jake decided the best thing to do was to try to be inconspicuous and act as normal as he could. *Remember, they don't know about you yet. Hopefully.*

"Howdy," Eddie said as the men entered the office. "What can I do for you fellows?"

"Morning, sir," the shorter one out front said in a formal tone as he retrieved his ID. "I'm Special Agent Donald Chaney from the National Security Agency"—flashing his old badge—"and this is Agent Eric Gonzales. The other men outside are also from my agency. We'd like to ask you a few questions," Chaney said as he stopped just in front of Eddie.

"Sure. What you fellas need?" Eddie asked.

"We're looking for someone," he said, removing a picture from the envelope and handing it to Eddie.

Eddie looked and squinted at the picture. "Never seen this person," Eddie said, handing the picture back. "Are you all chasing him? Must be a bad fellow . . . what'd he do?"

"That's classified, sir," Chaney stated, taking back the picture. "Here's my card. I'd appreciate a call if you see him around here."

"OK, we'll sure do it," Eddie said. "Why you think he'd be way up here, out in the middle of nowhere?"

"Oh, we know he's around here. We've been tracking him," Chaney said. "Anyway, we better get going," Chaney said, turning to leave. Then he spotted Jake.

"How about you, sir?" Chaney said, walking over to Jake and pulling the picture back out of the envelope. "Have you seen this person?"

Calling on his military training and his trial lawyer's skills, Jake stayed cool as he looked at the picture of the man he called "Jones." Chaney honed in on Jake's face, looking for any indication of knowledge or nervousness.

Jake remained composed, took his time, then said, "No, sir. Never saw this guy."

"OK, thanks," Chaney said, putting the picture away. "You live around here?"

"No, sir. I drove up from Asheville to meet some friends and do some fishing." Jake hoped that would do it as he sensed sweat seeping out of his underarms.

"I see," Chaney said, staring hard at Jake, looking for any hint of something not right. He turned to get Gonzales' impression, but Gonzales only shrugged. "OK, I guess we'll be going."

"Good luck," Eddie said as the agents headed out the door. "Hope you catch him."

"Thank you, sir," Chaney replied. The men talked for a brief time outside the office, got back into their vehicles, and drove away.

Jake took a deep breath, poured another cup of coffee, and headed toward the door, trying to leave quickly before Eddie could start a conversation.

"Boy, that was somethin'. We don't get people like that 'round here very much."

"Guess not. Well, thanks for everything," Jake said as he left the office.

. . .

Making sure the agents were gone, Jake headed west and entered the destination into his GPS: *Claytor Lake, Virginia, 105 Layze Road.* Maybe this meeting would clarify things and help him make up his mind on whether to go forward.

A little while later, his personal cell phone rang, interrupting his thoughts. He turned down the radio and checked caller ID. It was Florence.

"I'm just checking in on you to find out how things are going."

"Fine. Everything is OK," Jake said.

"Anything I can do, besides Max?"

"No, we're good. I'd better go," Jake said, ending the call.

Just over two hours on the road, he picked up his secure phone to call Jones. "One hour out."

"I see that. I'll confirm with him that you will be there shortly. I gave him your description—orally—so he will recognize you," Jones responded. "He is planning lunch for you at his place, by the way."

"Thank God. I'm starving."

"OK. Be careful," Jones said.

Jake kept watch for anyone following him. It all looked clear, but that didn't make him feel any better.

After a while, he saw signs for Claytor Lake State Park, and then for the town of Claytor Lake. Eventually he found himself on a gravel road heading down to the lake. A weathered sign hidden under a tree branch said "Layze Road."

The gravel clanked against the underside of his car. Finally, he came to number 105, a small, well-maintained ranch house. The view of the lake was restricted by an abundance of maple and poplar trees with a few pines and dogwoods mixed in. Beyond the trees, the water looked like a flat, dark green mirror. It was an inviting, peaceful place.

Jake pulled into the driveway and grabbed his satchel containing the documents and his weapon. As he looked around and walked toward the house, the front door opened. A small man with white hair, mustache, wire-rimmed glasses, and a pipe stood before him. Jake was amazed how much the man conformed to his own mental images of what a Polish professor should look like. He was also surprised that despite the summer heat, Collins had put on a tie.

"Good morning, Mr. Baird. Thanks for coming. Please come in," Dr. Collins said, his English permeated by a thick Polish accent. Collins slowly shuffled away from the door.

"Certainly," Jake said, moving into the room and extending his hand. "Jake Baird, Dr. Collins. Good to meet you."

"Good to meet you," Dr. Collins responded, shaking Jake's hand.

"Let's go out on the porch. It's a lovely day and it will provide us with a good place to talk. Please follow me."

Dr. Collins led him through the foyer and the living room—early 1970s, but tasteful—and onto a screened porch that allowed for a grand view of the trees and lake. It was more of a den than a porch, with cushy wicker furniture, a small television, and tables filled with magazines and newspapers.

"Sorry it is a bit messy, but neatness is not my forte. My wife was much better at keeping things straight than I am. The absent-minded, messy professor, you know," Collins said, smiling.

Jake was already taken in by the warm charm of this man. "I have the same affliction, but I've never had a wife to make me keep it straight," Jake said.

"Oh, she tried, but I was too much of a challenge," Dr. Collins smiled sadly, and his eyes became moist. "She never pestered me about it. She just kept going around behind me, straightening up."

"I think the women in our lives are much closer to sainthood than we will ever be," Jake said, seeing a picture of Mrs. Collins—an attractive, silver-haired woman—and thinking of his mother.

"That was true in my case," Dr. Collins remarked. "I miss her terribly. She was a beautiful woman."

Jake, looking at the picture, asked, "How long has it been?"

"Six years, eleven months," Collins said, without hesitation. He paused, then moved on. "Well, I promised lunch. Hope sandwiches are OK. Why don't you make yourself comfortable at the table, and I'll be right back?"

"Sure," Jake said, and moved to a seat at the table.

Dr. Collins returned with a tray holding two glasses of iced tea, lemon, sandwiches, and a plate of cookies. "The tea is mine and I prepared the sand-wiches, but I confess the cookies are from the market. I find them quite addic-tive, so please, eat all you want," he said, patting his round belly.

"Looks great."

Collins cleared his throat. "Captain Kemp has told me about the situation with your client."

Kemp, Jake thought. *That must be Jones. So the guy is a Navy captain.* That explained a lot.

"I believe, however," Collins continued, "that this matter has implications far larger than a single lawsuit. I will, of course, do whatever I can to help you." He then looked directly at Jake and said, "What you are doing is vital to the safety of US servicemen and women and to the security of this country! So, tell me what you need to know from me," Collins said, lifting his glass of tea.

"Uh . . . well, Dr. Collins—"

"Please, call me Sommer."

"OK, Sommer. I need an overview. Where did it start? How did your ver-sion get pushed aside? And why, and how, did this aircraft continue to make its way through the process? That would be a good start." Jake chose to keep his doubts about this potential lawsuit to himself.

"Those questions would take hours to explore, and include much that would ultimately not be useful to you," Collins counseled. "Besides, I am not sure I know all of the whys. I tried to stay out of the politics of the process and keep my focus on the technical aspects."

"Makes sense," Jake responded.

"But for your purposes," Collins continued, "you should know that the original design team I headed proposed a tilt-wing vehicle. That is because after a relatively short time of comparing the tilt-wing with the tilt-rotor, we became convinced that the tilt-wing was the better choice. It had a number of advantages over the tilt-rotor."

"How was it better?" Jake asked.

"In several ways. Most importantly, it had better aerodynamics—the propellers did not have the interference of the wing in the hover and transition modes. This alone gave it a vertical lift advantage, which then translated into a payload advantage. It could carry more. Second, it was more efficient, which meant that the propellers were smaller than the XV-11's rotors. This in turn gave it an advantage in search and rescue because it wouldn't beat up the person being rescued with air loads—downwash. Third, we believed that its development and production costs were less, which has been more or less proven by the tremendous development costs of the XV-11—in time and money. We also showed that its operational costs would be less and it was safer. There are other reasons, but those are the basics."

Jake thought for a minute, then asked, "With all those attributes, how did it get rejected?"

Collins put down his fork. "There seemed to be no reason or reasons for its cancellation. That is when I figured it had to be political. The current inferior design tells me my hunch was right."

Jake leaned back in his chair, "Do you have any documents that show the attributes of the tilt-wing? I have nothing on it."

"I suspect that is one of the reasons Captain Kemp sent you to talk to me." Getting up, Collins said, "Come with me. I will show you." Jake followed Dr. Collins as he headed through the screen door and into the yard.

"So not only does the XV-11 have problems of its own, the better solution never saw the light of day," Jake said as he walked with Collins toward the lake. "So it's doubly bad."

"Right again. You're a quick study, Jake. Your client is going to be well served."

"I hope so," Jake responded.

They arrived at the run-down boathouse. "Doesn't look so good, I know, but it is safe," Collins assured Jake as they stepped on the platform that led to the boathouse door. "I used to spend a lot of time around this boathouse and on the lake. Helen loved the peacefulness of the lake. But since she's been gone, I just haven't had much desire to come down here, you know."

"I understand," Jake responded.

"Sorry for the spiders' webs," Collins said, clearing them away as they entered the boathouse. It was dark and musty. Collins turned on the light, illuminating a canoe on a mechanical lift.

"How long do you think it's been since she's been in the water?" Jake asked.

"Six years and a month—I remember it exactly." Collins gazed at the boat. "My wife didn't like my fishing, you know. She didn't want to be a part of causing the death of any creature. She wouldn't eat anything I caught, either. I tried it for a while after she passed, but just couldn't do it. So eventually I just put the rods up there where you see them," Dr. Collins said, motioning toward the wall over the workbench.

Collins went over to the lift, unlocked it, and began lowering the canoe, the chains creaking and the pulleys screeching as the boat approached the water. He let it descend just into the water, and then went down the stairs to the lower level. Jake helped Collins remove the dusty boat cover, revealing boat equipment—preservers, lights, paddles, et cetera. "Just help me with these. Stack them on the bench, please," Collins asked.

"Sure," Jake said, leaning over to reach for a couple of life preservers. They worked together until the boat was empty, then Collins got into the boat. Jake watched Collins reach down to the floor of the boat, remove a couple of hidden fasteners, and pull up the floor. Jake was startled—he expected water to pour in. Then he realized that Collins was removing a fake floor.

"Very clever," Jake commented. Collins did not respond, but reached down and pulled out what looked like a black rectangular plastic case and a plastic tube.

"Hold these for me, will you, Jake?" Collins requested as he handed the items to Jake.

Jake watched Collins reattach the floor, then helped Collins get all of the gear back into the boat before Collins hoisted it back up to the ceiling. "OK, let's go up to the house," Collins said. "I will give you an orientation of what's there. You can then take everything with you and review it. What I say will have more meaning to you when you study the documents."

"Sounds sensible," Jake said.

"I'll not keep you too long. These lake roads get tricky once the sun goes down." Collins cautioned.

Collins led Jake to the dining room. "We'll spread things out here. I am guessing you can read English, so I won't start with the memos. But I assume that you don't read 'engineer'—you appear much too pleasant to be an engineer—so let's go over these for a moment," Collins suggested as he carefully laid out the drawings on the table.

"My God . . . what is that?" Jake said, leaning over the table, staring at the aircraft.

"This is . . . or was, the XV-20 tilt-wing. It was a cross between the LTV XC142A and the Chana CTW-409. You have probably never heard of either."

"You're right."

"Google them. You will see they were real. These concepts worked. In fact, the Canadians proved it with a smaller version, the CL-84. It sustained two crashes, but they were mechanical, not design-related. And no one died. The Japanese came up with a civilian commercial version, the Ishida TW-68. Seemed to have a good chance, but didn't make it."

"What happened?"

"That's what I asked. These were much further along than the XV-11, even though the tilt-rotor actually started first." He looked up from the table at Jake and smiled. "Tells you something, doesn't it?"

"Yes. I understand the foreign—"

"Of course," Collins interrupted. "NBH—not built here. There was strong sentiment at that time that only US-designed and -built products would be pursued. So the question is, why didn't the American versions of the tilt-wing go forward, at least to proof of concept?" Collins shrugged his shoulders. "Maybe you will find out why," he said.

"It's interesting. I don't know if it makes much difference to the Thorpe case, but I can see that—"

"Of course it makes a difference!" Collins said in a raised voice, hands trembling. "It's the truth behind why we have an inferior product! It's the truth behind why lives are being put at risk!" The tension slowly left him. "I know. I know. I get mad at myself when I get this upset about it. It means they are still winning. I try to get it out of my mind, and it comes back," Dr. Collins said, his voice trailing off.

"Maybe I should leave you, and let you get some rest. We can reconvene tomorrow. I can buy you breakfast?"

Collins wouldn't hear of it. "We must continue. I can get through the rest of these things fairly quickly. You're a smart fellow. You'll get it."

"OK, but you might be giving me more credit than I deserve."

They worked three more hours, into the late afternoon. "Well, that's about it," Collins said. "I think I have given you a fairly comprehensive overview. You now know about as much as anybody—more than the people actually running the program." He took off his glasses, leaned back in his chair, and rubbed his eyes. He was tired.

"It's a lot to absorb," Jake responded, "but you've done a good job laying it all out."

Collins started organizing all the documents into neat collections and put the drawings back into their tube. He handed them all to Jake and led him to the door.

"Protect those items I gave you," Collins said. "They're not all of them, but they are most of the important ones. I played hell getting them out. Study them. I'll answer questions you have anytime you call," Collins said, squeezing Jake's arm.

Jake smiled. "I will."

"Good afternoon, Mr. Baird." Collins closed the door as Jake said good-bye. It was obvious that Collins was in a hurry to get some rest.

Maybe this was all too much stress for him, Jake thought.

Jake got in his car and started down the dark road. He realized he didn't know how he was going to talk to Collins without a secure means. Maybe more trips to Claytor Lake?

The difficulties of this case pressed upon him. Collins's story was one of bad decisions that resulted in an inferior aircraft, but so what? What was done was done—Jake couldn't rewind the whole process.

· · ·

Jake headed toward the highway. He reached for his cell phone to call Madison, but his holster wasn't on his belt. He'd taken it off at the table when he and Collins were looking at the documents. It should be right on the seat of the chair where he left it. Damn!

He turned around and headed back to Collins's place, hoping the old guy had not gone to bed yet. There was still about half an hour of daylight left, and he should be there and gone by the time it got dark.

He pulled beside Collins's house where he had parked before and walked up to the door; it was open.

"Professor Collins? Sorry to bother you, but I left my cell phone," Jake called. No response. *Strange.* He went inside, calling again, more loudly. As he walked to the table, he noticed some bureau drawers pulled out and a secretary's doors opened. *Maybe Collins was looking for something else to give me,* Jake thought. He saw his phone and clipped it to his hip.

As Jake left the house, out of the corner of his eye he saw a light coming through the partly open door of the boathouse. As he approached it, he could make out two men in casual clothes talking to Collins. *Huh,* Jake thought—*I didn't see another car in the driveway. Maybe they're neighbors.*

"Hello?" Jake said as he got to the door. The two men turned quickly away from Collins and stared at Jake, saying nothing.

"Oh, Professor Kline, good to see you," Collins said to Jake. "Those texts you wanted are on the third shelf of the center bookshelf. You can go get them and I will be up there shortly. I am just showing these men the canoe."

Quick thinking for an old guy, Jake thought, deciding to play along. "Thanks, Dr. Collins, I can wait." Jake looked at the two men, neither of whom had taken their eyes off him. Jake wasn't about to leave him with these two guys, whose close haircuts and stern demeanors made Jake think they just might be the bad guys.

"Maybe you should go up to the house as Dr. Kolinsky—uh, Dr. Collins suggests," one of the guys said, but his tone wasn't asking. "We might want to take the canoe out on the lake."

"Really?" Jake responded, now combat-focused on the two men, slightly spreading his feet and slightly bent at the knees, watching for any move they might make. "I never heard of taking a test cruise at night."

"Well, now you have," the other man said.

"OK," Jake said, turning away, but he immediately swung around and cold-cocked the guy closest to him. The man dropped like a bag of rocks.

Collins grabbed a paddle and tried to hit the other one as he lunged for Jake, but he missed. Jake and the man exchanged punches and wrestled together, grabbing each other by the waist, banging against the walls of the boathouse. Fishing poles fell on the men and containers of fishing tackle fell off their shelves, crashing to the floor and breaking open. Just as Jake was about to finish the guy off, *thunk!* Something hit Jake's head and he started fading out. Right before he passed out, he heard one of the men say, "So much for your professor friend, '*Dr. Collins.*' Let's go for a little boat ride."

• • •

Nolan called Chaney. "Number two is done."

"Great. I trust all went smoothly."

"More or less. Some professor showed up and tried to be a hero but we took care of him."

"How?" Chaney asked.

"We knocked him out after he broke someone's jaw," Nolan said. "He's out cold."

"How do you know he was a professor?"

"Because that's what our friend called him when he showed up at the boathouse."

"This guy just happened to show up when you guys were there and was able to give you guys a fight? Didn't you think that was strange? Since he was out cold, did anyone think to check for some ID?"

"Uh, no," Nolan said.

"How about a license plate? Did we get a number, or at least a state?"

Silence.

Chaney sighed. "Well, at least you did what you went there to do. I hope this doesn't come back to haunt us."

12

"Rumor control" about deployment had been in full operational mode for days around Cherry Point. Major Gary Bennett had not said anything to his wife, Kathy; it was best not to bother her with gossip about deployments until the official word was out. He wasn't good at keeping things from her, though. Last night at dinner and again when the lights were turned out, Kathy asked him if anything was wrong. He truthfully replied, "No." He didn't add, *Not yet, anyway*.

Gary bumped into Major Bill Harris as he headed down the hall. "You ready, there, Mr. Pacifist? Looks like we all are going to get into the game!" Once the rumors started, Gary knew Bill had used all his contacts to find out what was going to happen. But down at squadron level, neither Bill nor anyone else actually knew what was going on in the two separate commands, NAVAIR and USMC Operational Command.

"Sure. Why not?" Gary replied, forcing a smile to hide the fact that his stomach was in knots.

They followed the rest of the aviators into the briefing room, some in flight suits, some in khakis, and some in civvies. The word for the pilots to assemble at 1000 hours had been put out just six hours before via telephone, e-mail, and text. The alert message had made it clear that they were to tell no one about this meeting.

"Attention!" the squadron's XO shouted at precisely 1000 hours. The men snapped to attention where they were. Immediately, Colonel Paul Dixon entered the room in camouflage utilities. The cammies spoke directly to Gary's fears about deployment. He knew it was just a matter of Colonel Dixon speaking the words.

As the colonel approached the podium, the XO announced, "Take your seats!" All quickly complied.

Dixon began, "Men, our squadron has once again been ordered to perform a great service to this nation. I have in my hand orders directly from Marine Corps Headquarters at the Pentagon that deploys our unit into Afghanistan to support the joint operations being conducted there by combined team of Army, Marines, Special Forces, and others. We're honored to go there to assist in wiping out terrorist training sites and personnel, including Taliban leadership. By these actions, we're going to make our own country more secure."

The announcement was met by a loud "OoooRah!"

"It will be our distinct honor to be the first unit ever to deploy the XV-11 into battle." The colonel paused. "Now, I want to address what I am sure is on your minds. We all know that the XV-11 has not yet completed phase six of the operational test plan, but the orders state that Marine Corps Headquarters has coordinated with Test Directorate at Quantico, which has given assurances that what has been achieved thus far in phase six testing makes further work on this phase unnecessary. So we can proceed directly into the combat test phase. Except in this case," he paused for emphasis, "we're going to conduct real, rather than simulated, combat exercises. We have been told the aircraft is ready . . . and I know my men are ready!" This brought another round of cheers from the aviators. They all liked their commander. Gary found him affable, unassuming, and a natural leader. It didn't hurt that he was not an academy graduate.

Dixon continued. "We leave in just under twenty-four hours. We will self-deploy to theater. All necessary logistics will be supplied en route and in theater. Just bring your standard combat and flight gear, your combat uniforms and, of course, a toothbrush." The men laughed. "You will load your personal gear into your aircraft. Crew assignments are posted on the ready board. Our heavy gear is being transported by cargo jets and C-130s. Our enlisted crews are receiving the same briefing at this very moment by First Sergeant Horace on the other side of the hangar," Colonel Dixon added.

"You may not—you will not—tell anyone the destination of this deployment. Just inform your loved ones you are being deployed overseas for extended exercises. When they inevitably ask where, your response will be that it is classified. You may tell them you'll see them in 150 to 180 days.

"Men, I'm giving you the rest of the day to get things squared away at home. Be here tomorrow at 0700 hours for a mission briefing and flight planning. A lot of the general planning has been accomplished, but you will need to integrate long-range flight planning into the overall plan.

"We'll conduct final mission brief at 0900 tomorrow and will depart at 1000 hours. Note this is twenty-four hours from now." He stopped, then asked, "Any questions?" He scanned the room looking for a hand in the air and listened for a comment.

Silence. It wasn't that the pilots didn't have questions. It just didn't appear to be smart to ask them. Questions might reveal some doubt about the aircraft, the unit, or one's self. This was way too macho an environment to ask anything in public. But Gary sensed that even the most gung-ho among them thought it was premature to deploy the XV-11 aircraft, especially with no combat readiness training.

"Hearing no questions, I will assume there aren't any. Good day, men. See you tomorrow," the commanding officer concluded, and the XO bellowed, "On Your Feet!" the minute the CO and S-3 stepped away from the podium. The CO, XO and S-3 were out of the room before all could get to their feet and shout "Semper Fi!"

Some of the aviators stood in the room, dazed. Others talked, but most, like Gary, just sat back down. Gary noticed that even Bill seemed taken aback. Some aviators headed out to check the board for crew assignments. Gary followed and was relieved to see that he had, in fact, been paired with Bill and Sergeant Theodore (Ted) Cook as crew chief. *It was as it should be,* Gary thought. *We will both be there to see if one of us will be proven right.*

When Gary walked back into the ready room, Bill was still sitting in his seat, calmly discussing the news with a couple of other pilots. When Bill saw Gary, his demeanor changed. "OK, Major Bennett, that look shows me that you got lucky and are going to get to kick the Taliban's ass with yours truly, right?"

"You are so right about both."

"See there, guys," Bill said, jumping to his feet and looking at his fellow pilots. "That's one Marine Corps aviator who knows his stuff!"

"Right, asshole," one of the other pilots shouted. "If he's so lucky, why aren't any of us trying to switch with him?" The group laughed.

"Because none of you are as smart as Major Bennett, right, good buddy?"

"Right," Gary responded.

. . .

First Sergeant Horace knocked on the open doorframe at the commander's office and Dixon waved him into the room. The colonel pulled a cigarette out of a pack on his desk and started to light it, but caught himself—no smoking inside buildings.

He looked up at First Sergeant Horace, who was still standing. "Have a seat, First Sergeant. How'd your briefing go?" he asked, putting the cigarette back into the pack.

"Very well, sir," Horace responded. "I think the men are ready. They seemed to understand the importance of this deployment."

"I wish I was as confident about the officers. I think some of them think this is too soon," Colonel Dixon said.

"Sir, candidly, they might have concerns, but they're Marines, sir. They will perform."

"I'm not really worried about them; I am more concerned about *this* air-craft in *that* environment," Colonel Dixon said, pointing toward the aircraft. "I just hope my worry didn't show."

"Understood, sir," Horace responded. "The troops all trust you, sir. I can't speak for the officers like I can for the enlisted, but they have confidence in you."

"That's the problem, First Sergeant. I've never led men into combat when I wasn't totally confident in them *and* their equipment. This is a first, and it's bugging the hell out of me." He looked down and tapped at the ciga-rette pack. "I hope those bastards who are sending us downrange know what they're doing. If one of those machines kills one of my men, there'll be hell to pay!" He paused, then said, "Thanks, First Sergeant. That will be all."

"Yes, sir." First Sergeant Horace saluted, pivoted, and exited.

Colonel Dixon decided to take a walk down the flight line so he could make sure all that could be done was being done. Plus, it would give him opportunity to visit with his men, which would help take the edge off his anxieties.

In a little over three days' flight time, the first of these aircraft would be in country—after one hellacious shakedown flight. He knew advance support crews, equipment and parts were already headed to Afghanistan. So far, that part of the operation had gone without a hitch. He was concerned about this part—the long flight to Afghanistan.

"Goddamn aircraft better work," he muttered. "They goddamn better."

. . .

When Kathy drove the SUV into the driveway of her two-story duplex on Tarawa Drive in on-base housing, she was surprised to see Gary's VW parked in the carport. "Gary?" she called as she exited her car, but she didn't get an answer. She put the grocery bags on the countertop in the kitchen and went to the foot of the stairs. "Gary?" she called again, and again no answer. She went upstairs, but all she found was a partially packed sea bag and a couple of open drawers on their dresser. The all-too-familiar dread instantly came over her. *Another deployment, this one out of nowhere.*

She went into the children's rooms, called again, but didn't see him.

Kathy looked outside in the yard and there was no sign of him. She picked up her cell phone and was about to call him when she heard the screen door open and close. She turned to see Gary dripping with sweat, in a sopping wet tank top and shorts.

"So there you are," she said, walking over to hug him.

"Here I am—watch out! I'm sweaty!" he warned.

"You've been sweaty before. I like it!" she flirted, hugging him and reaching up for a kiss.

"Oh yes, I remember now," he said, kissing her.

She held the kiss for a long time and then said, "You know, the children won't be home . . ." Gary didn't wait for her to finish. He led her up the stairs into their bedroom, where he playfully tossed her on the bed and started pulling off her clothes as they went after each other.

Although Gary was a great lover, this time there was something missing.

Kathy could feel the tension in his body. He was physical and caring as usual, but she sensed he was distracted. The usual intimacy wasn't there. Afterward, they lay there and she wondered and waited—for the right time to speak.

She rolled over to look at him. "You can't tell me, can you?" she said softly.

"No, I can't," he said, barely audible.

"It's OK, I understand," she said, rubbing his chest. "Just come home safe to us," she whispered as she moved over to kiss him.

He responded to her lips, but Kathy felt him hold back. She saw his eyes become moist, then watched as a tear rolled out of the corner of his left eye and onto his cheek. Kathy moved her face away from his and stroked his hair as she gently wiped the tear away without saying a word.

Gary was torn up inside, realizing what this mission could destroy. He didn't share these feelings with her because it would worry her. Maybe she would think he was sad because he would miss her and the children, and wouldn't sense he was terrified that this time he might not come back.

He rolled over and held her.

13

"A-h-h-h, Jesus!" Jake moaned, rolling over and reaching up to feel the back of his head. He found a huge knot under his wet hair; bringing his fingers in front of his face he smelled the metallic odor of blood, though it was too dark to confirm it. He sat up slowly, gathering himself, and holding on to the boathouse's doorframe, pulled himself up.

Remembering Dr. Collins, Jake stumbled out of the boathouse to look for him, but only made it a couple of steps before an overwhelming dizziness put him back on the ground. "Too fast," he said. He tried again, collecting himself on all fours, then carefully rising to his feet. He waited a moment and then started slowly toward the lake. In the moonlight, he could make out the canoe about seventy-five yards away against the shore. He scanned for Collins, didn't see him, and called out. Nothing.

Jake went back to his car to retrieve his flashlight. Weaving back down the hill, he came to the lake's edge and started a methodical search with his light.

"Damn!" he whispered. His light found the facedown body of Dr. Collins floating about twenty yards from the canoe. Jake moved toward a spot on the shore close to the body, walking in the water so as not to leave footprints that might make him a suspect. Once close to Collins, he waded into the deeper water and pulled him up, hoping for a pulse, but he knew already there wouldn't be one.

As he held Collins, he considered his options. Pull him out and go to the police? No, they'd suspect him, and it might blow the lid off why he was really there, bringing up the whole XV-11 issue, and possibly revealing Kemp's involvement. He hated leaving Collins in the water—maybe he could put him in the canoe? Of course not. People don't drown then hop back into their canoe. As distasteful as it was, he knew he had to leave Collins as he was, but at least he could pull him to the shore's edge.

He needed to get out of there. The cold water had brought him back to his senses, but his head still hurt like hell. He pulled his first aid kit from the trunk of his car and rubbed some ointment into the back of his head.

Jake started his car and went as far as he could without headlights. He didn't want to be seen by anyone—good or bad—who might be around. Once at the paved road he turned his headlights on and drove away from Claytor Lake.

He picked up his secure phone and called Kemp.

"How'd it go?" Kemp asked.

"Well, I saw him, and we had a good meeting. Problem was other people came to see him, too."

"What does that mean?"

"He's dead," Jake said.

"What? How?"

"I'll explain in person. Not now," Jake said.

"When can we get together?" Kemp asked. "Much we need to discuss."

"Give me the weekend. I've got to sort through all of this. I need to work up a plan."

"OK. But we need to push," Kemp said.

"I know that. Plan on Monday. Out."

. . .

"Goddammit!" he yelled, pounding on the steering wheel as he headed back toward Raleigh. "I'll get those sons of bitches for this!"

He was red-hot pissed off, but he knew that raw anger wouldn't bring Collins back or, for that matter, get these guys. He had to outwit the bastards.

Options raced through his mind, then it hit him. "Of course," he said. "Lisa Thorpe. I'll put their asses on my home turf—the courtroom—where they have no idea how to fight."

Jake knew what this meant. He had to draft a Complaint to start the lawsuit. But that wasn't enough to really get these people. He had to nail them with the documents. Then it hit him: draft a Requests to Admit, asking the defendants to admit the authenticity and the substance of the documents. This way he could tell the damning story of the XV-11 through their own words. He would spend all weekend in the office working out the details, drafting these pleadings, organizing the documents, and making the necessary copies. It wouldn't be easy—but it would be worth it.

. . .

As Jake headed to Raleigh, his thoughts alternated between the plan and his own personal safety. Surely the guys who took out Collins had looked in Jake's wallet for an ID or at least got the license tag number off his car. They must know about him now. How he could stay safe? The only thing that came to mind was to be smart, stay vigilant, get his plan together, and execute it as quickly as possible. And be armed at all times.

. . .

Raleigh, North Carolina
Friday, August 7, 2009
6:00 a.m.

Jake nodded off for a split second as he was driving. *Man, I gotta get home, quick.*

He chose an unusual route to his house—just in case someone was following him. When he got close he drove past his house, checking it out as he went by. Nothing seemed odd. Jake pulled his .45 out of his bag as he opened the garage door, just in case someone was waiting for him. Fortunately, no one was there. If the bad guys had ID'd him it was risky being home, but maybe they hadn't—yet. So far, there was no sign they were following him. At home, he had Max to warn him and he had his weapons. Plus, he knew the potential entrances and exits to his house—they didn't.

He shut off the engine and carried his bags into the house, Max greeting him with a deep bark. Jake gathered all the documents and engineering drawings and took them to his closet. He loosened a plumbing access panel hidden by his clothes and carefully tucked the classified information inside.

He set the house alarm, then took a long, hot shower, finding cuts and bruises from the fight and washing the dried blood out of his hair. *I'll grab a couple hours of sleep, and then figure out the rest of the plan.* He got his .45 automatic and his defender shotgun and laid them both on the bed beside him. He was asleep in seconds, with Max curled up on the floor by the bed.

· · ·

Jake had been asleep for a few hours when his personal cell phone rang. It was Florence.

"You doing OK?"

"Yes, fine. I'm home now, just taking a little rest."

"OK. I'm on top of things here."

"Anything I should know?" Jake asked.

"We need to arrange an appointment or a telephone conference with a client. Just tell me when and I'll set it up."

"Let me think about it." He understood Florence to be talking about an appointment with Lisa Thorpe.

"When will I see you?" Florence asked.

"Probably not until tomorrow." He wanted to decompress, take care of his head, and start on his plan.

"OK. So long."

She could have had a career in the CIA, Jake thought. He couldn't wait to see her light up when he gave her the secure phone.

Jake gave Madison a call.

"Does this mean you're back?" Madison asked.

"Sure am. How are you?"

"I'm great. How was the trip—did it work out for you?"

"Yes. Got it figured out."

"Terrific. You know, there's a good-looking blonde who happens not to have any lunch plans and would love to hear all about it," Madison said.

Jake smiled. "Really? Who?"

"You're smarter than that, Ja—"

"You're right, I am," Jake interrupted her once she started to say his name. "Look, I'd love to, but I'm beat. Let's get together for dinner instead? Something simple."

"Sounds great. Simple it is. Get some rest. Bye."

. . .

Jake couldn't wait to see Madison. She was beautiful, sexy, accomplished, caring, and smart. Very smart. In fact, he entertained the idea of practicing with her once she finally escaped her father's law firm. He knew she wanted to get out of the pressure cooker of litigation and slow her practice down. She would be a hell of a researcher and writer; he was going to suggest it to her sooner rather than later. Of course, her father, George Wright, would explode if she left his firm and went with Jake. Jake's leaving George's firm had been stressful enough on his relationship with Madison, but Jake got a bit of sadistic glee imagining George's reaction to her defection to Jake's one-person firm.

Jake and Madison had their moments where things got rough, mostly about differing views of where the relationship should be heading. He had no illusions that working together would be entirely trouble-free. Tonight would be no different, except after what he had been through, he *needed* to be with her. Going out in public could be risky, but he felt a visceral desire to see her, so he was going to do it anyway.

Everything in his life had seemed too uncertain, too unsettled for him to fully commit to her, and he remained concerned how this might affect their future. He wouldn't shortchange her. She deserved a full-time partner—not someone who was busy with a one-person law practice and Reserve duty. He also knew that part of his hesitation was the fear of losing another loved one, connected to the loss of his parents. But way down, he knew there was something else. Was he scared of failure?

The horror of the failed mission in the Hindu Kush region of Afghanistan was never far away from his consciousness. Jake had listened to the mission briefing and realized the plan was doomed due to the high concentration of enemy forces. He'd tried to talk the commander out of the mission, but the commander had insisted on "pressing on" and berated Jake for not being a team player. Jake had considered refusing to fly, which could have meant a court martial, but ultimately he'd decided to go in the hope he could make a difference.

Approaching the landing zone, enemy fire—machine guns, rocket-propelled grenades, and mortars—came at them from all sides. The other two helicopters were hit immediately and burst into flames, their troops lost. Jake's helicopter took fire and several people were hit, including him and his co-pilot. Jake knew he couldn't take any more troops on board but nevertheless hovered over to the burning wreckages of the other helicopters to look for survivors. He saw no one moving, so he flew his aircraft and his men out of the heavy fire—maybe he could come back.

He woke up in a hospital two days later and was told he'd almost bled out from a leg wound. Everyone said it was a miracle he made it back with the helicopter. But he didn't feel gratitude or relief. He was overcome with the feeling of failure—that he was unable to stop the mission, that he didn't abort en route knowing what awaited them, and that he couldn't save more people.

From that moment on, Jake had tried to avoid any situation where he could lose, especially where control was out of his hands. He never wanted to feel that type of failure again, where things spiraled downhill and he couldn't stop them. It wore on him, and he knew sometimes it affected him more than it should.

14

At a traffic light near Jake's house, Madison impatiently tapped her hand on the steering wheel. "C'mon, light, change!" she said.

Six years out of law school, Madison Wentworth Wright was moving rapidly up the legal ladder. She'd graduated near the top of her class from Harvard Law School and excelled in her first years in the corporate law world at Alexander, Johnson & Wright, LLP. Not only was she a quick study and a tireless worker, but she also had all the charm and refinement that Ivy League schooling brought. Of course, it didn't hurt that she was a very attractive, tall, athletic blonde, and that she worked in her father's firm, although she would bristle at any hint that either of the latter had anything to do with her rapid successes.

The pace at which she was conducting her practice—not to mention her activities out of the office—social work, charities, and her aggressive tennis schedule—was wearing on her, as the creases on her forehead indicated. At thirty-one, she was beginning to feel the pressure of her biological clock. She was eager to start a family and whittle down her schedule to part-time, where she could still do what she loved, but also enjoy nurturing a baby.

Jake was not easy. He could be headstrong and independent; his Army Reserve schedule and law practice kept him busy, not to mention his frequent workouts to keep in shape and ball games with his friends. He had a hard time letting people get close, even her. Still, he somehow made her feel comfortable. He was down-to-earth and logical, and his sense of humor cheered her up at the end of a long day with humorless corporate types. He could be thoughtful, even sweet. But he didn't seem eager to spend all his time with her the way she wanted to spend hers with him.

She knew Jake had felt awkward in the corporate work environment of her firm—it just wasn't him. He'd told her several times that having to please big corporate clients reminded him of the rigid structure of his small hometown, where being right didn't always matter, but having power and money did. She missed having him in the office—even now—though she understood Jake's reasons for leaving the firm.

Jake was so unlike the ambitious, suspender-wearing, go-along-to-get-along wannabes who permeated her profession—especially in corporate law. She knew what *she* wanted and what would make *her* happy—and it was not one of those inbred country-club kiss-asses. She wanted a man, not a boy, and Jake Baird was in every way a man. He was a military aviator and a proven combat veteran who exuded masculinity, and he was a hell of a trial lawyer. She just couldn't understand why Jake was withholding part of himself from her, and she was determined to break down the invisible wall between them.

• • •

Max's sudden barking interrupted Jake from outlining his plan. At first he tensed up and reached for his pistol. Then he remembered Madison was coming over, and when Max quit barking, Jake realized Max had recognized Madison through the front door sidelights.

"Well, hello there," Jake said opening the door. She was wearing perfectly fitted denim shorts, sandals, and a white cotton V-neck T-shirt that did not entirely conceal the lacy bra underneath it. Jake wanted to jump her then and there—it had been too long.

"Hi there, Max! I am not ignoring you!" she said, bending down to pet the jumping dog. "You sure are happy to see me." She stroked his back, but he just wanted more. "Poor pup, Jake's all over the place and you don't get any company, do you?"

She moved to Jake, and gave him a big hug and a kiss. "Great to see you."

She first noticed the fatigue on his face, then saw a bruise. "You look exhausted—my God, Jake, what happened to you?"

"I know. I know. Let's head down to Tussy's Café," Jake said.

"OK," she said.

"Just a minute . . . let me get my bag." Jake went to the bedroom, got his satchel and put his .45 and two extra magazines in it.

"You bringing work?" Madison asked.

"No, only my laptop, just in case," Jake responded.

Jake locked up and they started the three-block walk to the restaurant.

"So how was your trip?" Madison asked.

He took her hand, twining her fingers between his. "It's complicated. But I'll try to explain it as best I can once we're sitting down." Jake spoke quietly and looked around, even behind him.

"Jake, what are looking for?"

"Nothing."

"C'mon, Jake. I can feel the tension in your hand. What's going on?"

"Once we get there, Maddy."

Entering Tussy's, Jake asked for a table in the back by the kitchen door. He sat with his back to the wall, and asked Madison to sit beside him. He didn't even look at the menu—he kept looking around and outside the restaurant.

Madison made her choice and once the waiter left said, "We're at the table and I'm all ears."

"Look, some of it's classified, at least for now. So I can't tell you all the details. But I'll tell you what I can."

"Classified? OK, go on . . ."

Jake hesitated. Maddy leaned in closer and said, "Whatever it is, I don't want to add to your troubles. Just tell me what you can." She reached up to rub the back of his neck, and instinctively let her fingers wander into his scalp.

"Ouch!" Jake cringed, pulling away.

"My God, Jake, is that a knot on the back of your head? Let me see," she said sitting up to get a better look.

"It's nothing—"

"Yes it is! There's a huge bump and cut. What in the world happened? Did you fall?"

Jake decided to tell her the truth. "No, I didn't fall. Someone hit me on the head."

"What the hell? How did that happen?"

"Maddy, I've been through a lot worse—like working for your father," Jake deadpanned.

Madison kicked him under the table and gave him the most evil look she could muster, but she couldn't hold it. She burst out laughing, and so did he.

"Good, humor still works," Jake said, then got serious. "Here's the gist of it: you sent Lisa Thorpe to me. I wasn't going to take the case. But the morning after I met with her, some guy called me and asked me to meet him at the Waffle House on Hillsborough. When I got there, he gave me a folder with classified documents—obviously stolen—that showed lies and cover-ups in the XV-11 program—the aircraft Major Thorpe was flying."

Madison stared at Jake. "Keep going . . ."

"After he gave me the documents I saw some people looking for him at the Waffle House—looked like government agents. That's when I decided to get out of town—to take a good look at the file and get away from those guys, just in case they knew I was associated with him."

"Makes sense."

"It turns out the guy who gave me the documents is a retired Navy captain who is a real crusader against anything that he thinks won't help the Navy—or the Marines, in this case. Anyway, he tracked me to the mountains where we talked about the situation, and we decided I should go see a guy who knew all about how the program got off track—the chief engineer at the start of this aircraft program. He had walked away from the program and has been living incognito on a lake near Blacksburg, Virginia. I met with him—a great guy—and he told me all about the history of this program and alternative designs that would have worked better. He gave me more documents and some engineering drawings."

As the waiter dropped off their meals, Jake stopped and took a long drink of iced tea. "I left him and was headed back to Raleigh and started to call you, but I realized I had left my phone at his place. When I went back to get it, I saw him with two guys in his small boathouse. I could tell something wasn't right just by looking at these guys—they looked like government agents, and there was an edge to them. Dr. Collins tried to get me out of there by calling me 'Professor Kline' and telling me the books I came for were back at the house. But I couldn't leave him alone with those guys—"

"So you went after them?" Madison shook her head, thinking of two against one. "You couldn't just get away like Collins wanted and call for help?"

"It wouldn't have worked. Something had to be done right then. Anyway, I knocked one guy down and was working over the other when I got hit. A third guy. When I came to, I found Collins near his canoe in the lake—"

"Dead?"

"Yes," was all Jake could say.

"Oh, Jake. That must have been terrible," Madison said, rubbing his shoulder.

"That's apparently what they came there to do. I have no idea why they let me live. When I called Kemp right after it happened, I learned they have been looking for this guy a while to shut him up. I wanted to call the police, but that would have meant a lot of trouble for me and could have blown the whole thing open on Kemp, me, the documents—everything. We would have lost control."

"Control of what, exactly?" Madison asked.

"Well, it looks like we're going to use the Lisa Thorpe case to expose the cover-ups and fraud in the XV-11 program. That's apparently why Kemp gave me the documents and arranged the meeting with Collins, to convince me to do just that. But even after reviewing all of this material and meeting with Collins, I still thought there were too many problems. I knew the story, I knew what needed to be told—but much of it was in stolen classified documents that I had no right to have. On top of that, we lost a vital witness. Not to mention the inherent difficulties in a military product case."

"I understand, Jake. It sounds impossible. I'm sure Lisa will understand if you explain all of this to her."

Jake turned to Madison, a devilish smile on his face. "Oh no. It's not impossible. It's just *almost* impossible. But I'm not going to let them get away with killing Major Thorpe, his co-pilot and Dr. Collins—and who knows how many more? This is about much more than a defective aircraft. Besides, they hit me on the head—from behind. Now it's personal."

Madison thought a moment and then said, "This is about more than just righting this wrong, Jake. Losing could cost more than just time and money. It could cost your life."

"I've already thought it through. I have a plan that will work," Jake said.

"What?" Madison asked.

"Let me work out a few more details and then I can talk to you about it. You can let me know what you think and help me make sure I haven't missed anything."

"I'll try." Madison looked down and began moving the salad around on her plate with her fork. Jake couldn't quite determine her mood.

"It's going to be fine, Maddy," Jake offered.

"Fine? They just killed a guy for what he knew. What do you think they'll want to do to you for trying to get back at them? Of course I'm worried."

"I understand, but trust me. It'll all be fine." Jake gave her a kiss. "While this is going on, we have to be careful about phone calls and e-mails. Nothing about any of this. Of course we can talk about day-to-day matters. But we will probably communicate a lot person-to-person, just to keep the phone traffic down."

"Phone traffic?" Madison asked.

"Yes, people could be listening."

"Oh my God, Jake. That's scary," Madison said. "Does Florence know?"

"She knows some things. Not all. I need to protect her, also. Neither of you will know everything."

They left the restaurant to walk back to his house. Once at the front door, she turned to him again. "Jake, I love you." It was the first time she had spoken those words to him. She kissed him, gently at first, then passionately.

"I know, Maddy. I really do. I know how you feel," Jake mumbled against her lips. This was as close as he had ever come to saying he loved her.

"Oh shit," Madison said, "then I guess we're really in trouble." Jake laughed out loud with her, then took a long deep look at her. She *was* so beautiful. He kissed her again, and as the kissing became more intense, he decided the front porch might be a little too public. He led her around the side of the garage, through the gate, and into the backyard. Max saw them through the slit in the drapes and barked. After trying to silence him, Jake opened the back door and reached in to turn off the outside lights. The big, black Giant Schnauzer bounded past him and headed directly toward Madison, stubby tail wagging. Silently, Jake signaled to Madison to be quiet, and she greeted Max with a hushed voice. "Good dog, Max, good dog. Good to see you," she said, softly.

Jake pulled Maddy gently down to the grass and said, "Where were we?" He and moved his hand underneath her shorts . . . to find that she had no panties on.

"Did the big-time corporate lawyer forget her undergarments?" he teased.

"To the contrary," Maddy responded, "I *remembered* to forget to wear them, just in case."

"In case of what?" Jake responded.

"In case, you know, I met a lonely soldier."

"Well, how about a lonely Army helicopter pilot?"

"Guess you got lucky," she responded.

He began to rub her chest through her T-shirt and bra, but quickly took them off and began gently massaging her bare breasts with his hands. She moaned, sensitive to his soft touches. "I better investigate, you know, the underwear status. Did you really remember to forget your panties? You know, 'trust but verify,' as one of your presidents said." He moved his hand down her stomach to remove her shorts.

"This is one investigation I want you to make. Take your time and verify for as long as you want. Make sure—"

"That's very Reagan of you, Counselor." He got the button on her shorts undone and slid the zipper down, slowly.

"There's nothing Republican about this, my dear," Madison responded. "Right now I strongly embrace one of the fundamental precepts of democratic liberalism—you know: sex is good."

"See, I knew you were a Democrat at heart."

"Maybe not at heart, but my other parts certainly are. Now shut up and do your duty, Colonel."

"Yes, ma'am."

With her jeans fully unzipped, he was able to verify, visually and tactilely, that she had indeed remembered to forget her underwear. He slipped off her shorts then pulled his T-shirt over his head and tore off his gym shorts.

Madison lay back. "Oooh . . . this is a bit cold," she muttered. He put his T-shirt on the ground under her back.

As she lay completely nude under the full moon, Jake took a moment to take in this beautiful, sexy woman. She smiled and reached out her arms. "I hear you helicopter pilots are good with your hands. C'mon, flyboy, start moving those controls."

He lowered himself onto her. They intertwined and became one.

It was almost enough to make Jake forget everything else.

15

The flight line looked like an anthill that someone had kicked open. Gary had never seen so much activity, not even with his old unit in the big combat missions in Iraq.

Multiple people in an array of uniforms, civilian and military, were climbing on and through the aircraft that were going to self-deploy—one of which was his. And at every aircraft there was what appeared to be a supervisor, each reporting to a man in a tie who was scrutinizing the whole process. Obviously, he was some big shot with the aircraft's manufacturers.

On the other side of the ramp, Gary noticed a difference with the preparations on the aircraft that would be deployed by ship. They looked liked someone's stepchildren, not quite ready for prime time. These aircraft would be flown to the ship off the North Carolina coast for the long cruise overseas. No hurry here—they wouldn't reach Afghanistan for weeks

The time arrived for their pre-departure flight briefing, so Major Gary Bennett headed to the ready room. Colonel Dixon was already there, along with the operations officer. The pilots began to file in—none looked especially happy. Gary saw Bill walk in and waved. At precisely 1000 hours, the XO called the room to attention.

"You men are gonna get tired of hearing me talk about 'firsts,' so you might as well go ahead with the pool to see how many times I use that term in the next couple of months," Colonel Dixon said. The old man had a sense of humor, which was one of the reasons the officers liked him.

"OK, Lieutenant Colonel Meyers will go over the final details of the *first* self-deployment of the *first* XV-11 squadron to be deployed into combat, but I just wanted to generally outline the route for you now." A large map was unveiled behind him.

"Today'll be short, starting up the east coast to Halifax, where we'll overnight," he said, pointing to the route. "Tomorrow we fly the Great Circle Route from Halifax to the United Kingdom, with midair refueling around Greenland. Again, we'll not push too hard. We overnight at Boscombe Down in the UK, and then on Sunday we fly from there to Incirlik in Turkey, refueling over southeast Germany. After our overnight at Incirlik, on Monday we punch all the way into Afghanistan, to Bagram, with midair refueling over Iraq and Saudi."

Dixon turned to the flight crews as he put down his pointer. "The entire way we'll be shadowed by the C-130 tankers and cargo aircraft, which will have on board additional items we might need—parts, mechanics, rescue crews, rafts, et cetera. Just in case. Following the flight will be HH-53 helicopters, Super Jolly Greens, which will also have an array of equipment on board, including aircraft components and rescue equipment."

"OK, now I'll turn it over to Lieutenant Colonel Meyers, who will fill in the details. Give him your undivided attention. We want to be out of the chocks in two hours. That should allow plenty of time to iron out any final issues."

As he backed away from the podium, Colonel Dixon stopped and surveyed all of his aviators. He then moved back to the podium, stopping LTC Meyers in his tracks, and changing his tone to dead serious. "Marines, I am not only your commander, I am one of you. I know the concerns you men have. We all know this won't be a vacation. But I would not have agreed to undertake this assignment unless I knew you—we—could do it. You're as fine a bunch of aviators and Marines as I have ever been around. I am damn proud to be your CO. So let's go into this with your standard can-do attitude and we'll be just fine. Lieutenant Colonel Meyers, they're all yours."

As he stepped back to give way to the ops officer, the men jumped to their feet, whooping and clapping. He let it happen for a few seconds, then raised his hand in a quieting gesture and joked, "Too early, way too early. Just remember that for when we get back." The men laughed as they sat back down.

The Ops officer began in his official-sounding manner, "OK, giving some detail to the CO's overview, after we overnight in Halifax, our ten aircraft . . ." and went on for thirty minutes in "nauseating detail" as Gary described it later to Bill. He wondered if anybody remembered anything—other than the details about ditching at sea, which sent chills down his spine.

• • •

The briefing finally over, Gary and Bill headed to their aircraft to make sure all was OK. The aviators greeted their crew chief, Sergeant Ted Cook, and got busy readying their crew positions. Bill looked down the fight line, observing the other nine crews doing exactly what they were doing. It was quiet—no jokes, no banter, no loud talk.

"Nice and peaceful out here, isn't it?" Bill said. "Maybe it will be this way over there."

Gary looked at Bill to see if he was being serious, but couldn't read him. Finally Gary responded. "Is this your sick sense of humor, or are you serious? I hope it's the latter, so we can ground this bird for lack of crew while you go to the psych ward."

Bill gave his best impression of an insane man, rolling his eyes and bobbing his head, then started laughing. "Gotcha!" he said.

"Bill, you're an ass. Lucky me, I get to fly around the world with an ass. I get to bunk in the same hooch with an ass, and I will probably eat a good number of meals with an ass. Then it's combat with an ass." He stepped back from the cockpit, spread his arms out, and looked to the heavens. "You know, Lord, I have been good, and I've tried to be tolerant of Bill. But did you have to test me THIS much?" He stared into the sky for a moment longer. Bill watched.

"I understand, Lord, I understand. Thanks." Gary then lowered his arms to his side, stepped back to the aircraft and continued his preparations.

Finally, Bill couldn't help himself. "What'd the Lord say?"

"You don't want to know."

"Yes, I do. What'd he say?"

"OK," Gary began. "He said He thinks you're an ass, too."

"Yeah, right."

"Then He added He had intended to ship you to the Air Force, but it was already full of asses, so he made you a Marine. He said we didn't have nearly enough."

"Very fucking funny, Mr. Comedian," Bill said, trying to seem irked. "Maybe He'll feel differently as I keep your ROTC ass out of the shit in Afghanistan."

"I'll let you do just that, and I'll tell Him all about it," Gary responded.

Just then the public address sounded off: "Thirty minutes till gear up, men. Make your final preparations, man your aircraft, and start your checklists. Be turning in twenty minutes. Out."

As they climbed into the front, Gary called back to Sergeant Cook. "How's it look back there, Cookie?"

"Everything's great, sir," Sgt. Cook responded. "Can't wait to see the blue water!"

"You'll see it soon enough, Sergeant Cook," Bill said as he strapped in, "and you'll have a long time to look at it."

"Sounds good to me!"

"All cargo secure and are our passengers all accounted for, Sergeant?" Gary asked.

"Yes, sir. We're ready," Cook responded.

"OK, we're initiating the start-up check list . . ."

The pilots continued through the preparatory steps until they got to the end, ready to fire up the big aircraft's engines. They looked at each other while they waited for the call to start. Bill reached out his gloved hand.

"Good luck, man. Damn glad to serve with you," Bill said in all seriousness.

"You too, man," Gary replied. As the men lessened their grips, they gave a thumbs-up and saluted one another.

"Freedom Flight, check in," came the old man's voice through the headsets in their helmets.

"Dash Two, ready."

"Dash Three, ready."

"Dash Four, ready," Gary responded, and on it went until all ten aircraft called in.

"Roger flight. Start engines and wait for my call," the CO radioed, his Southern accent even stronger over the radio.

Whines of the big turbines could be heard through everyone's helmets. As the engines turned, ten groups of big, black, stubby rotors began their rotation about the tops of their engines, followed by their twins on the other side of the aircraft. It was a sight to behold: blades and engines pointing skyward and the fuselage pointing forward. *It just doesn't look right,* Gary thought.

"This is Six in Dash One. We're ready. Give me an ops check, flight."

All of the aircraft responded, in sequence, ready to go.

"Roger, Flight. Go to tower on one, but stay on squadron common on two."

"Cherry Point Tower, Freedom Flight is ready for departure."

"Roger, Flight. Wind zero-two-zero at ten knots, altimeter two-niner-niner-six, cleared for takeoff, runway five right, maintain runway heading, climb and maintain one point five thousand feet, contact departure control one two four point one."

"This is Freedom Flight, we copy."

"Roger Flight. Your big birds will be off right behind you. Good luck!"

"Roger. Thanks."

Slowly, the ten XV-11s rose off the tarmac, hovered, turned to runway heading, and angled into the sky. They climbed out as instructed, and, after the CO made the initial contact with air traffic control, they all heard ATC advise them to look out for the C-130s on their left. There they were, big gray monsters with four big turbine engines, their propellers spinning. Colonel Dixon also saw the HH-53 Super Jollies coming up on the flight's right and called them out. These giant helicopters couldn't keep up but would trail the flight to assist as needed. All aircraft headed northeast toward the Atlantic.

"There it is, Sergeant Cook," Bill called out. "Tomorrow it will be all that you'll see—hopefully at this distance, from above."

"Sure is something, isn't it, sir?" Cook responded.

"Don't fall in love, Sergeant. There are things in there that eat people—especially enlisted people!" Harris cracked up at his joke and turned around to Cook, smiling.

"I can't imagine they'd go for a tough old sergeant when they could have the delicacy of an academy-fed officer, sir," Cook responded.

"You're right! That's why I want to keep it the hell away from me. Why do you think I didn't go in the Navy?"

"Good point, sir." Cook said.

After six hours' flight time, they came to Halifax. All aircraft landed on time and passed their post-flight inspections. As he walked away from his aircraft, Gary felt fortunate. With a good measure of relief and a small amount of optimism, the crews went to dinner and bedded down for the night. Closing his eyes, Gary wondered what the rest of the trip would bring.

. . .

Thirty minutes after departure on the morning of the second day of the mission, it happened:

"Lead, this is Chalk Two—we got torque imbalance and number 2 engine has automatically shut down. We're too heavy for single engine operations: we can't hold it in the air!"

"Roger, Chalk Two. Follow ditching procedures."

"This is Boxcar 22. We got him and we're following him down. We'll report back," one of the cargo C-130's radioed.

"Easy, John, easy! Slow it down." The calls were coming from inside Chalk Two. Full of adrenaline, one of the pilots was squeezing his "push-to-talk" button too hard and was transmitting outside of the aircraft instead of over the aircraft intercom.

"Chalk Two, Lead. You're transmitting."

"Roger, Lead."

"You're looking good, Chalk Two. Just continue that down. We're orbiting overhead," Boxcar 22 broadcast.

"Roger. Seems to have stabilized. We have some power, but not enough to maintain altitude."

"Got time to go back to helo mode?" came the call from Lead.

"Rather not try it, sir," Chalk Two responded.

"Lead, understood." Colonel Dixon called to his adjutant and asked, "Felix, how many on that aircraft?"

"Just the crew, three souls," responded Major Ortiz, the S-1, "but they've got gear and a lot of parts."

"Thanks," came the reply. All who heard took note of the fact that the CO didn't ask about the equipment that was on board. He didn't care.

"Chalk Two, this is Chalk Eight." Everyone recognized the voice of the squadron's chief instructor pilot. "Get as slow as you can and when you get close, pull power back and feather, if you can. Better not to have blades striking the water at high speed."

"Wilco."

"Flight, this is Herc 21," one of the tanker KC-130s chimed in. "There is a fishing boat about five miles out. Looks like some kind of trawler. Might see if he can help. I'll try to reach him on guard frequency."

"Herc 21, Lead. Thanks. Let us know."

The sick Sea Eagle continued a fairly smooth descent into the water, but contact created a big splash. They went in hard. Fortunately, just before they hit the water, the crew had successfully stopped the blades from turning and becoming shrapnel. The impact was wings level, and the aircraft remained upright.

Boxcar 22 lowered its orbit to observe and saw that within three minutes of hitting the water, Chalk Two's crew had secured and exited the aircraft, deployed and boarded their life raft, with life jackets on. Knowing that even in the summer hypothermia was a problem in this part of the Atlantic, one of the trailing Super Jollies caught up quickly and extracted the crew. In a matter of thirty minutes, all were clear. Disaster avoided.

"Flight, you'll get a kick out of this one," Herc 21 began, "that's a Russian trawler—WITH antennas. I'm going to stick around until my relief and the fighters and recovery aircraft get here. Shouldn't be long."

"This is Boxcar 22. I'll stay for a while also."

"Roger. How are my guys?" asked Colonel Dixon.

"They're fine," responded the crew of the gigantic Super Jolly helicopter. "We are getting them into some dry clothes."

"Roger. See everyone at Boscombe Down. Out."

Gary relaxed knowing the crew was safe, but the aircraft's ditching brought his fears right to the surface. If it happened to that crew, it could happen to him.

16

Saturday was perfect for a funeral—overcast, drizzle, light fog, and cool. The undertaker couldn't have ordered a better day.

The service was conducted with full military honors, including a twenty-one-gun salute and Taps. The mourners were made up of a who's who of past and present United States Marine Corps, including the current commandant of the Corps and the present and two immediate past sergeants major. Admiral Lawrence also was there. The head chaplain at Quantico delivered the eulogy, calling Sergeant Major Hadley a "credit to his nation, his family, his faith, and the Corps." To those who knew him, it seemed like an understatement.

Trying to go unnoticed in the crowd were two men, both in dark suits and raincoats: agents Nolan and Freid, just back from Claytor Lake. They exchanged only minimal pleasantries with whomever they met and made no attempt to speak to the family.

But someone did notice them. Out of sight in the treeline at the gravesite was Stanford Kemp. He had been too close to Hadley not to show up. But he was there for another reason—he wanted to see who might be there for the bad guys. He figured they would be at the service, probably to look for him. Kemp got a good look at both men and even got the license plate number from their car.

Colonel and Mrs. Hartman were at Vickie Hadley's side throughout both services. At the end of the graveside service, Vickie said, "You both will come back to the house, won't you? Please don't leave just yet."

"Certainly," Charles Hartman responded. He and Betty walked Vickie to the funeral company's limousine. As they got to their car, Charles's breathing was labored. After opening Betty's door, Hartman got in on the driver's side, letting out an audible groan as he sat down. He sat still and did not try to start the car.

"Are you OK?" Betty asked.

"Yes, I am fine, honey. Just a bit tired from all of this," he said, regaining his breath.

Her eyes lingered on him as he drove, trying to detect the slightest hint of what was really going on.

As Hartman moved through the Hadley home speaking with all the guests, he noticed one uniformed young Marine, pacing about the room, sitting, then standing, then pacing again. Colonel Hartman walked over to find out why he was so agitated.

"Sergeant Tulver, I am Colonel Hartman," he said, reading the Marine's name tag and extending his hand. "I know you'll agree with me that this is a terrible loss."

"Yes, sir. He was a good man," Sergeant Tulver said in a heavy eastern Tennessee accent, shaking Colonel Hartman's hand.

"How did you know him?" the Colonel asked.

"I was in the Aviation Directorate, sir. Sergeant Major Hadley was my civilian boss."

"Well, you could have served under no finer leader, which I'm sure you know," Hartman stated.

"Yes, sir. He was like an older brother to me. I really respected him, you know. We even fished and hunted together some on the weekends. He's the one who got me interested in World War II jeeps. He was helpin' me restore one."

This got Hartman's attention. "Really?" Colonel Hartman frowned. "Well, learn from this terrible accident and get rid of the damn thing."

"I know, sir, but . . . well, sir . . . can I be truthful with you? Somethin's been buggin' me."

"What is it, Sergeant?" Hartman asked.

"Well, it's kinda private, sir. Maybe we could go outside?"

"Sure," Colonel Hartman said, wondering what could possibly require privacy as they walked onto the covered patio. "May I?" Tulver asked as he pulled out a cigarette.

Colonel Hartman nodded. "What's on your mind?"

"Well, you know, I was kinda curious when all this happened, so I went to the vehicle compound on base and checked out his vehicle. I didn't suspect nothing, just kinda interested, you know? I know the guys over there and they knowed that I was working on my own jeep with the sergeant major. I talked them into lettin' me take a look. I also thought about takin' a piece of his jeep to put into mine, you know, to remember him, how much he meant to me and all, like a tribute you know? That's OK, right, sir?"

"Sure," said Colonel Hartman, wondering where this conversation was going.

"Well, I was lookin' it over real good, you know, and when I crawled underneath I noticed it . . . well, it just looked kinda odd."

"Noticed what, Sergeant?"

"Well, sir, I don't know what you know about jeeps," Sergeant Tulver said, putting his cigarette on the patio table, pulling his phone out of his pocket and scrolling to a picture, "but right here, you can see that one of them tie-rods isn't connected to its attach point. It's supposed to be right there where that stud is stickin' up, right there, with a cotter-keyed nut on it. See?"

"I think so . . ."

"Here, sir. Here's a picture of the other side. See the rod attached there by that castellated nut?"

"Yes, I do."

"Only problem is that nut is loose and the cotter key is missing. So we have two loose nuts, one totally missing, and the other one ain't got its cotter key. That don't just happen, sir."

"Understood—certainly looks suspicious," Colonel Hartman agreed.

"I know'd it weren't right, sir, but I just wanted to check it agin' mine. So I took these pictures with my cell phone so I could compare it to mine when I got home—just to make sure, you know, the fasteners were the same."

"What did that comparison tell you?"

"When I crawled up under my jeep I seen it right away—see here?" he said pointing to another image on his cell phone. "Both my front end tie-rods have castellated nuts *and* cotter keys. Those things don't just fly off," he said, retrieving his cigarette.

"Anything else?"

"Yes, sir, look here at the sergeant major's jeep. See how the threads on the stud are shiny in places, and on the other side how the castellated nut has shiny marks on its ridges?"

"Certainly. I see that."

"Well that means somebody recently used a tool on them parts that rubbed off the dirt and corrosion." He took a drag off his cigarette, and looked right at Colonel Hartman. "Somebody screwed with the sergeant major's jeep, sir."

Heat flushed through Hartman's body. "Jesus!" Colonel Hartman exclaimed, "You're right!"

"There's one other thing, sir."

"What's that, Sergeant?"

"The rear bumper area showed kinda like a dent. You can see it in this here picture," he said, dropping the cigarette on the ground and rubbing it out with his foot, scrolling on his phone to bring up another image. "I scratched my head about this one for a long time, sir. I couldn't figure out how a rollover would cause this here damage to the back of the vehicle. Of course, if it tumbled end over end that might do it, but this was a side rollover. That got me to thinkin' . . . did Sergeant Major back into something before the accident or did somebody back into him in the parking lot? I mean, you can see some black paint right here," the sergeant said, pointing to one of the pictures. "For sure that weren't no tree or telephone pole."

"Good point, Sergeant." Hartman got close, and in a low, controlled voice said, "Have you told anyone about any of this?"

"No, sir. I was thinking of telling Mrs. Hadley about this, just so she'd know it weren't the sergeant major's fault. And then showing her these here pictures. Then I thought maybe go into the MPs or maybe even the CID. What do you think, sir?"

"Not just yet, Sergeant. Let me look into it first. I think I know some folks that might be able to get to the bottom of this. For now, it's important to keep this to ourselves. I don't want to stir anything up. Besides, if there was foul play, we don't want to tip anyone off that we're on to them."

"Yes, sir, I got you," Sergeant Tulver said solemnly. "Why would somebody do this to Sergeant Major? Who didn't like him? I sure would love to find those mother—"

"You've already done plenty. Just hold tight for now. Can you send me those pictures, Sergeant?"

"Sure, sir."

"Maybe it would be a better idea to put these on a flash drive than risk e-mail."

"Already did, sir, and I also backed 'em up to my PC. We're good to go, sir."

"Great work, Sergeant. Here are a couple of my cards with my home address and telephone number. Send them there. Keep one card and write your contact information on the other, then send it to me with the flash drive," Hartman said, "Now let's get back inside before we're missed." Just before they reached the house, the colonel turned to Sergeant Tulver and stuck out his right hand. "I want to thank you for this, son. You've done us all a great service."

"Thank you, sir, but it wasn't nothin' that the sergeant major wouldn't of done for me, or anybody else. It was the least I could do, sir."

"And if anybody gives you any trouble, or if anybody asks you any questions, you just tell them that Colonel Hartman ordered you to keep your mouth shut, and call me right away, OK?"

"Roger that, sir."

. . .

Eventually, the time came to leave and the Hartmans went over to Vickie.

"Thank you so much for coming. It means a lot," Vickie said.

"Oh, Vickie, you're so welcome. We're just so sad," Betty said. "We're all going to miss him."

When they got to the front door, Colonel Hartman caught movement out of the corner of his eye across the street. Focusing, he saw men in dark suits get into a sedan, which then sped away. Then it hit him—he thought he had seen one of those men in the crowd at the gravesite.

"What's the matter, Charles?" Betty asked.

"Oh, nothing," he responded.

Colonel and Mrs. Hartman got into their vehicle and headed to I-95. Driving up the interstate, the Colonel continuously looked around instead of just on the road ahead.

Betty noticed. "Charles, for goodness sake, what is it? You haven't been yourself since you talked to that man in the backyard. What's going on?"

"You can't say anything, Betty. This whole thing is taking on a different shape."

"What are you talking about, honey?" Betty asked.

"Well, that sergeant I talked to was a fellow World War II jeep fan who believes Ron's death maybe wasn't an accident after all," Hartman said, turning to look at Betty.

Betty gasped. "What? But you said it was the jeep."

"I know. But he showed me some pictures of his jeep compared to Ron's jeep that tells me someone messed with the steering on Ron's jeep."

"I don't understand."

"On Ron's jeep, one of the nuts that is part of the steering system is totally missing and the same one on the other side is loose. On the sergeant's jeep, both nuts are tightened down and secured by a cotter key. Then there's another picture that shows part of the rear section of Ron's jeep is bent inward."

"Are you saying somebody intentionally did things to Ron's jeep?" she asked.

"Not only that, but it looks like someone may have given him a little shove off the road."

Betty's fingers shot up to her lips. "Oh God, Charles, that's horrible! Why?"

"I'm not sure why, but I have a hunch. I'll tell you my suspicions, but not a word of this to anyone, including Vickie, OK?"

"OK, Charles."

"I think it has to do with the XV-11," Hartman said. "Ron wasn't a fan of the program and maybe somebody wanted to eliminate him over his opinions."

Betty just sat in silence, seemingly unable to take it all in.

Hartman was concerned about what might happen next. If Hadley had been hit, he could be a target, also. His military experience told him to have a backup plan. Over the years, he had become friends with Stanford Kemp and he knew Kemp was capable of handling whatever happened.

"You remember Captain Stanford Kemp?"

"Yes, I do. Why?"

"Well, if anything happens to me, I want you to give him a call and tell him what I just told you. I'll give you his contact information when we get home. He'll know what to do."

"Goodness, Charles, stop—you're scaring me. You really think something could happen to you?" Betty's voice rose.

"I don't know. But if any of my hunches are right, we can't be too careful."

When they got home, Colonel Hartman gave Captain Kemp's information to Betty and she put it in her purse. After dinner, Charles helped Betty clear the table and took a drink with him into the den to watch some television, but he couldn't quit thinking about Hadley—and what might be next. He got up several times to look through the shutters. He didn't see anything, but he knew that didn't mean no one was there.

Finally, Charles went into the bedroom and prepared for bed. Before he slipped under the covers, he took one more look out the bedroom shutters. Nothing. He then went to his dresser, opened the middle drawer, and pulled out the holster containing his military .45-caliber automatic pistol. He made sure the magazine was loaded, inserted it into the weapon, and set the weapon on top of his nightstand.

He got under the covers and saw Betty come into the bedroom. As Hartman reached for a book on his nightstand, he felt a sharp pain in his left upper chest. He quickly lay back on the bed, but the pain intensified. Hartman recognized the signs—it was another heart attack. He had forgotten to take his medicine when he got home.

"Betty, my medicine . . . !" he exclaimed, just before being overcome with pain. Betty took one look at him and hurried into the bathroom to get his nitroglycerin pills and a cup of water. She returned quickly, gave him the medicine and called 911. She held his hand, gently rubbed his chest, and waited for the ambulance. "Hurry, please God, hurry!" she pled. She had been through this before, and this time he looked a lot worse.

The emergency workers arrived and took him away in less than ten minutes. They wouldn't let her ride in the back of the ambulance—not a good sign. A neighbor took her to the hospital. On the way, she hoped, and she prayed. It was all she could do.

· · ·

The wait at the hospital for word of Charles's condition seemed like an eternity, but finally the cardiologist appeared. "I think he's going to pull through," the doctor told her. "He's a tough guy. He didn't suffer any collateral damage—no speech loss or anything like that. But I do think it's time to look at a different lifestyle. I'm going to order some significant changes," the doctor said.

"Agreed," she said, nodding.

"Good. You can go see him. He is sleeping, so please don't disturb him. But you're welcome to go to his side."

"Thank you, doctor."

"He's in room 2126. Sarah will take you to him."

"Right this way, Mrs. Hartman." Betty followed the nurse down the hall. She saw Charles lying peacefully on the bed as she entered the room. He had a oxygen mask on his face and an IV in his arm, and he was connected to several monitors. She stood by his side, worried about everything they'd just been through. She moved a chair over to sit closer to him.

She took a seat and watched him for a little while, then reached into her purse to retrieve her paperback book, hoping to distract herself by reading. When she pulled the book out, Charles's note with Kemp's information fell out onto the floor. She picked it up and held it in her hands for a few minutes, wondering what to do. She looked back at Charles to make sure he was all right, and left the room. Once in the hall, she wandered down into the distant corner of an empty lounge. She pulled out her cell phone and dialed.

"Kemp," the gravelly voice said.

"Captain Kemp, this is Betty Hartman."

17

When the Marines finally arrived at Bagram on Monday, the fourth day of the deployment, they and their security force were housed on one side of the airfield in standard USMC tents, and the XV-11 civilian contractors in temporary huts, some with air conditioning, on the other. The Marines' tents were hot during the day and cold at night. The officers were housed ten to a tent, while the enlisted were double that.

No running water meant filling canteens from a "water buffalo," a large water tank on wheels with spigots. And there were no toilet facilities. "One-holers" were placed outside the billeting area, nothing more than half of a fifty-five-gallon drum filled with jet fuel and placed underneath the "seat" opening. Afghans were hired to come daily, haul out the drums, and burn them, producing an unbearable smell. "Welcome to Afghanistan," Gary thought. He could only imagine what the chow was going to be like.

Aircraft hangar facilities for the XV-11s were nonexistent. The aircraft would have to be maintained in the open with all of the negatives associated with the sandy, dusty, windy environment. The talcum-powder-like sand would pass right through the particle separators designed to stop contaminants from entering the engines. It would not take long for engine erosion to develop.

Gary remained troubled by the aircraft problems experienced during the trip over and what it meant for the overall mission. It seemed that every possible thing that could go wrong with an aircraft was going wrong with the XV-11s: hydraulic leaks, which caused another aircraft to be left behind at Boscombe Down, oil leaks in engines and transmissions, fuel leaks, a myriad of software malfunctions that caused flight-control anomalies, multifunction display failures, and strange vibrations that couldn't be traced to their sources. No causes of these multiple problems could be identified. And now they had fewer pilots in mission rotation since two crews remained with the two aircraft that had been left behind.

All of this was taking its toll on morale. An epidemic of apprehension was spreading among the aviators. It was bad enough to go into combat with all of its risks, but now, on top of combat risks, the distinct possibility existed that the aircraft itself, and not the enemy, might kill its users. Every time a pilot pulled the trigger to start the engines in these monsters he wondered whether he would make it back.

Gary was beginning to sense that Bill was finally concerned as well. Ironically, Bill's bravado had buoyed Gary's own confidence before, but now Bill's actions and his demeanor indicated to Gary that the aircraft's staunchest supporter was dubious.

The crews had barely begun to settle in when the first briefing was called. Every pilot reported to the CO and operations officer's tent, which doubled for now as the operations tent. Waiting for the aviators in the tent were several people dressed in native clothing but with what appeared to be Western faces. They were armed with an unusual assortment of weapons, only some of which appeared to be American-made.

"Take a seat where you can," Colonel Dixon instructed. "Before I introduce you to some of the people you'll be working with while you're here, I need to tell you to remove all insignia from your uniform and replace it with muted insignias and camouflaged unit patches. We don't want to advertise our rank structure. Be careful how you address one another when the locals are around. Understood?"

A collective "Yes, sir" emanated from the assembled crews.

"They're all yours," Colonel Dixon said to the tallest native-dressed individual.

The individual walked over to the podium and began with the routine,

"Good afternoon. Thanks for coming." The crowd chuckled. "Oh, you didn't just wake up and decide to respond positively to an invitation? This wasn't your idea?" A few individual "No"s could be heard—even one "Hell no!"

Then he continued, "I'm Colonel Putnam of the United States Marine Corps. That's the last time you'll hear me or anyone else say that. Again, we want to make sure we don't reveal our rank structure to the locals."

So convincing was his look, Gary wouldn't have believed he was American if he hadn't heard his voice. And he was shocked when the guy said he was a colonel.

"I have been in special operations all of my career. One of the other people over there in native attire is Lieutenant Colonel Burnside, one of our SEAL team leaders. The two gentlemen you see seated to Lieutenant Colonel Burnside's right are . . . well, actually you don't need to know who they are—for now.

"You'll be flying us where only your machines can do the job. Most of your work here will be directed through the normal chain of command, but when we're on your aircraft, you will take your orders from us. In the tactical environment we're your chain of command. Of course, we will rely upon your expertise to keep us informed about the capabilities of your aircraft, but we have authority on go-no-go, at least as far as the tactical situation is concerned." He paused, looked at Colonel Dixon, and said, "Confirm that, Paul?"

"Confirmed," Colonel Dixon.

"We have seen the enemy change tactics recently as they have been uncharacteristically utilizing en masse tactics, overpowering our special ops teams." Putnam stated. "Now, to counter this, we are going to descend upon them with great force and power to wipe them out. That's why you're here. You will get us to where we need to be quicker than a conventional helicopter and with more personnel and equipment. Between our special ops folks and your leathernecks, we'll kick their asses."

This brought a round of raucous cheers and "Semper Fi!"

"All the markings on your aircraft, except for a number, are being removed and changed as we speak. We're not trying to fool anybody that you're an Afghan XV-11 squadron"—his comment brought a gush of laughter—"but we just don't want to make it easy to identify units and personnel.

"To assure surprise, you will not be able to prefly the potential combat routes that you might be flying on an actual mission. You will do your recon using the terrain maps and tactical 3D maps, computer images projected on our big screens to get a real good idea of the topo features. "We hope to use you suddenly and with complete surprise, which will produce the most dramatic results. If that happens, we'll all be home sooner rather than later."

Fat chance, Gary thought. *If we're as successful as he thinks we can be, we'll go from here to some other part of this godforsaken land.*

As Colonel Putnam left the podium, Colonel Dixon said, "Keep your seats."

First time I have not stood for a departing colonel, Gary thought. *This is going to be different.*

Colonel Dixon continued. "Now, about the threat. Our intelligence says that neither Al-Qaeda nor the Taliban have shoulder-fired SAMs. Once they know you're here, however, they may get them. That's why our plan is to have this over quickly—at least your involvement.

"We must be combat-ready in twenty-four hours," Dixon advised. "A rotational crew list will be put on the Ops bulletin board in two hours. Check it. You may expect heavy activity once we begin. We plan to nail the enemy quickly, before they find out we're here. The ruses to draw them out are already underway. Early indicators are that they are buying into our traps. Any questions?"

"None, sir," Bill shouted.

"Anybody else?" Colonel Dixon asked, looking around the tent. There was silence, so Colonel Dixon told everyone to go back to quarters and continue to prepare.

"Looks like there is going to be a lot of on-the-job training over here," Gary said to Bill as they headed back to their tent.

"No shit, Sherlock," Bill fired back. "Let's just hope a lot of it's prior to getting into the crap. I don't have a clue about this place, and being directed around the countryside by Harry and the Hoodlums doesn't give me the warm fuzzies. Where are OUR guys? This is bullshit about not being controlled by our own command! It's not the way we do it!"

"Whoa there, Mister Mean Marine! They gotta have some operational hot-shot to brief us on flying in this environment. Surely you're not suddenly of the opinion that the military doesn't know what it's doing?"

"Have you seen such a person? NO!" Bill shot back. "They figured since we flew '46s in Iraq, we can figure this out. There are only two problems with that—this ain't Iraq, and these ain't '46s!"

"Don't be shocked, Bill, but this time I am going to agree with you," Gary said. "Screw it. Let's go to the hooch and get settled in."

"Yeah. Let's do that. What a treat!" Bill said, sarcastically.

"What a treat, indeed." Gary responded, as the two men walked back to their tent, resigned to their situation.

18

"Baird Law Offices."

"Hello, Florence, it's Lisa Thorpe. Is Mr. Baird in? I really need to talk to him."

"Not yet. But he should be here any minute now. Can I have him call you when he gets in?"

"Sure, I'm on my cell phone."

"Thank you."

Moments later, Jake walked in, dressed in his standard khakis and starched oxford cloth shirt, but this time wearing a navy blazer.

"Good morning, Florence."

"Good morning, Mr. Baird. What's the occasion?"

"Oh, you mean the jacket? Well, I made it to church yesterday and my keys were still in the pocket, so I just threw it on," Jack said. He pivoted as he passed her desk on the way to his office to hide the back of his head from her. He didn't want to get into it.

"Well, that explains it. By the way, I tried to straighten up your office a bit before you got in. What in the world were you doing in there over the weekend?"

"Just trying to catch up a bit," Jake said.

"Before you get onto something else, Lisa Thorpe called and asked that you call her on her cell. She seemed anxious."

Jake went into his office and made the call.

"Hello?" Lisa answered her phone on the second ring.

"Hi, Lisa. It's Jake Baird. How are you?"

"I'm fine. Thanks for calling so quickly. I've got a few things for you. First, I had a meeting with Colonel Freeman; he was Sam's commanding officer at the time of the crash. He told me something very strange, and told me I should ask you about it."

"What's that?" Jake asked.

"Well, first he said this wasn't Sam's fault. That was a relief, but I already knew Sam was an excellent pilot. Then he said that there were two investigations, one that I could see, which he gave to me. I can mail it to you."

"That would be great. That one is called the Judge Advocate General's Manual Report, or JAGMAN," Jake said.

"The other one," Lisa continued, "he called the Safety Board Report. He said that the Safety Board Investigation is more thorough but that I won't be able to see some of it? He says it's privileged—whatever that means."

"Right, unfortunately. The military will black out most of it."

"What do you mean, 'black out'?"

"They have a Judge Advocate General's Corps officer, a military lawyer, who decides what is releasable information and what isn't, based on that officer's interpretation of the regulations. Then he or she takes a big black marker and marks through the unrealeasable portions of the document."

"But Colonel Freeman said that's the one that says what really happened."

Jake tried to explain. "Every military branch conducts two investigations. The one where the defense contractors help is the second one, the Safety Board Report, sometimes called the mishap report. For some reason, the services feel that if the public knew what really happened, it would jeopardize safety."

"That seems like backward thinking."

Jake agreed. "Of course it does, and it's not the way our civilian agency, the NTSB, does it."

"It's unfair not to let the family members of those who died see it," Lisa said.

"I agree. But they are very serious about protecting their secrecy. Occasionally a congressman will challenge this ridiculous rule for a constituent such as yourself, but they always back down once the military tells them that Congress should keep its nose out of the military's business."

Jake moved on, being careful about what he could tell her. "Lisa, I need to be candid with you. Any military case is tough. Judges have issued decisions that say we can't sue the government for wrongful death, even if it's their fault. Other rulings have limited our ability to sue military contractors. Simply put, a person in the military does not have the same rights a civilian does. So it's an uphill, almost impossible battle."

"Does this mean you're not going to take my case?"

"No, it doesn't. I am going to take your case. I just want to set your expectations," Jake said.

"Thank you for being honest with me." She sighed. "It looks like Captain Kemp was right."

There was that name again. "How do you know him?"

"Only a little bit. He visited us a couple of times, passing through. He was a friend of Sam's father. I saw him again at Sam's funeral. I think he worked in aviation, but I seem to remember something about his being in intelligence work, also."

Now Jake understood why Kemp was operating as he did.

"Once I told him I'd hired you, he told me I made a good choice," Lisa added.

"Well, you'll have to thank him for me," Jake said.

He changed the subject. "Tell me, how are you doing otherwise, and how is Samuel?"

"I'm OK during the day; it's the nights that are a problem," she admitted. "Sometimes it's so hard, so so hard." Jake could hear her voice break, then silence, but finally she continued. "You know, I think the news of the XV-11 squadron's deployment is also causing a lot of emotions to resurface."

Jake felt his stomach lurch, but his voice stayed calm. "Deployment? Really? I'm sure that doesn't help," he said.

"No, it doesn't."

"I'd better go. I'll send you that report, and we'll talk soon. Good-bye, Mr. Baird."

Florence walked into Jake's office when she saw that he'd hung up. "Pardon me for overhearing, but it sounds like you've decided to take her case. Good for you—and her."

"Yes, and there's a lot more to it that we have to talk about, but not right now," Jake said. He stood up, grabbed something from his satchel and motioned for Florence to follow him. He led her down the stairs onto the street, then whispered, "Remember the guy at the Waffle House who gave me the secret file?"

"Yes, of course, Jake."

"Well his name is Stanford Kemp—*Captain* Stanford Kemp, United States Navy, Retired."

"Okay," Florence responded, waiting for more.

"I have a present for you from him," and Jake handed Florence the phone he had pulled from his briefcase. "It's a secure phone, and you and I will use it to communicate. Its number is 222-410-4878. It will only be secure with another secure phone—like mine. My number is 222-410-4877 and Captain Kemp's number is 222-410-4875. Don't write them down. Just remember them, OK?"

"Certainly," Florence said, examining the phone. "This is getting exciting—secret documents, covert hand-offs, high-tech gear—I could get used to this."

"You don't want to get too used to it. There are reasons for all of this that I will explain when I get back. Right now, I've got to make a call," Jake said, moving away from Florence and pulling out his secure phone.

"OK, I'm ready to meet. How about eleven thirty?" Jake asked.

"That works. Let's say the place where you went after our first meeting."

"Roger. Out." Jake wasn't surprised anymore by what Captain Kemp knew. Jake was surprised, however, that with all the suits crawling all over the area after their original meeting, Kemp had stuck around to see that Jake made it. Earlier, Jake had found the small tracking device Kemp had attached to the rear end of the passenger door. "Kemp will know when I get close," Jake thought.

Jake headed to his car. Adrenaline raced through his body—no turning back now. His mind was a cyclone of thought. *One thing at a time,* he told himself. *Stay cool.*

. . .

Jake saw no sign of Kemp when he got to the college. He parked and started toward the library steps when his secure phone rang.

"Go into the woods behind the library," Kemp instructed.

As soon as Jake got about twenty feet into the woods, Kemp called to him, "Over here." Jake moved to Kemp's location.

Jake noticed a different look on his face. He couldn't tell if Kemp was tired, weary, or bothered.

"You first, Jake. What the hell happened in Virginia?" Kemp asked.

"After our talk, I headed out but realized I forgot my phone. When I got back, two guys had Collins at the boathouse. I fought them, but a third came up and hit me on the head, knocked me out. When I came to, they were gone and Collins's body was floating in the lake near his boat."

Kemp's face got beet red. "Those bastards! You should have blown them away—weren't you armed?"

"My weapon was in the car. When I pulled up there was no sign of anyone else. I didn't see the two goons until I got to the boathouse. Then I did what I could."

With a deep exhale, Kemp dropped to one knee, and waited for Jake to continue.

"Look, dammit, if I had known that he was in danger, I would have been carrying. But I broke one guy's jaw and had the other one reeling until the third one came up from behind. I did all I could. So don't give me any crap, OK?"

"It's not you. It's the fact that somehow they've penetrated my security measures. I thought I had devised a pretty airtight plan, but they found him anyway. With all the problems they're having and their file missing, they wanted to shut him up so he couldn't come out and talk about the better design."

"Don't be hard on yourself. Even a great plan can break down."

"It's not just one. They got to a retired Marine Corps sergeant major, also."

"What? Was he involved?" Jake asked.

"Deeply. As much as me and you."

"When did this happen?"

"Last Wednesday. They loosened the steering on his jeep and then gave him a shove off the road. Name was Ron Hadley."

"Damn," Jake said. "Does anything tell you they know about me?"

"No, we have no proof they know about you—yet. I think if they had known you might not have made it here today."

Jake smiled. "Collins's quick thinking worked."

"How's that?" Kemp asked.

"When I showed up at the boathouse Collins called me 'Professor Kline' and said the books I was looking for were up at the house. He knew the third guy was searching his house. Guess he figured if I went back there, I could handle him and maybe come back. Should have listened."

"Forget it. He protected you there and maybe they're still trying to figure out who and where you are. Anyway, we still have a mission to complete. Now you're the guy who has to be protected at all costs," Kemp said.

Hearing this didn't give Jake any comfort. If Kemp thought he was the most important person in this equation, it was just a matter of time before the other side thought that too. If they'd found Collins, they would find him, sooner or later.

"We have to move before they get anyone else," Jake said. "I worked on this all weekend—drafted pleadings and made copies. Before all of this happened, I was going to use the information in the documents secretly, as a roadmap to bring out the truth in the lawsuit. But now things have changed—these killings—and now the deployment—everything's moved too fast. We can't wait for the litigation to take its course. The documents and my talk with Collins have given me the background I needed. We have to use the documents now to do what needs to be done."

"Yeah, I heard about the deployment." Kemp said, then smiled and nodded. "Looks like that wimp got left behind and the courageous combat officer came through."

That was a low blow—wimp. "I'll let that slide, Captain. I can't stand by and let Hadley's and Collins's deaths go unavenged. Oliver and Beech are going down, and their murdering friends with them. Lisa Thorpe will get to see these guys squirm in a courtroom, and the others who are currently flying that piece of shit will be protected."

"That's the man I thought you were," Kemp said, slapping Jake on the back. "Before we talk about your plan, there's one more thing." Kemp continued, standing up.

Jake's eyes widened. "There's more?"

"Yes. Admiral Lawrence, head of NAVAIR, is going to testify on the Hill in two days. I can't let him go up there and give false information," Kemp said. "I was hoping to have the lawsuit filed well before Lawrence went before Congress, and get the information to him that way, but they pushed up the Senate briefing. Now the information he presents will be compiled by the current staff, without the info in the documents or the assistance of the program manager, Colonel Hartman, who has a bad heart and is in the hospital. Losing Sergeant Major Hadley was a real blow to him. So Oliver and his cronies now have no one in their way—except us."

"The Assistant Program Manager? That Oliver? I thought Beech was directing it all."

"Beech is minor league. Oliver is the primary player. He's the one controlling the hits . . . we know this. Beech wouldn't have the guts—or the resources."

"How does Oliver have the resources?"

"I watched that slick SOB operate for years. I always had a hunch he was skimming funds and befriending people outside of NAVAIR, but I never could prove it. Well, now I have evidence he's been funneling money away from programs and using that to buy favors," Kemp said.

"The best way to defend ourselves and get these guys is to go on offense. I have to finalize a couple of things, but I think you'll like the plan," Jake said. "But first, I need to know something—why are you in this?"

"Let's just say it's in my DNA to shoot down weapons programs that don't work. But this is personal, too. I encouraged that boy, Thorpe, to go to flight school. And then they gave him that piece of shit to fly? I feel like I owe it to his family." Kemp shook his head. "Enough on that. What's the plan?"

"One more thing—how the hell did you get that file out of the Pentagon?"

"It helps that I got to know the guards at a small entrance special ops people used. So when I walked in and out with a big briefcase full of papers, they didn't think anything of it. They looked inside on the way in and out, but my papers covered up a leather flap at the bottom where I stashed Oliver's file."

"But how did you even know about the file?"

"My friends at the Test Directorate and inside the Pentagon have been watching Oliver for months. They knew someone in the program was changing the info after it left the Test Directorate before it got to NAVAIR. It was a process of elimination. We had a hunch he was the guy at the center of the cover-up. So we merely broke into his office and searched his desk to see what we could find. Picking that Mickey Mouse lock was easy."

"So when did you think of the lawyer angle—specifically, me?" Jake asked.

"We were waiting for the right circumstances. When Lisa Thorpe told me she had hired you, it all came together. An innocent widow represented by a military hero lawyer. Lisa gave us credibility we might not have had without it. Getting to the truth through a lawsuit would avoid the messiness of directly disclosing classified files. But all I had was a concept that might get us somewhere. You're the one who has to come up with the plan that will make it work—and then execute it."

"I've already started. I've roughed out a draft complaint with allegations based on the documents. I also sketched out a set of Requests to Admit, asking the defendants to admit the authenticity of the most important documents and what they said, thereby telling the story. All will be finalized in a few hours."

"Sounds good."

"But before actually filing the lawsuit, I'm going to give them—the military and the contractors—a chance to do the right thing by sending them copies of these documents and telling them we won't file the papers and go public, *if* they will agree to fix the aircraft's problems."

Kemp smiled. "I like your moxie, Colonel, but you know they'll never do it. You'll wind up filing."

"Probably so, but I want to play this as fair as I can. And from what I've seen, there's at least a chance that the damning information in those documents never even got to the top of either the military or those mega-corporations. Admiral Lawrence is a case in point, right? Maybe they'll be shocked by what they didn't know and want to look into it."

"I think you're dreaming, Colonel, and I don't know if there's enough time for all of that."

"Sure there is. I was thinking twenty-four hours or less. If they believe what they're reading, they'll move quickly," Jake said.

"Any thoughts on what to do with the originals?"

"We should secure them somewhere. Treat them as an insurance policy," Jake suggested. "And I have just the place for them. As long as the originals are missing, those assholes can't scream about a security breach, because they'll have to *explain* the security breach, which might result in revealing what's in those documents. They don't want any of this out. So they'll think twice about what to do about the breach. They'll keep trying to fix it without reporting it."

"Maybe," Kemp said.

"In the meantime, the CEOs and the military brass will get copies of everything I intend to file. At the very least, they'll do something to start covering their asses. Assuming they really don't know about any of this, they'll try to find the rotten apples, which will squeeze the bad guys. The top brass will understand that if we're sending them around, we won't be afraid to actually file the lawsuit and let the general public see them."

"Right," Kemp said, still sorting it all out.

"On the other hand, if the military and the CEOs don't do the right thing, then I'll file the lawsuit, which I have decided to do at some point for Lisa Thorpe anyway."

"Looks like you have it all worked out. But you'll need some cover to keep working, and that's how I can help. They've been chasing me for so long, I'll just get them to chase me some more. But I'll need to make some noise to get *all* of them after me."

"Be careful—you know they won't play nice," Jake said.

"No, they won't. But they have to catch me first. Even if they do, killing me would cause them more problems than it's worth. This isn't a slick road or an isolated lake situation. You, and others, will know I am captured and by whom. And in case that happens, I have something else in the works that you don't need to know about. Anyway, they can't do anything to me I haven't already experienced."

"Just don't get caught. I've gotten used to you."

"No guts, no glory." Kemp responded, and slapped Jake on the back. "You just leave that part to me."

"If you say so," Jake said.

"By the way," Kemp began, leaving the joking aside, "remember I started to tell you that Admiral Lawrence would be testifying this week before Congress? I didn't finish. *You'll* need to prep him."

"What?"

"Yes—there's no one else. I've already talked to him about this potentiality. Plan on being in DC tomorrow afternoon, the day before he testifies. I'll get you the details later. This means you have to get your stuff done here pronto."

"Good thing I got that head start," Jake said.

"You're right." Kemp began to walk away.

Jake watched and wondered: *So is the admiral involved? Who else? Would the admiral be Kemp's safety valve?*

Kemp stopped and turned around. "By the way, where are the documents?"

"Secured where no one can find them," Jake responded.

"I'll trust you on that. Better I don't know," Kemp said. "See you around."

Jake watched him walk away, then headed out.

19

Just after 2200 hours, the XO came into the aviators' tent and shouted, "Majors Harris and Bennett, grab your flight gear and follow me. The old man needs to see you, ASAP." He didn't wait for them.

"This doesn't sound good." Bill said as he scrambled off the cot.

"No, it doesn't. I can't think of anything we did," Gary responded, gathering up his stuff. "I wish we had done something. I'm afraid it's something worse," Gary said as he looked around for his charts.

"What?" Bill demanded.

Gary was shoving his gear into his flight bag. "I have a bad feeling we're going flying."

"Maybe so." Bill wanted to reassure Gary. "Don't worry, we'll be fine. Probably just a test hop." Bill zipped up his flight suit and grabbed his helmet.

The XO jerked the tent flap open and yelled, "Now, gentlemen, NOW! In the operations tent, NOW!"

"Understood, sir. On the way," Bill said.

The XO glared at the two men and then disappeared. Bill and Gary raced out the door behind him. "Test hop my ass!" Gary said to Bill, as he jogged toward the operations tent.

They entered the operations tent, where the CO, the XO, the S-3, and Lieutenant Colonel Burnside from the SEALs were all gathered in front of a large map of Afghanistan. Gary and Bill both noticed that no other aviators were there.

"Come in and sit down, men," their commander, Colonel Dixon said, pointing to two chairs by themselves in front of the assembled group.

"We have a little situation down in Ghor Province. That's here," the CO said, pointing to a place on the map. "It is about an hour's flight away. You're as good a crew as I've got, and your aircraft is in great shape. Mr. Burnside will brief you men on the details of the mission."

The CO moved away and the man they saw for the first time only days ago fully made up in native clothes, now dressed in full SEAL combat uniform, stepped up onto the podium in front of the map.

"Good evening, I'm Patrick Burnside, Commander of SEAL Team Four. About thirty minutes ago, we got a report from our local operatives that a meeting had taken place here, near Chaghcharan, that involved many known Taliban leaders. The meeting ended about an hour ago. A lot of the lower-ranking attendees disbursed and headed back to their villages, but most of the top leaders, five total, stayed, apparently to eat their evening meal together. According to our intelligence, their activity suggests that they are planning to stay the night.

"They probably know the XV-11 is in theatre, but they don't understand its capabilities. Your aircraft is perfect for this mission, and they won't be thinking we can move our forces that far that fast."

Burnside looked at the two aviators and saw apprehension.

"I can see it on your faces, gentlemen: why not an air strike, maybe a drone strike? Good question. Normally that would be an option, but these guys are in three houses on the east side of the village. We can't take a chance—too many civilian casualties. Plus, if possible, we want them alive for intel purposes."

Bill and Gary nodded. They understood what Burnside was saying, but weren't eager to hear the rest. "Got it," Bill said.

"You're going to fly this route to here," Burnside said, pointing to a green line on the map. "Your approach route will bring you up over the reverse side of a slope to flat ground at the edge of the village," Burnside continued, "and you will insert our twelve-man team here, right on top of the enemy." Burnside pointed to a circle on the map. He added, "You will not shut down. The team will conduct a rapid raid designed to capture or kill. After dropping off the troops, during the raid, you will reposition here"— once again pointing to the map—"and orbit. Tactical air support will be available via A-10s and fast movers and will be orbiting, here, in this vicinity, and here, both two minutes away." He stopped and looked at Gary and Bill. "Questions thus far?"

"None, sir," Bill said.

Burnside continued the briefing. "The actual assault will take no longer than fifteen minutes. Upon the team's call, you will return to the LZ and retrieve the team and any prisoners. Any seriously wounded will be taken directly to Kabul Air Base and the hospital there. Your whole time on the ground, inserting and extracting, should be less than five minutes. You should also know that we have friendlies in town who will block any attempted escape by the Taliban cadre.

"In addition to our twelve team members, you will also carry a squad of Marines with heavy personal automatic weapons. This is for contingency reasons only. They are not part of our team. They are for backup only."

He stepped away from the map. "OK, that's the overall mission. You will depart at 0200. Again, gentlemen, any questions?"

"No," the two pilots responded in unison.

"OK, then. Mr. Landis will go over flight planning. Be here by 0130 with your crew chief." He stepped off the podium and walked to the two pilots, who stood up. He extended his right hand. "I am sure you'll do a great job. I'll see you at 0130."

Burnside briskly left the room as the SEALs' operations officer mounted the podium, moved to the map and gave his briefing, which was clear except for his omission of critical information about the landing zone.

"What's the altitude of LZ?" Gary asked.

"Approximately 8500 feet msl," Landis responded.

Gary and Bill moaned in unison. They knew a fully loaded aircraft would have performance problems at that height above mean sea level. Landis blew it off. "You'll be fine. Other questions?"

"Uh, with all of the fuel, troops, and equipment, we are going to be heavy going up. We'll burn off some fuel, so I guess it will be OK. But I am just wondering about POWs. How many, potentially?" Gary asked.

"As you indicated, fuel burn-off should take care of any additional weight due to potential POWs," Landis replied. "Don't be concerned—my personnel know how to secure them in your aircraft." Then he added, "Personally, however, I would be surprised if there are any POWs other than the five leaders."

Gary looked at two SEALs who had entered the tent. They shook their heads, confirming to him there would not be any POWs—maybe not even the leaders.

"OK, if no questions—"

"Just one more," Bill began.

"Yes, Major Harris?"

"Well, I have no doubt about the great skill of the troops, but . . . well, uh, I am just wondering—"

"Yes, Major Harris?" the impatient Landis interrupted, leaving the podium to walk down right in front of Bill.

"Well, what if it takes longer than expected? What if we don't get a call in fifteen minutes? How long do we hold? Fuel could be an issue."

"From what I have been briefed," Landis responded, "I am confident the call will come in fifteen minutes. But if it doesn't, you wait until it does come. We don't leave our men on the ground."

"Yes, I wouldn't—"

"OK, if neither of you have any other questions you can go get ready. I am sure you have a lot to do," Landis said. He straightened up, took a big breath, and with a smile said, "This will be a great mission. Now we can do what we need to do. Dismissed!" Landis marched out of the room with the two SEALs, leaving Bill and Gary alone.

Bill turned to Gary and said, "Well, that's that. I didn't hear a recovery option, did you?"

As Gary stood up, he replied, "Sure did. We fly our ass in circles until they tell us not to or until we run out of gas. Great mission planning."

"Then you and I better figure it out now, before the shit hits," Bill said, poking Gary in his chest.

"The only thing we can do is call ops at the fifteen-minute mark if we don't hear anything from the SEALs. But first, we go see the old man. He heard the briefing. He's not going to let us run out of gas up there," Gary said.

They found Colonel Dixon by himself, outside the tent smoking a cigarette.

He knew what they wanted. "I understand your concerns, men. You'll be fine. You two are my best. But if things get out of hand, let our recovery team know and work out a back-up plan with Burnside before you depart. Seems like a smart guy. Screw the OPS officer."

"Thanks, sir," Gary said. "We'll go find Burnside and our recovery team."

"Good luck, men. I know you'll do great," Colonel Dixon said, taking a draw off his cigarette.

Bill and Gary headed out to their aircraft to pre-flight, but not before they looked for the SEAL team mission leader, Burnside, and their own recovery team to set up a plan.

20

Raleigh, North Carolina
Monday, August 10, 2009
1:00 p.m.

He'd worked out his plans with Kemp, and now Jake wanted to play the media card—or at least have it ready. He had a friend at the *Raleigh Observer*, Jeff Noe, whom he'd gotten to know when Jeff had used him as an aviation source. Jeff had won several awards reporting on Department of Defense fiascos. One was about the poisoning of the drinking water at Camp Lejeune that caused devastating illnesses and birth defects. The other exposed a botched Air Force procurement program, which caused the Air Force Procurement Office brass to fly down to Raleigh to let Jeff's bosses know that they didn't appreciate the negative articles.

Jeff had written two articles on the XV-11, but they had not gone deeply into the aircraft's flaws. The critical information was almost impossible to dig out. Jake wanted to give Jeff copies of the court documents he was drafting in a sealed envelope that Jeff would open only if the case was filed. The question was whether there was a way, ethically and professionally, for Jeff to hold on to them and not use them until Jake said OK. Then, what if all went well and there was no filing? Would Jeff just give them back?

A meeting with Jeff might answer Jake's concerns.

"So how's the newspaper business, Jeff?" Jake asked as they met in the park across from Jeff's office.

"Busy. I'm glad this worked out, though. It's been a long time." Jeff, who

Jake thought was a bit older than he and prematurely gray, took off his glasses and let out a sigh.

Jake got down to business. "I really need to talk to you about something urgent."

"Oh? What's up?"

"Let's sit over here," Jake said, moving to a park bench. "I would like to drop off some lawsuit papers, a Complaint and Requests to Admit, at your office sometime in the next day or so. They will be in a sealed envelope and addressed to you. I just need for you to hold on to them—unopened—until I say it's OK. That will happen when, and if, they are filed, or under some other conditions I won't go into. When you read them, you'll know what this is all about."

"OK . . ."

"There's plenty of solid information to back up what's in these documents. Some of it will be attached to the requests. For right now, though, I ask that you take my word on the rest of it."

"Jake, you know I have to do the right thing under our ethical rules. I can't just take the word of a lawyer about some court filing . . . even if it is you."

"I understand that. The legal papers will lay it out. You'll see—this is right up your alley," Jake said.

"Well, I'll have to see for myself, you know," Jeff cautioned.

"Of course," Jake said. "Look, I wouldn't ask if it weren't important, and I wouldn't ask if I didn't think you could do it. Besides, I'm fairly certain it will benefit you—and the paper."

"OK. I'll stand by. I'll have to run it by the boss, especially if it is big as you say."

"Your editor will jump at it. It's simple. All you're doing is reporting on the facts of what's been filed in court. I'm giving you a head start and need for you to give it your best shot—maximum play, wire services, front page if at all possible—after it's filed."

"But what if it's not filed? What do I do with the envelope?" Jeff asked.

"We'll handle that if it happens. Just keep it sealed until I say so," Jake advised. "My bet is it will be filed. When it is, I may not be immediately reachable for comment. Just wanted you to know."

"Can you at least give me a *little* hint of what this is all about?"

"Like I said, a wrongful death lawsuit that happens to involve a certain aircraft . . . assuming it qualifies as an aircraft," Jake said.

Jeff nodded. "Yeah. Seems like no matter how bad the press gets, the program continues. And all we do is report on the facts. Those associated with the program just don't like their own facts."

"It's a strange world in which we live, Noe. Truth becomes fiction and fiction truth. It's amazing what's being sold to the American public. But they're proving that if you tell a lie often enough with sufficient force, it displaces the truth," Jake said.

"May I quote you on that?" Jeff asked rhetorically.

"Sure. You can even claim that as your own, if you wish."

"Thanks. I'll save it for a slow day." They both laughed.

They stood up and shook hands. "Good seeing you again, Jeff."

"Same here. I'll look forward to getting your package," Jeff replied. "When do you think that might be?"

"Not long. In the next couple days," Jake said.

. . .

Raleigh, North Carolina
Monday, August 10, 2009
2:30 p.m.

Jake walked back into the office and said, "Florence, let's take a little walk."

They headed down the stairs, turned the sign hanging from the doorframe so it read "Closed for Lunch," and locked the door. After a brief walk, Jake found a bench in the shade and motioned for Florence to sit there.

"Florence, things are getting dangerous," he said as he sat down beside her. "People have been killed—"

"I know, Jake. I know Lisa Thorpe, remember?" Florence said.

"I'm not talking about Major Thorpe. People who knew about the papers I receive killed a Marine sergeant major, then they drowned Dr. Collins—the man I went to see on my trip. He was the sweet older guy who explained the aircraft program to me."

"Oh shit!" Florence said, covering her open mouth with her hand.

"They'll do it again. You, and I, are in danger. And I don't want to be responsible for anything happening to you. So you have to do exactly what I tell you, understand?"

"I understand," Florence said, staring at Jake. "So what's the plan?"

"I'm not going to tell you the whole plan, but here is what you need to know for now. I've drafted a Complaint and Requests to Admit to be filed together in federal court. I'm going to attach some of the stolen documents to the Requests to Admit, which will tell the entire story. I'm going to send copies to other places."

"You don't need me to help with that?" Florence asked.

"Not with that—I don't want you to see the pleadings or the attached papers. But there is one very important thing," he continued. "You will need to file the papers when it's time because I won't be here to do it." He looked for a reaction from Florence, but she just nodded. "There is risk, as I said. I doubt if they would hurt you, but I can't deny there is a risk."

"I can tell you this is surely more interesting than working at my previous corporate law firm," Florence replied, grinning.

Jake shook his head. *Typical Florence.*

"In the meantime, especially at the time of filing, as hard as it's going to be for you, you're going to have to play dumb. But then, as smart as you are, I know you are very good at playing dumb—when you want to."

"I think there is a compliment in there somewhere," Florence said.

"Of course."

"You can't work for attorneys who represent big corporations and not learn how to play dumb. Working for you, I've never had to do that, until now."

"Well, thank you, Florence. I think there's a compliment in there somewhere."

They both smiled. Their banter helped to at least take a bit of the edge off the situation.

"Now, I don't want you to be caught with that phone. Hide it somewhere where it will be safe and where no one can find it except for you. But don't take it to the courthouse when you file."

"Understood," she said.

"Come on, Florence, let's head back. I've got a couple more things to do and then I'll be back to finalize everything. You can close up right after you get back."

They rose off the bench and headed back to the office.

. . .

Raleigh, North Carolina
Monday, August 10, 2009
4:00 p.m.

Jake pulled up Irwin Thompson's cell number. "Got a minute for a meeting?"

"Certainly, Counselor. You know I wasn't doing anything else on this Monday afternoon at my busy law office except waiting for your call."

"Good. See you at Caribou Coffee in ten minutes."

Jake beat Irwin to the coffee shop.

"Thanks for coming Irwin, and I apologize for the short notice," Jake said when Irwin came in.

"You seem especially steeled for something, Counselor. What's got you so tuned up and turned on?" Irwin asked.

"A lot. The easiest first. They're deploying a squadron of these XV-11s before they're ready. This whole program is flawed and needs to be stopped."

"You've said as much to me before. What's changed?" Irwin asked.

"They just killed a Marine sergeant major who was trying to help bring this issue out of the shadows. Then they killed an engineer who I met with to school me on the alternative designs and the start of the program."

Irwin flinched. "Good God, Jake! That changes things. I don't know who *they* are and I don't want to know. But I do know you need to get out of this situation, now!"

"Exactly wrong, Irwin. Now *we* have to push it," Jake responded.

For once Irwin was speechless.

Jake pressed. "When you're about to be ambushed, you attack. It's the only way to survive. So we're going to attack before they have a chance to ambush us. We're going right after these assholes."

"Have you gone loco?" Irwin leaned across the table and glared at Jake. "You're a smart guy. You have to know once *they* find out about you—if they haven't already—you won't be too far down the hit list. And I, well, I have a family to think about. A bunch of munchkins running around looking for someone to keep them eating chicken nuggets with an endless supply of Vineyard Vines rugby shirts."

"That's right, Irwin, you do have a family to think about, and not just your immediate family." Jake was referring to Irwin's brother, who had been killed in a military accident. He wanted to drive his point home. "I can't wait for the discovery process to complete its sluggish journey." Seeing the apprehension still on Irwin's face, Jake opened up. "Look, I've got top-secret documents that tell the story of this piece-of-shit aircraft. I wasn't going to use those documents up front—just keep them as back-up to guide me through the lawsuit. But now I've figured out a way to use them as a spear instead of a shield. I need you to figure out all the legal defenses once I use them." Jake paused. "How long will it take for you to get me some answers?"

"Well, I guess 'now' would be the answer you're looking for," Irwin said. "But actually, a day or two for a preliminary answer, anyway. Airtight response—if there is such a thing in this area—in about a week," Irwin offered.

"You've got twenty-four hours for the initial and forty-eight for the final," Jake said.

Irwin shook his head. "You know, Counselor, I can see why you were such a combat hero. All you require is superhuman effort from your troops. You're only looking for a miracle. Let me see if I've got any left."

"Isn't there someone at your office that can help?" Jake asked.

"Ordinarily, Counselor, yes. But since my ass, and might I remind you, your ass, could be going to Leavenworth for a long time if we don't do this right, I think I'll do the research myself, if you don't mind."

"Got it," Jake said.

"And you will be prepared to pay for my legal defense for the divorce action my betrothed surely will file when I tell her I need to spend the next couple of days at the office for reasons I can't explain?" Irwin was only half joking.

"Sweet Julie wouldn't do that," Jake argued.

"Oh yes, she would, Counselor, especially since her adoring parents are in town this week," Irwin said.

"Oh," Jake replied.

Irwin looked resigned. "Just make sure you set up my legal defense fund and the fund for my children's college, since I'll be unable to provide for them from behind bars."

"Irwin, that's not going to happen. I have faith in you. You'll figure it out."

Irwin shook his head. "You know, it's times like these I wish you didn't have such a remarkably high opinion of me."

"How can I not, Irwin?" Jake said, a smile sneaking onto his face.

"Ah, the voice of reason and enlightenment returns. True, Counselor, how could you not?" Irwin lifted his coffee cup to toast in agreement.

"OK, we both have work to do," Jake said, finishing his coffee. "I truly appreciate your help here, buddy." He patted Irwin roughly on the back.

"Where are you going now . . . in case I need to talk to you?" Irwin asked.

Jake dodged the question. "I'll be on my cell. Just don't say too much. And get me some answers, pronto."

"Yes sir!" Irwin responded, firing up a salute.

. . .

Raleigh, North Carolina
Monday, August 10, 2009
4:30 p.m.

Jake was in the foyer of Madison's office building when he called her.

"Hi, Jake. What's up?"

"How about an early beer?"

"What a treat. When?"

"Well, now, as a matter of fact. I'm in the building lobby."

"I have an important call in about an hour. I can't stay long."

"That's perfect. See you shortly," Jake said, storing his phone.

Madison met him a few minutes later in the lobby. "How are you, babe? How's your head?" She kissed him gently on the forehead.

"Everything is fine. Look, I lied. I don't really have time for a beer. I've got to go back to the office and finish up the pleadings in the Thorpe case."

"Then why did you lure me down here?" she asked, leading him over to a corner of the lobby.

"The suit papers are almost ready to file, but before I file them I want to send them to the military and the contractors to see if they will respond and fix the aircraft. If not, I file," Jake explained.

"Seems fair," Madison said.

"They'll only have twenty-four hours. I am planning to file on Wednesday, so I have to get the papers into FedEx tonight."

"Can I help?"

"That's why I'm here. Your research skills are better than mine. I need some information that I think you can get—and I need it quickly."

"What, exactly?"

"The precise office addresses and direct phone numbers of some important people. The CEOs of Apex Helicopters and Vertical Aerospace, the secretary of defense, the chairman of the Joint Chiefs of Staff, secretary of the Navy, the chief of Naval Operations, and the commandant of the Marine Corps.

Silence, then, "Jeez, Jake. Those people are unlisted for a reason."

"I know, but I need to send papers to their specific business addresses so they'll get them quickly, and be worried that I know more than maybe I do. They can't sit around in the mail room for hours."

"Assuming I can do this . . . how do I get this to you?"

"If you could have it hand delivered that would be great. Otherwise, fax it. But don't use your office fax—go to the one at the library. And you might want to do your research there, also. I don't want anything that'd be traceable back to you."

"I will do what I can. When do you need it?"

"Now. Well, within the next couple of hours."

Madison laughed out loud. "Ha! Thanks for thinking of my busy schedule, Jake."

"It's just come down this way. But I gotta go—much appreciated."

Jake stood and gave her a kiss suitable for an office lobby, then hurried back to his office.

21

Back in his empty office, Jake got busy with the legal documents. He did not know if the bad guys were close, or if they even knew about him, but that was irrelevant now. He had to finish what he had started. After working for about an hour, he heard a knock on his office door. It was a clerk from Madison's office, holding a sealed envelope marked *For Jake Baird, Esq. Confidential*. It was the information he'd asked Madison to get—all there.

Jake got the Complaint off the office printer. This was the legal document that set out the facts and started the lawsuit. He carefully reviewed it, paying special attention to the opening:

Lisa Thorpe, through undersigned counsel, Jacob C. Baird, complaining of Defendants, alleges and says as follows:

Lisa Thorpe, Plaintiff, is the widow of Major Samuel Ward Thorpe, the Executrix of His Estate, and the Mother and Natural Guardian of his son, Samuel Wallace Thorpe, a Minor.

Defendants are the co-designers, co-fabricators, co-assemblers, co-manufacturers, and co-sellers of certain tilt-rotor aircraft known as the XV-11 "Sea Eagle," serial number 08-645362, Bureau Number (BuNo) 455616, which crashed on April 22 of this year near Patuxent River Naval Air

*Station, Maryland, causing the deaths of all occupants on board, including
Samuel William Thorpe, Plaintiff's decedent herein.*

The Complaint went on to allege that the "defendants designed, manu-
factured, assembled, marketed, and sold an aircraft that was inherently defective, unable to perform its intended purposes, and that was unreasonably dangerous, all of which made it completely foreseeable that this aircraft would
crash, causing fatal injuries to all on board."

Jake also alleged that since its very inception, the XV-11 had been
plagued by severe aerodynamic problems, which in turn produced control
problems, which could occur at anytime, without warning, and for which
there was no corrective action or emergency procedure. This rendered the
aircraft fatally defective and unreasonably dangerous.

Then Jake finished the second pleading, Requests to Admit, attaching
the classified documents in a logical narrative sequence. Now completed, the
Requests were a veritable road map showing the development of the XV-11,
its problem-plagued history, and the current fatal flaws, which had not been
fixed but excused.

Requests 33 and 34 showed that the aircraft could not meet the man-
datory military requirements, including carrying its full load of men and
equipment for extended distances and then operating at high-density altitudes. Requests 42 and 43 showed the aircraft could not meet the design
requirement that it be capable of autorotation in case of loss of engine power,
a failure that placed the passengers and crew at risk. Third, Exhibit 38 set out
the scheme by which the agents and employees of the defendants, working
with their individual counterparts in the US Marine Corps and at NAVAIR,
defrauded and misled the United States Marine Corps and NAVAIR leadership about the aircraft's inability to meet this design requirement by down-
playing this shortcoming, claiming autorotation was essentially "unnecessary"
in this aircraft.

He also attached a secret memorandum, authored by Oliver and sent
to Webb and Beech, in which the potentialities of nonrecoverable engine
failure modes were quantified, and which shockingly predicted the number of deaths that could be anticipated as a result of the aircraft's inability to
autorotate.

Finally, Jake hammered on the Vortex Ring State issue. He showed that certain individuals at NAVAIR, the Department of the Navy, and the aircraft's contractor knew at least fourteen months before the fatal crash at Patuxent River that the design of the XV-11 made VRS an inherent problem, rendering the aircraft uncontrollable in certain combat flight maneuvers, including, but not limited to, rapid descents, shipboard operations, and high-pressure altitude situations. The documents also showed that VRS could occur at any time, without warning, under certain flight conditions, especially in the maneuvers required in combat operations. They also showed that there was no adequate cockpit indication or warning system alerting pilots to this condition, nor was there any corrective action that would enable flight crews and their passengers to escape this condition.

It had taken four hours and too many cups of black coffee to finish the Complaint and the ninety-six Requests, and to attach the relevant documents. Jake was both exhausted by the effort and hyper from the caffeine.

He finalized the pleadings and then ran fifteen copies of the originals, signing each one. He knelt down on the floor right in front of Florence's desk and carefully assembled the documents. He put each set into an envelope: plain white envelopes for the hand deliveries to Noe, Irwin, Florence, and Admiral Lawrence; FedEx packages for delivery to the chief executive officers of the two defendants and to the secretary of defense, the chairman of the Joint Chiefs of Staff, the secretary of the Navy, the chief of Naval Operations and the commandant of the Marine Corps. He prepared the FedEx shipping labels, silently thanking Madison for supplying him with direct office addresses, office room numbers, and all of their direct phone numbers. Prior to closing, he placed the following note into each FedEx package going to the corporate and government recipients:

To: Chairmen of the Boards and Chief Executive Officers of the Defendants Named in the Enclosed Litigation Documents and to the Secretary of Defense, the Chairman of the Joint Chiefs of Staff, the Secretary of the Navy, the Chief of Naval Operations, and the Commandant of United States Marine Corps

Re: XV-11

Gentlemen:

I represent the family of Major Samuel Ward Thorpe, who lost his life in the crash of an XV-11 on April 22, 2009, near Patuxent River Marine Corps Air Station, Maryland. The enclosed documents are copies of the pleadings for a Wrongful Death lawsuit which will be filed in federal court on Wednesday, August 12, unless the conditions set out below are met. The enclosed documents show the flaws inherent in this aircraft which are un-remediable, which will continue to kill Marines, and which have been concealed by your commands and your corporations.

As stated, these documents will be filed in Federal Court on the indicated date unless word is received by 5:00 p.m. on Tuesday, August 11, that you all personally and directly have made contact with the undersigned admitting that these defects exist and agreeing to halt production until these flaws are fixed. If such acknowledgment is not forthcoming by the required time, these papers will be filed and copies released to the press.

You may call my office with your answer. 919-555-4500.
Be advised: I will release copies of these papers to the press should there not be a timely response or if I or my staff is harmed.

Sincerely,

Jacob C. Baird
Attorney-at-law

In the envelope going to Jeff Noe, he put another short note:

Jeff: Here they are. Since you have now opened this package as we agreed, my primary plan of getting these companies to voluntarily address this aircraft's problems has failed. The enclosed documents are to be filed on Wednesday, August 12, at 9:00 a.m. You may use these as we discussed after that date and time. Thanks. Jake.

It was nine thirty p.m. He put all of the FedEx and other envelopes in a large briefcase and headed out the door. The FedEx facility at the airport would accept packages until 11:00 p.m.

The die was cast. All that was left was to file—if that became necessary.

As he got to his car, his secure phone rang. "You all ready?" Kemp asked.

"All done. Headed out." Jake replied.

"Great. I have confirmed the meeting tomorrow where we talked about. Bring a suit."

"Got it. I am packed."

"OK. Be there by 1500."

"Roger."

Before going to FedEx, Jake turned off Hillsborough to stop by Irwin's house in Cameron Park. Irwin came to the door in a seersucker bathrobe and the rattiest leather slippers Jake had ever seen.

"Well, Counselor, come on in! I should've known it was you. Who else would come by at this hour but the police, the fire department, a burglar, or you?"

"Sorry, Irwin. I've got one more thing for you."

"OK, shoot—uh, excuse me—tell me what you need."

"Here is a set of pleadings, a Complaint and Requests to Admit, that must be filed Wednesday morning at nine a.m. if you don't hear from me," he said. "For God's sake, don't open them until then. You're my back-up. Got it?"

"What's going on, Jake? You didn't say anything about filing when we met earlier today. You gave me the impression we were a few days away from filing this thing," Irwin said.

"You're right, but everything is on a need-to-know basis. Just file this and then get back to the research, OK?" Jake responded.

"I guess you aren't going to be here do it yourself, is that the idea?"

"Right," Jake said.

"And I know better than to ask you where you'll be."

"Right again."

"OK, then, I implore you to be careful. Use all of your guile, your smarts, and your experience to keep yourself safe, my friend," Irwin urged.

"Thanks, Irwin, but it's going to be fine."

"When will I hear from you?" Irwin asked.

"Check with Florence on Wednesday. And look in on her for me, please.

I'm driving her set by her house. I didn't want to leave them in the office."

"Not at the office? OK, never mind . . ." Irwin turned to close the door and go back inside. But then he stopped. "Is Florence going to file, also?"

Jake hesitated. "Look, Irwin, Florence is plan A. But you file . . . regardless. Worst that can happen is we have duplicates on file and we dismiss one of them."

"Well, I trust you know what you're doing, Jake. Godspeed."

"Thanks, my friend," Jake said, as he turned to head down the walkway, looking at his watch. *Just enough time,* he thought. He started his car and did a U-turn to head to Florence's house on the way to the airport.

He called ahead of time on the secure phone. "Yes?" Florence answered.

"I'll see you shortly," Jake responded, and hung up. As things got tighter, he was more cryptic on the phone. No names, places, or times.

He pulled in front of Florence's house and grabbed another white envelope with the filing documents. He didn't have to ring the bell—Florence opened the door as soon as he walked onto her porch. She didn't say a word, but led him quickly toward the back of the house. Jake motioned her outside. He figured the bad guys might have somehow learned about Lisa Thorpe's visits to his office and might be watching or listening inside Florence's house.

Florence turned on the outside floods. Jake grabbed her arm to get her attention; she flashed a look at him and immediately turned them off.

"Stupid," she whispered.

Jake shook his head and mouthed, "It's OK."

Florence opened the French doors leading out to the patio. Jake followed her out and raised the envelope. "Take this to the courthouse on Wednesday morning and file the enclosed documents at nine a.m. sharp. Don't open it until you are at the filing desk ready to file on Wednesday morning."

"OK," she said.

"You're plan A. If anything happens—who knows, they could come to the office, whatever—there is a plan B," Jake said.

"And you're not going to tell me for my own protection," Florence offered, keeping her voice low.

"Yes, that's right." He stopped and moved inches away from her. Still whispering, he said, "Florence, I have planned this the best I could. I don't want anything to happen to you. What I have set in motion should keep everyone safe."

"Including you?" she inquired, looking in his eyes.

"Yes," he said, smiling, and reaching out and holding both of her arms in his hands. "Including me."

He hugged her. He had never done that before.

She didn't say a word but hugged him back, tightly.

"Gotta go. You'll see me in a couple of days."

"Be careful."

"You, too."

Jake headed to his car. It was now ten thirty—he had to hurry. He picked his cell phone off his belt and called Madison.

"Hi there," she answered.

"Hello. Look, sorry it is so late, but would you mind if I came over in a few minutes?"

"Of course not. Want a cold beer when you get here?"

"Actually, that sounds great. How did you know?" Jake asked.

"It's in your voice." She paused, and added, "You can't stay, can you?"

He could hear the disappointment. "No, not this time."

She moved on. "When should I pour the beer?"

"Give me about thirty minutes."

"See you then."

He pulled in front of the airport FedEx office. It was ten fifty. He grabbed the seven packages and gave them to the man at the counter.

"You want all for early delivery tomorrow?" the man said, looking at the packages.

"Yes, sir."

"We'll have them at each place by eight a.m. Our earliest delivery time."

"That'll be great. Thanks." Jake responded and headed out.

. . .

Jake pulled into the driveway at Madison's Cape Cod–style house. Even at night, the place shone. Where did she get the time to take care of this place? It always looked right out of the pages of *House Beautiful*. He walked up the brick sidewalk to the front door and rang the bell.

Madison opened the door in her pajamas. Her hair was up and she was obviously ready for bed. She looked tired.

"Hi, Maddy," Jake said, giving her a hug. "Long day?"

"Yeah—pretty rough. Come on into the kitchen," she said, closing the door.

"What happened?" Jake said, following her.

"Just that my jerkiest client tried to top his previous record for world's worst behavior today. I think he's going to make it all the way to the jerk hall of fame." She poured his beer into a glass and handed it to Jake.

"That sucks, Maddy. I'm sorry. Thanks for the beer," he gave her shoulders a quick rub to help ease the strain of her day. "And thanks for finding that information I requested. Everything's already with the good folks at FedEx."

"Glad I could help," Madison said, sitting down at the kitchen table. She pulled a chair out for Jake, patting the seat. "Sit down," she said, then rested her chin in her hand.

Jake did as she requested, then placed the envelope on the table.

"What's that?" Madison said, perking up a bit.

"I need for you to take this over to the *Observer* on Wednesday and give it to Jeff Noe, the reporter. You know him." He saw Madison was confused. "You know, the guy who wrote about Lejeune—the one who uses my basketball tickets sometimes . . ."

"Yes, sure. What time?"

"He must have it by eight a.m."

"OK. By eight. Will he know what this is?"

"He knows it's coming. Be sure to tell him he can open it at nine o'clock Wednesday morning and not before."

Madison nodded, then yawned, her eyes barely open.

"Has to be Wednesday morning, without fail. OK, sleepy head?" Jake said, rubbing her arm.

"I got it," Madison said. "Sorry I'm so sleepy." She crossed her arms on the table, then lowered her head onto them. Then a thought hit her and she looked up. "You're going somewhere, aren't you?"

"Yes. I gotta head out now."

She leaned over and spoke softly, "I know better than to ask where. But don't come back with any knots this time, OK?" she said, reaching across the corner of the table and holding his hands.

"No knots. This isn't that type of trip. I just gotta go help somebody get ready for a talk—a very important talk." Jake said, kissing her on the forehead. "I should be back on Saturday, Sunday at the latest."

"OK. Anything else I can do in the meantime?" she asked.

"Just get that to Jeff, and could you look in on Max, please?" Jake asked, standing up with her. He was concerned that in a worst-case scenario, Florence might be prevented from doing so.

"Is Flor—never mind. I'll do it, of course," she said, holding his hands, and. "C'mon, I know you have to get going, and I just have to get to sleep," she said, leading him to the front door.

They stopped at the door. Despite their exhaustion, they exchanged a kiss so passionate Jake almost couldn't bear to leave. Finally he pulled away.

"See you soon, sweetie," Jake said.

22

At 0200, the sounds of engines and rotors turning swept over the flight line. Bill looked toward the rear of the aircraft at the SEALs, their equipment and the squad of Marines.

"The SEALs and Marines sure look ready, even eager," Bill said to Gary.

"Let's hope we're as ready as they are," Gary replied.

"Here we go, Burnside," Gary shouted to the back.

"Let's do it, guys!" Burnside responded.

The flight crew went through the pre-takeoff checklist. All was perfect. *Maybe this thing will work after all*, Gary allowed himself to think. He was in the right seat and was going to navigate. Bill was going to fly the aircraft in the left seat. They went with their strengths.

The launch signal came from the operations hut. Bill moved throttles to wide open and Gary felt the aircraft get light on its gear. The aircraft shook and struggled to get airborne. The noise was deafening. After checking gauges, Gary allowed himself a look around the field. Everyone had come out to watch. *I hope they're looking at the launch of the most successful mission ever*, Gary thought.

"Bagram tower, Oscar 22, ready for departure."

"Roger, Oscar 22. Clear for takeoff when ready."

"Roger." Gary put on his night-vision goggles. Bill had put his on just before engine start. As Gary's eyes adjusted to the bright green world, Bill continued to move the power controls to get the aircraft airborne. The XV-11 crawled slowly into the air.

Gary radioed, "Oscar 22, departing pad Charlie."

"Roger, Oscar 22," the tower responded. "Good luck!"

They were on their way. From here on out, there would be radio silence and blackout.

As the XV-11 accelerated, its big engines and their rotors eased forward into airplane mode. Gary was always amazed at the transition that put those huge blades right out his window, rotating at 300 rpm, five circular trips per blade per second whizzing by his head. He knew this produced a terrific centrifugal force that could send the blade through the fuselage like an artillery shell. He hoped they stayed where they belonged.

The first twenty minutes were uneventful. The barren landscape was beautiful in its own way. Both Gary and Bill noticed the steep terrain and the lack of good forced landing areas. Fortunately, there was a bright moon in a cloudless night sky that enhanced the effectiveness of their night-vision goggles. Unfortunately, this would silhouette them against the night sky, making them easier to detect. Although the XV-11 was loud, its speed and their low altitude made the aircraft's sound reverberate over a broad area, making it difficult to tell where they were coming from.

"Man, I sure hope the LZ is flatter than this," Bill said.

"It looked fairly flat on the recon photos," Gary responded. "Let's hope it's just as lonely."

When they made the turn at RP Alpha and prepared for the transition to nap-of-the-earth flight at RP Bravo, all on board got more alert. The turn signaled to each man that they were now headed directly into combat. No detours, no going back. This was it: the real thing.

That wasn't the only reason the cockpit crew was becoming anxious. "There is some slop coming into the controls—not nearly as responsive as before," Bill said.

"No! Let me see," Gary responded.

"You have the controls," Bill stated, in the formal exchange language that had become ingrained in every military aviator.

"I have the controls," Gary said in response. "You're right. Very loose. The

aircraft isn't responding to the inputs like it should. You have the controls."
Although the people in the back wouldn't notice the control problems, it
could lead to things they would notice—vibration and maybe loss of control.

"I have the controls," Bill replied, taking the aircraft back.

"Let's pray it doesn't get any worse. Let me take a quick look at the
NATOPS—I don't remember any procedure for this—"

"Be quick. We're almost at Bravo. If it gets much worse, I can't fly this
thing. It's very difficult to maneuver now. If we have to maneuver to avoid
ground fire, we're in trouble."

"Understood," Gary responded while flipping through the emergency
section index of the NATOPS manual. "There's nothing in here except some
reference to shutting down hydraulics."

"This is bullshit! We need to call base. What's this 'radio silence' crap?
What's wrong with our secure radios?" Bill was getting more aggravated.

"Beats me. Some genius thought that one up," Gary said. "Let's just hope
the indigenous forces are there as forecast or that the Taliban nation is on
vacation."

They continued for another three minutes and were now at RP Bravo
flying nap-of-the-earth, as low as they could go, just over the treetops. As
they started their final approach, Bill manipulated the controls to check the
condition. "This is really bad. Any worse and we abort."

Gary was surprised at Bill's willingness to give up the mission.

"Crap! Out here on our own with a sick fucking aircraft!" Bill added.
"And all NATOPS tells us is to shut down the hydraulics. That might be
next . . ."

Bill then stopped talking. Gary thought maybe he was trying to concen-
trate. He waited for feedback.

"This thing is really bad, Gary. Get on the controls and follow me."

"OK—two minutes out!" Gary announced over the aircraft PA system
as he placed his hands and feet on the cockpit flight controls. The men in
the back checked their gear and readied their weapons. "Just over that hill,"
Gary said, pointing through the front windscreen to a spot out in front of the
aircraft.

"Roger," Bill responded, his full concentration focused on just flying
the aircraft. Just as he began to apply power to clear the final hill, the aircraft

shuddered and drifted to the left. Bill applied right cyclic, but it had only a marginal effect. He made a greater input, but it didn't help. They barely cleared the last hill, just above it, as Bill lowered the collective for descent to the LZ below.

Bill and Gary could now see the buildings in the village 2000 meters in front of them. They saw a few people coming out of their houses in response to the noise. Thus far, at least, the quickness had worked. They weren't being shot at. The Taliban were probably just now stirring and the good guys would be on top of them in seconds.

"I'm not sure we're gonna make it to the LZ," Bill said. The effect of lowering the collective for landing had slowed the left bank but was increasing their rate of descent. He now had applied almost full right cyclic and a lot of right pedal, so he had very little sideward control movement remaining.

The aircraft was tilting left and crabbing right, but somehow staying over the course. When Bill pulled in power to slow the descent for landing, the problem got worse. It was now in a serious left bank. Bill did the only thing he could—reduced power—although he knew the aircraft would slam down in the LZ—if they made the LZ.

It didn't work. The roll to the left continued; the aircraft was beyond the tipping point. The Afghan ground was rising up rapidly, at an angle. Gary knew there was no hope of impacting anywhere near upright; it was now only a question of what degree they'd be inverted.

"We're going to hit, dammit! We're—" Bill screamed.

"Hang on!" Gary blurted through the PA system.

The aircraft slammed into the dirt, almost fully on its left side, and rolled, sending pieces of rotor blades and aircraft shooting through the air. As the aircraft's exterior came apart, the inside was smashed inward, pieces of equipment flying through the cockpit and cabin, smacking metal and men. The impact and roll meant bodies were being broken, and the loose equipment caused cuts, concussions, and puncture wounds. The aircraft rolled off the level ground and down the hill, continuing to tear itself apart, scattering parts and equipment as it went. Finally, it settled in a small ravine, smoldering. People were crushed and trapped, but there was no fire.

Moans and cries rose above the hissing and creaking aircraft sounds. As shock wore off and the men in the back slowly came around, the pain became real.

Bill was still in his seat. He reached up and cut off the fuel and electrical switches then struggled to get out of his seat restraint system. Gary, seated in the right front seat, had the worst of it. His helmet had been ripped off and it looked like he had a bad head injury. He was bloody, but still breathing.

"Gary!" Bill called out. "Gary! You there, man?" Getting no response, he called to the crew chief, "Ted, you back there?"

"I'm here, sir. I'm OK," Cook replied.

"How is everybody else?"

"Can't tell, sir. Can't see. Equipment's everywhere," Cook yelled.

"Looks like my team is all alive, but a couple are in bad shape," Burnside responded.

"Sergeant Brooks, how are your Marines?" Bill yelled.

"I got a couple hurt bad. But the rest are mostly OK," Brooks shouted. "We'll get out and set up a perimeter."

Bill was relieved to hear this. "Great. See if you can raise anybody on your radios. We gotta get some help." Still looking around, Bill said, "Burnside, see if your radio works . . . we've gotta get somebody to us! And no lights—keep it dark."

"Roger. Gibson, get who you can outside and work with the Marines to set up a perimeter," Burnside shouted to his assistant team leader.

"Roger that, sir," Gibson said, extricating himself from the tangled mess. "Martinez and DeLapp, orient up the hill. Jackson and Preston, to the east, and Hackney and Valens to the west. I'll take the south for now. Hurry! Everybody got his weapon?" Not all of his men responded.

"Delta base, Delta base, this is Delta One, do you read?" Burnside started barking into his radio. He shouted, "Anybody got a count?"

As Burnside was checking his men, Bill was calling through his helmet, "Night Bird 66, Night Bird 66, this is Oscar 22, do you read?" Bill unkeyed the mike and waited. Again, "Night Bird 66, you read?"

Ping! Ping! Plat-plat! Bill heard the unmistakable sound of small-arms rounds hitting the airframe. "Jesus!" Bill yelled as a round zipped by his head. "Gotta get out of this cockpit! The aircraft was still pointing uphill, right into the gunfire. Bill managed to get out of his harness and reached over to Gary and to loosen his. "C'mon buddy! I'm getting you outta here!"

Bill looked back to see if he could drag Gary into the back of the aircraft, away from the incoming rounds, but his view was blocked by the gear that had slid forward off their moorings during the crash.

The gunfire increased. Bill wondered why he hadn't been hit—rounds were zipping and ricocheting all around. He had no idea how close the Taliban were. Suddenly, he heard much closer gunfire. The SEALs and Marines who had made it out of the aircraft were returning fire from their defensive positions.

Bill finally pulled Gary just behind the cockpit seats when he heard the crackle of radios.

"Oscar 22, this is Night Bird. We have your location. We're inbound, hot."

"Roger. They're all around."

"Are your guys all with you?" Night Bird asked.

"Right by the aircraft . . ." He hesitated, then yelled back to the ground forces commander, "Right, Burnside? Your guys all here?" Bill yelled. "Brooks?"

"Yes, except for two men in front of the aircraft!" Burnside responded while firing up the hill. "Got eight SEALs and seven Marines with me. The rest are inside," he added.

"Roger, two of us are ten meters in front of the aircraft," came a shout from the dark area out front.

"We're all in close," Brooks answered.

"OK! Everybody stay where you are. Keep your heads down!" Bill shouted out of the aircraft.

"Everybody hear that? Can't go get them yet!" Brooks repeated.

"Roger that!" Burnside and Gibson responded through the chaos.

A second later the area in front of their downed aircraft ignited with a tremendous *ka-bloom!* Another blast, and the areas on both sides of the aircraft were ablaze. Seconds later, another bomb, and the area a little farther in front exploded, then the sides again.

They must have Nighthawks up there, Bill thought.

"We have wounded. Can you guys call in some help?" Bill radioed to the fast movers.

"That's on its way along with some other aircraft," one of the fighter pilots responded.

"Thanks," Bill said.

"The hogs will be here in about one minute. You'll like their stuff." The A-10 Warthog, which had been designed as a tank buster, was perfect for close air support.

"Yours seems to be pretty good."

"Thanks. Here you go again."

Another *ka-bloom!* This one bigger. The ground shook even more. The SEALs' and Marines' firing had slowed down; they seemed to be looking for targets. The Taliban fire now was only an occasional round. But Bill knew that wouldn't be for long.

"What's the story?" shouted Burnside.

"Help is on the way," Bill responded.

"When?" Gibson shouted back.

Before he could answer, Bill felt intense pressure and the air sucked out of his lungs. Then a deafening *g-g-g-r-r-r-r-r-r-r!* filled the air. Bill knew it was the A-10 Warthog's 30-millimeter cannon letting go. The ground all the way up the hill was churned by the explosive shells as if ripped up by a massive grinder. Then *ka-bloom!* A second A-10 had dropped two bombs farther up. This was followed by another A-10 that did the same to the area to the east. Then one came around and destroyed the area to the west.

"How's that look, Oscar 22?" came a call from a husky voice, one of the Warthog pilots.

"Great, man. Keep it up!" Bill responded.

"Roger. Relief is about ten miles out! We'll stick around until you guys are gone."

"Thanks."

Gary groaned. Bill looked at him, holding him. There was no response from Gary to anything that was going on, but at least he was still breathing.

Blam! A shell exploded just meters away from the front of the aircraft. "Mortar!" one of the SEALs yelled.

"Hog 41, they're popping mortars."

"Yeah, we saw that. I think I have the muzzle flash. Let me see what we can do."

Blam! Blam! The mortar rounds were being walked in closer. Bill saw the SEALs coming back from in front of the aircraft with two injured troops, hit by shrapnel from the mortar rounds. "They're going to zero in soon. We gotta move!" Burnside said.

A *whoosh* sounded over Bill's head, and an area inside the village exploded. The men waited, and they heard no more mortars. One of the A-10s had successfully fired a precision AGM-65 Maverick anti-artillery missile that took out the mortar.

But then *rat-a-tat, rat-a-tat* came from behind. Taliban forces were approaching from the rear, spraying the downed aircraft with machine-gun fire. "Auuuggh!" Bill cried out, holding his leg. He had taken a round in his thigh. Then *blam!*—a dreaded RPG round exploded at the rear of the airframe.

"Hog 41! They're at our rear!" Bill screamed. "They got RPGs!"

"OK. Gotta do a quick turn. How far back?" the Warthog pilot asked.

Just then another machine-gun burst tore through the wreckage. "Augh!" Bill cried. He took another round, this time in his shoulder. He had been trying to spot the Taliban when the shots were fired. "Close! About 100 meters about directly to our rear," Bill groaned into his mouthpiece. He was losing blood.

"Rolling in close! Get your heads down!" The A-10 pilot radioed.

B-r-r-r-r-r-r-r-r-r-r-r-! The men in the aircraft wreckage felt the concussion and the heat of the rounds over their heads. Immediately after the rounds flew by, the A-10 roared just feet over their heads, rattling the wreckage with its shock waves and jet thrust. It was no more than twenty feet off the deck.

Just then the ground exploded at the rear of the wreckage. Before the dirt settled, they heard the other A-10. It had climbed higher and had made a vertical dive, dropping ordnance. Perfect hit. Right behind it was the other A-10, spraying the area with its cannon fire.

The small-arms fire was back again from the front, and then *blam! blam!* More mortar rounds. Bill labored to make another call to the Warthogs as the SEALs returned fire, joined by the Marines with their mixture of M16A4, M4, and M4A1 rifles. One Marine even was letting go with his Mossberg shotgun. Through the fire, Bill could hear the faint hum of rotor blades. The sound got louder and clearer. The men on the ground could hear several hums. Sounded like UH-60s—Army utility helicopters. But there was another rumble—Apaches! The SEALs knew that sound. Army gunships! Thank God!

The inbound aircraft were six UH-60s carrying a company of Army Rangers, three medevacs, and two AH-64 gunships. When the reinforcements hit the ground, they were immediately met by scores of crack Taliban fighters armed with rocket-propelled grenades, mortars, and heavy machine guns.

The full-scale battle lasted until just after daybreak, when the superior firepower of the US combined arms team—Army troops, Army gunships, Marines, and Air Force tactical air support—finally pushed the Taliban out of the village and back into the hills. But at a heavy cost. Although the US forces counted over sixty Taliban bodies, combined forces suffered twelve killed and thirty wounded, some seriously. There were also twenty-two dead villagers.

Bill and Gary, along with the other wounded occupants of the XV-11, were extracted quickly after the reinforcements arrived—as soon as a medevac LZ could be secured. Twenty-seven personnel had started out in the aircraft; three died in the crash impact, and four were killed by enemy fire. Of the twenty other aircraft occupants, all sustained injuries in the crash, with eight also wounded in the firefight.

23

"I thought you'd like to know we're getting closer," Agent Chaney said into his secure phone.

"Good news," Oliver responded, "but I need *great* news."

"You'll get that shortly. Twenty-four hours, tops," Chaney replied.

"Why the optimism after all this time chasing him around the country?" Oliver asked.

"Direct contact made a little while ago. He got careless."

"He doesn't get careless." Oliver said.

"He did this time." Chaney said, "We still need guidance. Do we have approval to eliminate the problem?"

"NO!" Oliver shouted. Oliver knew Chaney was angry at Kemp since he had led him all over the place, making him look inept, but Kemp was too well known and too important to too many people. "The other situations were one thing. This is another," Oliver said.

"Roger that. It's your show," Chaney responded.

"Just get him and the documents. Find out what you can and the why and who. That may give us some options."

"Will do. Out."

Chaney turned to Agent Eric Gonzales in the front seat. "The guy's a coward. He let us knock off the little fish but won't let us finish the big one."

With the help of cash he had embezzled from some defense projects that he had previously planned on keeping for himself, Oliver had been able to call in favors from three of his long-time acquaintances who were retired from the NSA. He hadn't gotten to where he was in Naval Acquisitions without doing some "horse trading" with people all over government. Once Kemp was captured, however, Oliver had to come up with a reason why he should be prosecuted other than by proving he stole the XV-11 documents, because there was no way to prove that without revealing their content. He needed something that would overcome the Captain's unblemished reputation without revealing the XV-11 breach.

Then it hit him. One of the super-secret stealth programs, the XD-40 Unmanned Remote Airborne Strike System, was being run out of the office next to his. Jokingly known as "URASS," the program was now going well after a rocky start and would soon produce an efficient, low-cost, solar-powered, stealth anti-terrorist aircraft that could stay aloft for extended periods of time. Kemp had openly opposed it at first, when it was failing and horribly overbudget.

If I can manage to get a classified document from the XD-40 program into Kemp's possession, that would give me the breach I need, Oliver thought. A security breach in the secret XD-40 program would be more serious than one in the public XV-11 program. Not only would it solve the Kemp problem, but it might get rid of Oliver's most hated competitor, Commander Ben Miller, NAVAIR's golden boy. Oliver knew that if Miller's program sustained a security breach, his career would be scarred forever. *They might even give that program to me,* Oliver thought. The question was how to get into the XD-40 computer file—Oliver didn't have access.

He picked up the secure phone and dialed Chaney.

"Got something else for me?" Chaney asked.

"Yeah. I remember a while ago you sent me someone with computer security expertise. I can't remember his name or where he worked."

"But I didn't actually know the guy. I knew someone who knew someone who sent him to you. Where's he needed?"

"Here," Oliver said, "as soon as possible."

"OK. Let me see if I can find my contact and set it up. But it's a little late in the day."

Oliver had met this computer guru when the XV-11 breach occurred. The guy was known as sort of a "fixer" when it came to IT security issues around the Pentagon. He'd helped Oliver clean up the computer so there wouldn't be any way to electronically trace the damning XV-11 files back to him. But he still needed the documents—they were the only hard copies that showed what Oliver, Webb, and Beech did and when they did it.

There was a knock at Oliver's door. "Come in."

"I'm Wiggins from IT security. I got a call that said you needed some help—something about a computer problem?"

Oliver stared at the guy. He hadn't seen this man before. "Hi. Thanks for coming up so quickly, Mr. Wiggins. Yes, I can't seem to get to a file I need. I know it's on here somewhere."

"The guy who helped you the last time—Olenik—isn't in today. I was just out the door when I got the call. This almost had to wait until tomorrow," Wiggins said.

"Sorry to have called so late." Oliver said. "Is your office nearby?"

"I'm with Security—just like Olenik. Not too far away." Wiggins said.

Wiggins grabbed a piece of paper and wrote "File?"

Oliver wrote, "XD-40."

Wiggins looked up at Oliver with raised eyebrows. Oliver nodded in confirmation of what he had written. Wiggins shook his head and slipped the paper into his pocket. He looked around the room and saw Oliver's stereo system. He approached it. "Would you mind if I turned this on? I like to listen to music while I work."

"Sure, whatever you want," Oliver said as the man approached him, leaned over, and put his hand on Oliver's shoulder. "It blocks any listeners," he whispered.

"Right." Oliver whispered back.

"Mind if I sit down?" Wiggins said, his voice returning to normal volume.

"Of course not," Oliver said, moving out of Wiggins's way.

Oliver got busy with other things at the table in his office as Wiggins worked. In about twenty minutes, Wiggins motioned Oliver over and whispered, "Look at these—tell me what you're missing."

Looking at the screen, Oliver couldn't believe his eyes. There before him was the entire index of the XD-40 program. He reviewed it for a moment and wrote, "Section B, 'Tests and Evaluations,' and Section I, 'Capabilities.' OK?"

Wiggins nodded, made a few keystrokes, and shortly thereafter, the download flag came up on his computer, followed by the "Download Complete" message.

"Where do you want it?" Wiggins asked.

"Here, put it on this," Oliver said, handing the man a flash drive.

Wiggins inserted the drive and began the copying process. He held up two fingers, pointed at the computer, and mouthed the word "back-up." Oliver nodded in agreement and got another flash drive.

Now Oliver had two flash drives containing the Tests and Evaluations and Capabilities sections of the XD-40 files. He put one of them in the lining of his jacket for delivery to Chaney and the other in a lockable drawer in his desk. He would worry about exiting security later.

When the screen went back to Oliver's desktop, Wiggins walked over and turned off the stereo. He took a piece of paper on the desk and began to write as he spoke, "Glad I could help you out with that missing file. It just got in the wrong place in your filing system. Anything else?"

"No, thanks. That's all I need for now," Oliver said, as the man held up the paper that read, "All cleaned up. Never happened."

Oliver smiled and nodded. Wiggins nodded back, got up, and exited the room without saying good-bye.

Well, that was easy, Oliver thought, laughing at how simple it was. Now he just had to get the flash drive into Kemp's possession.

Back in his office, Wiggins pulled out his secure phone. "He wanted the URASS file. Knew you would want to know."

"Thanks," said the gravelly voice.

. . .

Near Dulles Airport, Virginia
Monday, August 10, 2009
11:00 p.m.

Kemp was now on the Virginia beltway heading toward the Dulles Toll Road. He planned to head west to the little farm he had outside of Clifton,

Virginia, but with the bad guys close, he knew he couldn't outrun them. He had to switch cars to confuse them and get some distance between them.

His plan included getting caught, but not this soon. He needed to give Jake a few more hours, maybe a whole day. This time, he had, in fact, gotten careless, lingering around Raleigh where they had spotted him.

Kemp parked the car in back of the Hertz facility and moved quickly to the counter.

"It's a Gold return. You have all the information," Kemp said to the man at the counter.

"Thanks. Bus is waiting. Fred will take you right over."

Kemp ran to the bus. "Hello, Fred. We need to get moving, OK?" he said, handing Fred a hundred-dollar bill. "Step on it, please."

"Sure thing, sir." Fred folded his newspaper and put it behind his seat and stashed the bill in his pants pocket. Kemp looked back through the bus's windows for his pursuers. He saw them get out of their car and go into the building.

"Kill the inside lights, will you, Fred?" Kemp asked. Fred complied.

"OK, Fred, got another little request of you," Kemp said, flashing his identification.

Fred looked at the ID and said, "Yes, sir. How can I help?"

"When you get to the stoplight, kill your engine."

"Say again?" the bus driver responded.

"Turn off the engine at the stop light," Kemp said, putting his ID away. "Those guys in the sedan behind us are chasing me. No time to explain. It's national security."

"OK . . ."

"Just turn off your engine, get out, and open your hood. After you do that, call and report engine trouble to your people and to the airport police. Tell them you need the cops here for safety and you need a tow truck," Kemp said.

"OK, buddy. But you'd better not be jiving me—I could lose my job," Fred insisted.

"I promise, Fred, but you have to trust me." Kemp saw the sedan racing out of the rental lot toward the bus.

"Do it now!" Kemp said. "And leave the bus door open."

Fred turned on the emergency flashers and got out of the bus. He radioed in engine trouble as he moved immediately to raise the engine cover. He looked to the back of the bus and saw a sedan come to a screeching halt.

Inside the car, Gonzales asked Chaney, "What's this?"

"Don't know. Stay alert. I don't like this at all," Chaney advised, as they exited the car.

"What's the matter?" Chaney yelled to the driver as Gonzales raced to the bus's open door, gun drawn.

"Sorry, fellows, engine trouble," Fred said. "I've already called for help. I can clear you around me and you can be on your way," Fred said to Chaney, who was looking around him at the bus, ignoring Fred's suggestion. Gonzales was already inside, moving quickly through the bus.

As Fred watched the agents, he heard the sound of the airport police car siren.

"What you got?" Chaney yelled to Gonzales.

"He's not here!" Gonzales hollered as he raced back down the aisle of the bus.

Chaney didn't wait. He holstered his weapon and reached for his handcuffs. Gonzales was hurrying toward them, aiming his weapon at Fred.

"What's all this?" Fred said, arms raised. "I got help on the way. You guys go . . ."

Chaney grabbed Fred and threw him against the back of the bus. "We're not going anywhere right now—and neither are you, sir," Chaney said, placing his handcuffs on Fred.

"Whoa . . . wait a minute—"

"Shut up!" Gonzales screamed at Fred. He pulled out his government badge and ID, and thrust them in front of Fred's face. "I'm Agent Erik Gonzales of NSA, and that's Agent Chaney. Where did your passenger go? Where is he?"

At that moment, the Dulles Airport police appeared, lights flashing.

"What's going on here?" Officer Boneta said, drawing his weapon and crouching behind the squad car driver's door. The other officer, Sergeant Jackson, was out of the car with the shotgun braced on the roof of the car, in firing position.

"You OK, Fred?" Sergeant Jackson yelled, but Fred didn't answer.

Chaney held up his badge. "You officers back off. This is a federal matter—national security."

Officer Boneta rose up from behind the door and said, "Put your weapon down and I'll come over and take a look."

"OK," Chaney responded, looking over at Gonzales. Chaney released Fred, and Gonzales holstered his weapon.

Boneta approached Chaney and looked at Chaney's identification. Then he called to Jackson, "Looks OK, Officer Jackson. Stand down." Jackson got out of the firing position, but remained ready.

"OK, what's this all about?" Boneta asked.

"We're pursuing this man's passenger," Chaney replied.

Officer Boneta looked around as Officer Jackson approached the bus.

"What passenger?" Boneta said. "I don't see anyone, so why is Fred in cuffs?"

"Nobody in here," Officer Jackson yelled back from the bus's door.

"He's not in there. He got away. And we want to ask this driver how that happened," Gonzales said.

"OK ..."

"Look, Officer, this driver needs to be held for questioning. We gotta get after our suspect. He can't be far . . . especially on foot," Chaney said.

"OK, we'll take Fred and see if he knows anything," Officer Boneta said. Gonzales removed the handcuffs.

"C'mon, Officer Gonzales, let's go," Chaney said. They had lost valuable time dealing with Fred and the Dulles Police.

. . .

Back at the rental car counter and out of breath, Kemp flashed his badge again to the same fellow who was there before—to remind him. "Look," Kemp said, "this is unusual. I need another car, quick. Just take the info on the one I just turned in, please. You know those guys are chasing me. I just left them at the rental car bus."

"Look. I can't get in the middle. Those guys showed me IDs, too. How do I know . . . I mean, I could lose my job."

"You can lose more than that if this thing goes bad. Once everything is explained your boss will understand. Just tell him I didn't like the car I had before."

"I . . . I . . . just don't know . . ."

"Look, here's one of my cards. Put this where no one else will see it, only you. Call me if you get in any trouble." He leaned across the counter. "This is important."

The guy thought for a minute. "OK, well . . . I guess. I didn't like those guys, anyway," the agent said, handing Kemp a set of keys.

Kemp ran to the door. "Thanks again. By the way, there's nothing wrong with the bus—the bus is fine . . . and give Fred a raise!" He started the car up and moved quickly out of the lot, toward home.

Chaney and Gonzales drove around the area in ever-increasing circles, trying to locate Kemp. Nothing. He could already be gone. They passed the rental car facility a couple of times, looking in to see if they saw anything suspicious.

Chaney was pissed. "We're grabbing the son of a bitch the next time we get the chance, whatever it takes," Chaney vowed.

"We have to catch him first," Gonzales answered.

"OK, Gonzales, so we screwed up," Chaney admitted. "But you have to hand it to him. We, emphasize *we*, fell for the oldest trick in the book."

When they passed the rental facility for the third time, Chaney suggested, "Let's see if that agent knows anything. Maybe a search and a little persuasion will loosen up our young friend."

"It's worth a shot," Gonzales replied.

They pulled in and walked up to the counter; the same guy was still there. They were right: after a forceful interrogation, the employee gave them all the information on Kemp's second rental—and his business card.

· · ·

Near Clifton, Virginia
Tuesday, August 11, 2009
12:01 a.m.

After rushing through the back roads and being sure he had lost his pursuers, Kemp finally came to his farm about a mile outside of Clifton. No one knew about this place—not even his neighbors knew who he was. He had bought some time.

Kemp drove the rental car into the dark garage. No longer in immediate danger, he realized he was exhausted. He headed down to a concealed, windowless bunkroom he had built in the basement. It would take a long time for them to find it, but even if they did, the room had a hidden escape tunnel that would take them even longer to find. He turned on his external and internal security systems and visual monitoring system, which also had audio, night-vision capability, a far-infrared component, and a vibration monitor. He could do everything but smell them.

His secure phone buzzed.

"How are you?" Jake was concerned.

"Fine. You get it all done?"

"Yep. They're done and on their way. I'll head up tomorrow, as you asked."

"That will work. I will try to check in with you in the morning. In case the situation is such that I can't talk, I'll just send a quick text that I'll pre-load," Kemp said. That was as close as he was going to get to telling Jake he planned to be caught to keep the focus on him.

"You going to be OK?"

"It's all under control. Don't worry about me. Just do your job."

"I will. Take care," Jake said.

Kemp rolled over and set his alarm. About five hours rest was all the situation would allow. He hoped he got it.

24

Bagram Air Base, Afghanistan

Tuesday, August 11, 2009

10:00 a.m. (1:30 a.m. EDT)

The deep-grooved tires on the desert tan humvee screeched as the vehicle slid to a halt in front of the main entrance of the Craig Joint Theater Hospital at Bagram Air Base, raising a cloud of sand that engulfed the vehicle. Colonel Paul Dixon and First Sergeant Vernon Horace jumped out of the vehicle and rushed through the hospital's doors.

Inside, Dixon grabbed the first person he saw wearing a medical uniform. "Where can I find personnel brought in from the XV-11 crash near Chaghcharan?"

"Sir, I am not sure—"

"Then who is sure?" Dixon responded, still holding the arm of the young nurse as he looked around for someone else who might help.

"Sir, I suggest that you follow the signs to the emergency room," she said, pointing to a sign hanging from the ceiling and pulling her other arm from the Colonel's grip. "They should—"

"Thanks," Dixon said, not waiting for the nurse to finish her sentence. He and Horace ran under the first sign and toward the next one. After a few turns, they arrived at two large doors with a sign overhead: EMERGENCY ROOM—AUTHORIZED PERSONNEL ONLY.

They didn't hesitate and pushed through the doors into a room full of chaos. Medical personnel in scrubs, some with bloodstains, raced around, bumping into one another. Screams of pain pierced the air over the shouts of instructions coming from the docs and nurses treating the wounded. Momentarily stunned at the horror he observed, Dixon wondered if any of his people were doing the screaming.

"Can I help you, Colonel?" a woman dressed in surgical scrubs asked as she removed her cap.

"Yes, thanks," Dixon responded. "I am looking for three of my men that were involved in an XV-11 crash near Chaghcharan. I was told they were brought here."

"Stay right here, Colonel. Let me see what I can find out. May I have their names?"

"Major Bill Harris, Major Gary Bennett, and Sergeant Ted Cook. They're Marines."

She smiled. "Yes, Colonel, I assumed they were Marines," she said as she looked at Colonel Dixon's uniform. She disappeared through a set of doors.

Moments later a male nurse approached, took off his surgical gloves and tossed them toward a large trash can. "You the people looking for the flight crew of that helicopter?" he asked.

"Yes," Dixon replied, agitated at the wholesale lack of military respect. *It's an emergency room. Let it slide.*

"OK. Follow me." After passing several rooms with medical personnel and patients who were either silent, moaning, or crying out in pain, the nurse slowed down. "One of them is in here," he said, pointing to a room with an open door. "Just go on in while I look for the other one."

"There were three crewmembers, not two," Dixon said, restraining his temper. "Do you know anything about the third one—anything?"

"I was told two," the nurse responded, matter of fact. "You want me to look for a *third*?"

Dixon had had it. "That's exactly what I want you to do," Dixon said through clenched teeth. Then he got right in the nurse's face. "And remember, these are MARINES, goddammit, not just anybody. Show some respect!"

The nurse recoiled. "Right, sir. My apologies. Please go in and I'll come right back when I find out more."

Dixon and Horace entered the drab, dark room. The first two bays were empty, their green privacy curtains pulled back against the wall. But from the sheets wadded up on the bed tables, trash cans full of bandages, and some fresh blood on the floor, it was apparent they had not been vacant long.

The curtain on the third bay was pulled all the way around, making it impossible to see who was on the gurney behind it. The two men gently pulled the curtain just enough for them to enter but couldn't tell at first who it was—tubes, adhesive tape, bandages, and the bed covers concealed the identity of the patient. They moved closer, quietly, but the patient heard them and slowly turned toward them.

"Hello, Colonel," he groaned. "Thanks for coming."

Faint as it was, Dixon recognized the voice. It was Major Gary Bennett.

"Damn good to see you, Major." Dixon placed his hand on Bennett's shoulder. "How are you feeling?"

Bennett instinctively tried to reach his right hand toward the colonel's hand, but couldn't. He was too weak. "Fine, sir. Just a bit banged up."

"Just a bit, I'll say. You'll be on your feet in no time," Dixon said, turning and nodding at Horace.

"Sir," Gary moaned, "what about the others—Bill and Ted? And . . . did we get everybody out?"

"I am checking on your fellow crewmembers. But everybody got out— thanks to the Army Rangers, the Apache gunships, and our friends at Air Force tactical air support. Everybody except the bad guys, that is. They got hosed."

A small smile grew on Gary's face. "Great . . ."

"Sir, I found Sergeant Cook," the nurse blurted out. He had come into the room without either the colonel or First Sergeant Horace noticing. "I can take you if you want to go see him now."

"I'll go, sir," Horace responded.

"Yes, please do that. Tell Cook I'll be down in a minute."

"You can come back and get the colonel, can't you?" Horace said, turning to the nurse.

"Certainly." The nurse and Horace left the room.

"Sir . . ." Gary said, pulling the colonel's attention back to him.

The colonel leaned over to hear Gary's faint voice. "Yes, Major Bennett?"

"Sir . . . it wasn't enemy fire . . . we lost control on the way in to the LZ. We both tried to hold it but we slammed in short . . . it was the aircraft, sir. We did all we could. We both got on the controls to try to hold it level, but nothing we tried worked."

"Understood." Dixon leaned back. "Now listen, Major. You just get some rest and don't worry about the whats and the whys. I'll make sure the right people hear what you said. We'll find out what happened."

"Thanks, sir." He was growing weaker. "Could I ask one more thing?" Gary said, gathering strength to extend his hand up to Dixon.

"Name it."

"Could you get in touch with Kathy and tell her I am OK?"

"Immediately, if not sooner." Dixon smiled and squeezed Gary's hand. "Now, you take care. I'll be back when I can, but you'll probably be out of here and on your way home by then."

"Roger, sir. Thanks."

Dixon placed Gary's hand back on his chest and saw he was dozing off. Dixon headed for the door at the same time Horace and the nurse entered the room. Dixon feared the worst and grimaced as he waited for the news.

"Don't worry, Colonel," Horace said. "Cook's fine. They just had to take him back in for a minor adjustment—they said—on his broken leg. But he's alert and in good spirits. He said to say hello to you."

"Great news." Dixon relaxed, but then immediately felt a cold rush as he realized they hadn't heard about Major Harris. Dixon turned to the nurse. "What about the third crewmember, Major Bill Harris?"

"Sir, I checked. He's not here. They have no information on admitting or treating him."

"Could they have taken him somewhere else—maybe to Kandahar?"

"I am checking on that, sir. Let me take you both back to the waiting area outside the emergency room and get back to you when I find out."

"That will work. Thanks," Dixon said.

. . .

Once seated in the waiting room, Horace said, "Sergeant Cook said something else, sir. I didn't want to mention it until we were alone."

"What's that, First Sergeant?"

"He said the crash was not caused by ground fire. He said they started losing control on short final, and he remembers everything the pilots said."

"Major Bennett said the same thing." Dixon's jaw tightened and he shook his head. "I never should have let them talk me into this deployment. But I thought if we were careful—single ship operations—we could do it."

"Not your fault, sir. You—we—never should have been put in this position," Horace responded.

Colonel Dixon nodded, but he didn't buy the fault part. *A unit commander is responsible for everything his unit does or fails to do* had been pounded into him in officer training, and he had lived by that rule. He wouldn't give himself a pass.

Just then the nurse came back. "Gentlemen, if you will come with me."

Colonel Dixon and First Sergeant Horace followed the nurse out of the waiting room and down another hall to a barren office close to the emergency room. "Colonel Carson, the hospital commander, will be with you shortly. Please have a seat," the nurse said, closing the door as he exited.

Colonel Dixon's stomach felt like he had been run through by a bayonet. *This will not be good news,* he thought. The toughness he had acquired through years of service never protected him from feeling the loss of one of his Marines.

"Maybe they're going to tell us he is at another facility in country—or maybe on his way to Wiesbaden for treatment," Horace offered. The major medical facility in Germany was where the seriously injured were taken for more extensive procedures.

"Maybe, but I don't—"

The Colonel was interrupted by a knock on the door and the entrance into the room by a shorter man with graying hair and glasses. He stuck out his hand. "Good morning, gentlemen, I am Charlie Carson, the hospital director—er, commander. Please have a seat."

He sat down in the seat behind the desk, placed a medical record on the desk, folded his hands on top of the record, then looked at each of them individually.

He spoke softly. "I understand you are inquiring about the status of Major William Harris."

"That's correct." Dixon responded.

"Well," Carson began, "I can't give you a definitive answer on his condition. He was in terrible shape when he arrived here, you see. We did what we could, but decided his best chance for survival would be at Kandahar. So we medevaced him there. There was so much blood loss . . ." Carson added, looking down at the records on the desk.

"Any word from Kandahar?" Dixon asked.

"I understand he is there and they are working on him. I know that much. We should hear back at any moment. You are welcome to wait in my office upstairs. This can't be easy for you, Colonel."

"Thank you. No, it sure as hell is anything but easy. We'll be glad to accept your hospitality."

Carson walked them to his office and offered them coffee. Once served, Colonel Dixon noticed what he recognized as a Department of Defense telephone on Carson's desk.

"Colonel Carson, is that a DOD phone?" Dixon asked.

"Why yes. Direct to the states. Do you need to use it?"

"Yes, if I could," Dixon said, standing and moving toward the phone.

"By all means. Access instructions are right there beside it," Carson said. "Would you like for me to step out?"

"Yes, please, if you don't mind. It's a need-to-know type of thing."

Once Carson left, Dixon took out his cell phone and retrieved the number for NAVAIR. As the phone rang, he looked at his watch—it was one thirty a.m. on the east coast.

"Naval Air Systems Command, Petty Officer Perez speaking, how may I help you, ma'am or sir?"

"Petty Officer Perez, this Colonel Paul Dixon calling from Bagram Air Base, Afghanistan. It is urgent I speak to Admiral Lawrence right away."

"Uh, yes, sir . . . uh, I just don't know if I can . . ."

"Look, Perez, I understand that you normally don't get calls at 0130 for the NAVAIR commander, but either you find him or put someone on the phone that can."

"Yes, sir. Just one moment."

Dixon could hear muffled voices followed by a new voice on the line. "This is the duty officer, Commander Doggett. I understand you want to speak to Admiral Lawrence, is that correct?"

"Yes, it is," Dixon responded, speaking slowly for emphasis.

"Sir, I am not sure that . . ."

"Look here, Commander, I am sure if you call Admiral Lawrence he will be glad to take my call. I am at a hospital in Afghanistan. I have just left two of my injured men and I have been informed that another one may not make it. So I think you will understand that I am not interested in any answer but yes. Get hold of Admiral Lawrence, NOW, before I come through this line and choke the living shit out of you—got it?"

"Uh, yes, sir. One moment."

After a series of clicks, Dixon heard the familiar voice. "Paul, it's Wilson Lawrence. Sorry to hear about the crash. How are your people?"

"Thanks for asking, Admiral, and my apologies for waking you. Two are in relatively good condition. Major Bennett and Sergeant Cook. We are told the other pilot, Major Harris, is in bad shape. We just don't know."

"Sorry to hear that. I will say some prayers."

"Thanks. Sir, I was able to speak with Bennett briefly, and he made a point of telling me it wasn't ground fire that brought them down. Said they lost control on the way in, before enemy contact. First Sergeant Horace spoke to Sergeant Cook, who told him that both pilots were wrestling the aircraft to maintain control well before the first shots were fired. Said he heard the whole thing on the intercom and remembers it all. Admiral," Dixon said with determination, "if it wasn't obvious before, it sure as hell is obvious now. We need to put this aircraft on the ground—over here and back there."

"Understood. I was hoping it wasn't the aircraft, but in my gut I felt that was what you were going to tell me." Lawrence paused a moment. "I owe you and your men an apology, Paul. Although I wasn't part of the deployment decision, I should have put up more resistance when I first learned about it. This was too early. The aircraft had too many unresolved control problems, despite what I was briefed. My fault." Lawrence couldn't tell him about the knowledge he had obtained from Kemp's efforts. Not now or ever.

"Not all your fault, sir. The whole damn system failed. Just put 'em on the ground, sir. We gotta sort this out."

"Don't worry, Paul. This will be addressed quickly." Changing tone, the Admiral continued. "You take care of your folks. Let me know if you need anything. Meanwhile, I'll request priority orders to get you and your people home as quickly as possible by air. We'll bring the aircraft back by ship—not your worry. Anything else?"

"Thank you, sir, but I want to make sure my men are OK before I pull out of here. We'll await orders." Then Dixon remembered Major Bennett's request. "Sir, one more thing. Major Bennett asked that someone call his wife, Kathy, to let her know he's OK. They're in on-base housing at Cherry Point."

"OK. I'll make sure it's taken care of. What else?"

"That's all, sir. Appreciate your taking my call."

"Thank you, Paul, for all you've done. I'll see you when you get back."

"Thank you, sir. Out here." Dixon looked at Horace, who nodded and gave him the thumbs up. The message had been delivered. They both knew Lawrence would handle it.

They stood up and moved out of the office to look for Colonel Carson and saw him walking slowly down the hall toward them. When he got close, Dixon saw his long face and feared the worst.

"Just heard back from Kandahar. It's not good." Carson looked at the floor, hesitating to utter the words. "Major William Harris died on the operating table at Kandahar Combat Hospital about twenty minutes ago. I am deeply sorry."

Dixon slumped against the wall and his voice cracked. "Thank you for letting us know. I am sure you guys did all you could." He stuck out his hand to Carson.

"Thank you. My sympathies to your unit and to his family."

Straightening up, Dixon said, "We'd better get back to our unit. Here's my number. Call me if there are any developments with Bennett and Cook, please."

"Will do. Safe travels."

Dixon and Horace headed back down the stairs and toward the hospital exit. Neither man spoke.

As they got into the Humvee, Horace said, "We lost a fine Marine, sir. A damn fine Marine."

"We sure did, First Sergeant," Dixon said as he got into the vehicle. "And if I have anything to do about it, that's the last one we are losing in this fucking aircraft."

· · ·

A few hours later, a cell phone rang in the middle of the girls' clothing section at the Cherry Point MCAS Base Exchange. Kathy Bennett laid the clothes she had been examining for her daughter Paige across the cart and dug the phone out of her purse, having to move aside two-year old Mason to get to it.

"Hello, this is Kathy," she answered, looking at the unfamiliar number on the phone's screen.

"Is this Mrs. Kathy Bennett?" the official voice asked.

"Yes, this is she," Kathy replied, pausing at the official tone of the caller. Her heartbeat sped up.

"This is the United States Marine Corps calling from Washington, DC, ma'am. We need to confirm that you are the spouse of Major Gary Bennett of VMX 42."

"Yes, yes I am." Kathy said in a small voice, fear twisting her stomach into knots. She gripped the handle of the shopping cart and tried to breathe . . .

"Ma'am, there has been a crash of a XV-11 in Afghanistan, and your husband—"

"NO!" Kathy screamed, stopping people around her. "NO!" she cried out again as she bent over, sobbing. This was the call military spouses dreaded.

Kathy reached for Mason and held him as she regained some composure. "What's wong, Mommy?" Mason asked. She just shook her head and held him, unable to speak.

"Sorry to have alarmed you, Mrs. Bennett, but I was going to tell you that Major Bennett is injured, but fine. He's in a hospital in Afghanistan with some wounds, but he is going to be OK."

"Oh thank God!" Kathy said, wiping the tears from her face. She began to breathe again and noticed several people were staring at her. "It's OK," she blurted out as she waved to them all, nervous laughter coming through her happy tears.

"Is he . . . I mean, what about his injuries?" she asked.

"I do not have all of those details, ma'am, but I understand a few broken bones and a concussion, but nothing life-threatening," the caller responded.

Kathy was still trying to regain her composure. "Can I speak with him?"

"They are trying to set that up. Hopefully within twenty-four hours. But according to the folks at the hospital, he was insistent that we let you know."

Kathy laughed. "That's him! Well, I'll wait to hear. Thanks so very much for calling."

"My pleasure. You take care."

Kathy picked up Mason from the cart and squeezed him. "Daddy's coming home! I can't wait to tell Paige!" She picked up her purse and raced out of the store, leaving the cart, clothes and all, right where it was.

25

The vibrating alarm on Kemp's watch went off at 0500. He lay still a minute, listening for any noises. It was quiet. If they were out there, maybe they had dozed off. He moved to the alarm panel and disarmed the system.

At the top of the basement stairs, he listened again . . . nothing. His exterior and interior alarms were state of the art and had not been tripped. Kemp was confident that they could not be breached, at least not by these people.

Kemp opened the basement door and maneuvered across the kitchen floor in a crouch to stay below window level. He downed a tiny GPS tracking device that would provide his location for seventy-two hours. Then he moved to the garage, still in a crouch.

All was now set. When Kemp raised the garage door he thought they would burst in, but nothing happened. He started his car and headed out of the driveway, turning on the headlights at the end of his road. He placed his secure phone on the seat beside him, programmed it to send an alert to Admiral Lawrence, with whom Kemp had coordinated the entire plan of his capture and rescue. It also had a short text to Jake: *All good.*

Kemp headed for the Dulles Toll Road and DC. Now he *was* surprised. Would they actually not catch him after chasing him all over North Carolina and Virginia? "What the hell are they up to?" Kemp muttered to himself. "Are they going to just let me go?"

WHAM! Suddenly his car was rear-ended by a large sedan just before he got onto the toll road ramp. He hadn't seen it. It was operating dark. *WHAM!* again—but this time the car maintained contact. His car was being pushed over to the side of the road. *Just like Hadley,* he thought. "Goddamn you!"

Suddenly another car pulled alongside his, someone inside shining a bright light into his car. "Pull over into the shopping center at the next road to your right!" a man shouted though a bullhorn. Kemp then saw another car whip out of a side street in front of him. He was boxed in.

The light was extinguished, and he followed their instructions. He grabbed his secure phone and pushed the Send button, then rolled down the passenger window, hit the Clear button, and threw it out into the woods. It then shut down as programmed, but not before it erased all data.

In the parking lot, his car was surrounded by agents. "Out of the car," one of them said, opening the car door and pulling Kemp from the car. He was slammed onto the hood of his car and handcuffed.

As the two men searched him, another man approached. "Captain Kemp, I am Officer Chaney of the National Security Agency. You are under arrest for theft of classified documents. You have the right to remain silent. You have the right to an attorney. Anything you say can and will be used against you in a court of law. Do you understand these rights?"

"Yes," Kemp responded.

He was then pushed into the back of one of the sedans. Agent Gonzales was in the front passenger seat and turned to Kemp. "You have led us all over hell. We have some questions for you. You don't deserve no fuckin' attorney. Forget that crap."

Kemp just looked at Gonzales.

"You're ours now."

Kemp saw two other agents search his car then drive it across the lot toward a truck with its back open. As his rental car approached, its headlights illuminated a ramp at the rear of the truck. In a moment, the car was up the ramp, the truck's rear doors closed, and the truck was driven away.

Another agent approached Gonzales in the front seat of Kemp's car, and the men talked to each other in hushed voices. As the driver entered the car, Gonzales turned and said, "Where did you think you were going?" Kemp glared at him and said nothing. "You'll tell us later, old man. The only question is when," Gonzales said, grinning at Kemp. Another agent got in the back seat with Kemp and put a blindfold on him. "Let's go," Gonzales told the driver.

After several miles he felt the car leave the road and stop. Agents Freid and Gonzales pulled Kemp from the car. They opened the back doors of a windowless van and pushed Kemp inside. Agent Nolan stepped from a waiting sedan and got in the back of the van with Kemp. He leaned over and attached Kemp's handcuffs to a chain on the wall of the van, then attached Kemp's ankles to shackles bolted to the floor.

After what Kemp guessed was about a thirty-minute drive, the ride got rough.

"Almost home now," Nolan said.

Finally, the van came to a stop. Kemp again heard other car doors open and close, followed by the doors of the van opening.

"Well, here we are at last," Chaney said from outside the van. "Welcome to our little facility."

Kemp was pulled out of the van and led into a building. He heard a sound like an elevator door opening. He was led forward, felt a descent, and smelled the air get musty. Once the door opened he was guided into a room, pushed down onto a seat, and his blindfold was removed.

As his eyes adjusted, he made out the contours of a cell. It wasn't as bad as he had feared. Ten by eight, amply lit, no windows, a cot, a toilet, and a sink. *I've seen worse,* he thought.

"Put on these clothes, and give us yours. Shoes, too," one of the two men inside the cell said. "We'll wait."

Kemp began to do as instructed. After he undressed, the men went through his clothes and his shoes looking for anything suspicious, even an electronic signaling device. Of course, they had no way of knowing that Kemp had swallowed a GPS locator.

"You hungry? Thirsty?" One of the men asked.

"Neither," Kemp responded.

"OK, suit yourself."

What's going on? He thought. *This is too nice.*

He was right.

. . .

The Pentagon, Arlington, Virginia
Tuesday, August 11
9:00 a.m.

From his office, Alex Oliver called NAVAIR. "Lieutenant Colonel Beech, please. This is Alex Oliver from the Department of the Navy Aircraft Acquisitions Office."

"One moment, sir," the receptionist said.

After a few moments, Beech picked up. "Lieutenant Colonel Beech here, sir or ma'am. How can I help you?"

"Lieutenant Colonel Beech, it's Alex Oliver. How are you?"

"You tell me," Beech said.

"Oh, you're better than great. It's done."

"God, that's fantastic. I can't believe it." Beech felt a wave of relief.

Oliver smiled, "Yes, the genie is back in the bottle. Get back to work, Colonel."

"Right away. I owe you a drink," Beech said.

"Yes you do. Anytime," Oliver replied.

"You got it."

Oliver hung up and leaned back in his chair. He'd kept to himself the fact that the documents weren't with Kemp. Beech might freak out.

Now the next step: dealing with Kemp. Getting rid of him suddenly seemed the only viable course.

. . .

Kemp, left alone for a while, lay on his bunk, resting. Suddenly, large guards, both about six foot five, with huge chests and arms, burst into Kemp's cell, ending his rest.

"On your feet!" one of them said.

Kemp started up, only to be jerked to his feet by the two goons. One of them put a hood over Kemp's head as the other man pulled Kemp's arms behind his back and re-applied handcuffs. After another elevator trip, Kemp's blindfold was removed and he saw he was in an office, directly across from a desk, behind which was Agent Chaney, with another agent a couple of feet behind him. He also noticed that the two goons were still there, along with some other people in the shadows. The lighting was obviously set so he could see only those whom they wanted him to see.

"Understand you got some rest, Captain," Chaney began.

"Yes," Kemp said.

"Good." His host hesitated, then, in a more serious tone, said, "I am Agent Chaney. We met before."

Kemp nodded.

"Captain Kemp, I know who you are. You have done a lot for this country. We have a great deal of respect for you." He rose from behind his desk and moved to the front, where he sat on the edge. "But we have a little problem here. You took some classified documents, and we still don't know where they are. We did, however, find this flash drive containing classified XD-40 documents in your clothing," Chaney said, holding up the flash drive he got from Oliver.

"We need to know where the documents are, who you got them from, and how you got them out of the Pentagon. If we can get answers to those questions, sir, two things will happen. First, your stay here will be short, and second, depending upon what information you give us, your career might be unharmed. You know, retirement pay and benefits, your rank, that sort of thing. Now, doesn't that sound better than any alternatives?"

Kemp didn't say a word.

Chaney waited a moment, arms folded, and then walked slowly back to the chair behind his desk and sat down. "You know how these things go, Captain Kemp. I don't have to draw a picture for you. I'll give you thirty minutes." With that, he got up, pushed his chair away, and hurried out of the room through a door behind his desk, followed by Gonzales and others in the room. Only the goons stayed.

Kemp sat there, wondering about the time and the progress Jake was making. His plan was to draw this out as long as he could to allow Jake's packages to arrive at their destinations and give Jake and the admiral time to meet. Additionally, it would frustrate the hell out of these jerks.

Chaney re-entered the room. It hadn't felt like thirty minutes. More like ten. Chaney pulled up a wooden straight-backed chair in front of Kemp. He undid his tie, and leaned over to Kemp. "Look, Captain Kemp, I want this to go smoothly," Chaney said in a friendly tone. "But I've got a lot of pressure on me: some people want your ass. Help me help you," he urged. "Tell me why, tell me who, and we can get this over with."

Kemp didn't say a word.

Chaney stood up and moved to the edge of the desk, removing his coat. "Look Captain, no one knows that the XV-11 file was taken. No one knows we have you. So this whole episode never happened. And if you never reappear, well, you were into so much shit over your career people will just think that one of your old enemies finally caught up to you. So, the cavalry isn't coming, Captain. Plan B isn't going to work. You're ours. The program will go on, but you won't be around to see it. That's lose-lose, isn't it, Captain Kemp?"

More like win-win, Kemp thought. *Did these fools not think the documents could be made public? And the XD-40? He had a witness to the whole thing.*

"Guards!" Chaney called out as he stood up. "You're down to fifteen minutes, Captain." He left the room.

This time, they made him wait. Kemp figured it was around thirty minutes. That was part of it, he knew—never do what you say you are going to do. It keeps the prisoner wondering and hikes up his stress level.

The door behind Kemp suddenly opened and he was surrounded by four guards, who re-applied the blindfold and guided him back onto the elevator. After a few seconds, the doors opened, and he sensed deep cold. He was led down a hallway and into a room where he heard other voices.

They removed his blindfold, holding onto him. When his eyes adjusted, he could see in front of him a few two-by-twelves that had been joined together side by side into the shape of a table, about six feet in length, tilted slightly down at one end. The room was black—the only light was directed onto this "table."

"Seen this before, Colonel?" a deep voice said from the shadows, followed by a laugh. "Hell yes, you have! You've used it before, haven't you, Colonel? Strap him down!" The speaker moved into the edge of the light, and Kemp recognized him as one of the agents from Hadley's funeral.

The big guards threw him onto the board and strapped down his wrists, feet, torso, and neck. They placed a hood on him. He didn't struggle, conserving his energy.

"Well, Captain, I am told I have to ask you one more time if you want to cooperate. Do you?" the man from the funeral asked.

Nothing.

The man got right down to Kemp's level, placed his mouth right at Kemp's ear. "Good. This will be more fun than Hadley and Kolinsky," he whispered to Kemp.

Kemp couldn't hide his reaction to knowing who killed his friends and jerked his head away as much as he could, his hands tightening into fists.

"Guess you *can* hear me, old man! Well, I ain't got all day. You had your chance. Don't matter to me. I love this. I used to drown kittens for fun when I was a boy—until they made me stop. Now, I get paid to do this!"

He reached out and took a bucket of water from one of the other guards and poured a small stream of water on Kemp's chest. Kemp winced.

"Cold, ain't it, Captain?" the man said.

Kemp didn't respond.

"Well let's see if it's any colder somewhere else." He moved the bucket over Kemp's hooded face and began pouring the water slowly onto the hood at Kemp's nose and mouth. First a little at a time, then more each time.

Kemp had been through this before—at his own request, to know what it was like. During that process, he had learned a few tricks to endure it. He knew that panic would set in, and about all the physical symptoms. This knowledge wouldn't make him immune to the torture's effects, but it would help.

Still, it was torture. Kemp felt the water go up his nose. He couldn't breathe, and had to open his mouth for air. They were waiting. The man poured water down his mouth whenever he saw the pocket appear in the hood that showed Kemp was breathing through his mouth. Kemp coughed and choked, barely able to breathe.

I'm getting too old for this, Kemp thought.

Immediately after Kemp got his breath back, torrents of water were poured into his nose. Kemp feared this time he might not get his breath back. But he did. The guards let him recover for a minute, then resumed.

This went on for an hour. Several times he came close to losing consciousness. Finally, he was removed from the board, soaking wet. They re-shackled his legs and arms but left the hood on. They led him out of the room and to a cell on this same level, where they removed his hood. No light, no window, no cot. Just a cold cement floor.

"We'll be back. Enjoy your rest," one of the men said, laughing.

As they left the cell and closed the door, Kemp was already beginning to shiver. He would remain there for an hour—until the start of the next session.

After the third boarding of the day, around one o'clock, he was brought back before Chaney—wet, cold, and at the point of exhaustion. They placed him in the same chair as before and left him alone.

Although not aware of the exact time, Kemp figured by now the legal documents had been delivered to the corporate chiefs and military leaders and that Jake was near, if not in, Alexandria. His captors hadn't said anything about the legal documents Jake sent, so Kemp figured they were too isolated to hear about it. And since the legal papers were sent to legitimate principals of the program and not to rogue operators like Oliver, it made sense that these guys wouldn't know about it right away.

Chaney re-entered the room and lit a cigarette from the pack on his desk. After taking a deep draw, he blew out the smoke and spoke. "I have ordered the process stopped for a couple of hours. You can trust me on that. You will be returned to your room, where you will find some dry, clean clothes and some food. Get some rest."

Another drag on his cigarette and he moved closer to Kemp, bending down so they were eye to eye. "We'll meet again, Captain. Then we'll talk some more. Meanwhile, give this some thought. It's done, Captain. The birds will be made, they will fly, the corporations will make money, and workers will have jobs. The world will go on. This little exercise in hide-and-seek has already cost two lives—and maybe another. I understand Colonel Hartman isn't doing so well." After delivering that last shot, he waited for Kemp's reaction.

There was none.

He walked back to his desk and snuffed the cigarette into the ashtray. "Guards!"

As Kemp was led to the elevator, a slight smile broke onto his face.

"Something funny, Captain?" one of the goons asked.

Kemp said nothing, but smiled because Chaney was right, except he hadn't gone far enough. Not today, but tomorrow, it *would* all be over. He couldn't wait to see the look on their faces when they realized they had lost.

But in the meantime, the process would be repeated the remainder of the day and into the night, with waterboarding and a cold cell, challenging Kemp's physical condition, but not his mental fortitude. As tough as this was, Kemp was tougher.

26

In Pennsylvania, at Apex Helicopters, the company responsible for the XV-11's fuselage and cockpit, including its instrument packages, Chief Executive Officer Donovan Ross's assistant was already opening the mail when Johnny from the mailroom brought in a FedEx package.

"Good morning, Monica," Johnny greeted the secretary. "This FedEx addressed directly to Mr. Ross marked 'personal and confidential' came in first thing, but no one gave it to me until a few moments ago. I didn't think it should wait so I brought it right up."

"Thanks," Monica said as Johnny left. She opened the envelope and read the cover letter, then quickly scanned all the enclosed documents. She gasped, and quickly pressed the intercom. "Mr. Ross?"

"Hold it, Tom," Duncan Ross said to his caller. Covering the phone with his hand, he replied, "Monica, I am on the phone. Can't you see the light?"

"Yes, sir, but I have something you need to see. May I come in?"

"Yes." Getting back to the telephone, Ross said, "Tom, where were we?"

Ross motioned for Monica to come in and pointed her to one of the two leather chairs in front of his oversized desk, then held out his hand for the envelope. He squinted at the papers and looked around for his reading glasses. He put them on without removing the phone from his ear, cocking them awkwardly on his face.

Monica saw Ross's face turning red. "Uh, Tom, sorry to interrupt, but I'm afraid I have to go. May I call you back later? OK. Great. Thanks."

"Monica, ask Steve Robinson from legal to come up right away, please."

"Yes, sir." She started to turn, but was stopped by his additional request.

"And call Glenn Laker's office in Texas and see if you can reach him. Tell him it's urgent."

"Yes, sir. Anything else?"

"Touch base with the COO and the CFO and tell them to plan on a meeting in my office this morning at ten."

"Will do." She headed out of the door.

Ross started reading the documents in earnest, and after a few moments Monica called on the intercom.

"Sir, Mr. Robinson is here to see you."

"Great. Tell him to come in and hold my calls. Did you get hold of the others?"

"Yes, sir. They will be here at ten a.m. I'm still trying to reach Mr. Laker."

"Thanks, Monica."

Steve Robinson came into the office. "Good morning, sir."

"Good morning, Steve. Let's sit at the conference table," Ross said, getting up and heading to the seat at the head of the table.

"Steve, this is the damnedest thing I have ever seen. It's a threat from some lawyer down in North Carolina telling me he is going to file these papers if we don't do what he says," Ross said, disgusted.

"That's not all that unusual for us, sir," Steve said.

"You're right . . . but most of those don't have highly classified government documents attached to a Requests to Admit," he said, sliding the envelope across the table to Robinson.

"What?"

Ross watched as Robinson looked through the pleadings. Even this experienced corporate lawyer couldn't maintain his poker face.

"I can see you are impressed," Ross said.

"More like dumbfounded."

"Yes. There are some *pretty* bad things in there . . . if any of it is true," Ross responded. "This guy might just be grandstanding to get some attention. Why would anybody in his or her right mind attach classified documents to a public document?"

Robinson shook his head. "Don't know. Maybe he's some sort of crusader."

"Maybe. Let's see what we can find out. Also, just to cover our asses, we need to look into the allegations this guy is making. I never heard of any of this stuff. But I do seem to remember that we did have someone on the payroll in the liaison role. I think his name is mentioned in there . . . Webb," Ross said pointing at the documents. "We need to talk to him sooner rather than later."

"Yes, sir. I'll get right on it."

"Thanks, Steve. I'll see you at ten."

. . .

Fort Worth, Texas
Tuesday, August 11, 2009
8:30 a.m.

The telephone rang at the large home of Vertical Aerospace CEO Glenn Laker in the Rivercrest section of Fort Worth on Tuesday morning. Vertical Aerospace had primary responsibility for the XV-11's wings, rotors, and landing gear in this joint, two-company program. It would be a major revenue source for years to come—not to mention the civilian tilt-rotor spin-off projects that were already being planned.

"Laker residence," Maureen, the housekeeper, answered.

"Good morning. It's Donovan Ross's office calling from Apex Helicopters. Is Mr. Laker available? " Monica asked.

"One moment, please," Maureen said, then headed to the sunroom.

"Yes, Maureen, what is it?" Glenn Laker said, not looking up from his paper.

"It's Mr. Ross from Apex Helicopters for you, sir," Maureen said.

"OK," Laker said, holding his hand out to receive the handset from Maureen. "Hello, Donovan, how are you?"

"Glenn, good morning. Hope I am not disturbing you."

"Just playing hooky. I decided to have a leisurely morning at home," Laker responded.

"That's about to change. Did you get a FedEx package this morning?"

"Yes, someone did call from the office advising me I had an early morning FedEx delivery marked 'personal and confidential.'"

"Well, it will probably turn out to be nothing, but some lawyer down in North Carolina is threatening to sue us in a wrongful death case involving the XV-11."

"Donovan, my friend, I don't think that a wrongful death suit regarding one of our products is news," Laker interrupted.

"I agree. But this one came with a Requests to Admit that has what seem to be classified documents attached. They don't paint a very flattering picture of our companies, our product, or of the military for that matter. I don't have to tell you this program can't handle much more bad press."

Laker sighed. "Agreed. Guess I'd better get to the office and look at those papers."

"Good. I'm going to meet with my managers at ten eastern. Let me suggest that you spend a little time with this and we talk around noon eastern. We need to nip this in the bud. I sure as hell don't want to see a vital multi-billion-dollar program put at risk."

"You say he hasn't filed this thing yet?" Laker asked.

Ross flipped through the documents. "No, apparently not. He has some strong demands in here about fixing or halting the program, and says if we don't agree to them by five p.m. today, he will file first thing in the morning."

Laker laughed. "Well, you've got to hand it to him. The guy gets hold of some secret documents and has the nerve to go public with them and threaten two of the biggest aerospace contractors around into shutting down a fifty-billion-dollar program. Maybe he just wants money . . . .and a little notoriety," Laker responded

"Not from what he says in these papers."

"We'll see. Thanks for the heads-up," Laker said.

• • •

The Pentagon, Arlington, Virginia
Tuesday, August 11, 2009
9:00 a.m.

In the private exercise room adjacent to his huge office, Secretary of Defense Melvin Harrell saw his assistant, General Yates, come into the room with a FedEx package.

"You need to see this, Mr. Secretary. I think it deserves some urgency," General Yates said.

The secretary opened the door of the small refrigerator in the corner and retrieved a bottle of water. He sat down on the small bench, took a swig of water, wiped the sweat from his face with a hand towel, then held out his hand to receive the package.

"Who in the hell is Jake Baird?" he asked as he strained to see the label. "What in God's name is this?" Harrell examined the contents of the envelope. "A lawsuit? About the Sea Eagle? The damn thing has been deployed and is almost in full production—what does this lawyer know about it?"

"Sir," General Yates said, "look at the attachments to the Requests to Admit—it's after the Complaint."

Secretary Harrell fumbled with the documents until he got to the Requests. "I don't believe this! The son of a bitch has attached classified documents—are they real?"

"It appears so, sir," Yates responded.

Secretary Harrell rose from the bench. "This program is far too important for the country to let some crackpot lawyer derail it. I need for you to find Chairman Cohen, Secretary Parris, Admiral Tanner and General Kimball and tell them I need to see them in my office at 1100 hrs. If they are unavailable in person I need them on the phone. Top priority. Got it?"

"Yes, sir. I'll get right on it," General Yates replied.

"OK. Thanks. Brief me on the status in fifteen minutes," Harrell said, heading for his shower.

. . .

The Pentagon, Arlington, Virginia
Tuesday, August 11, 2009
11:00 a.m.

Secretary of Defense Harrell entered the conference room off his office. The uniformed members of the group as well as the secretary of the Navy stood up as Secretary Harrell moved toward his seat.

"Good morning. Please, take your seats. We need to discuss this package that I, Chairman Cohen, Secretary Parris, Admiral Tanner, and General Kimball got this morning. Right now, I don't care so much about how we got here; we'll get to that in a moment. I've had many calls from the press already today about the crash in Afghanistan and I will address the press at 1530 hours today about that matter. I don't want to be handling an additional press conference tomorrow regarding *this*," he said, holding up the FedEx envelope. "We have to come up with a legitimate, effective response to this potential lawsuit and its consequential bad publicity." He looked around the group and said, "OK, I'm all ears—Admiral Tanner, let's hear from you first."

"Thank you, sir," the chief of Naval Operations began, "We all know the XV-11 has had some problems and is way behind schedule. As I understand it from my legal folks, Baird is under no compulsion to file this lawsuit due to any statute of limitations. So we ask him to hold off because we are dealing with the early reports of an XV-11 down in Afghanistan. We then assure him that the events in Afghanistan will lead to a thorough investigation, and he won't help that process by filing. I have discussed this preliminarily with the chief of NAVAIR, Admiral Lawrence, who will be going on the Hill tomorrow to address the Senate Armed Services Committee, and he concurs."

"So we talk to him?" Harrell asked.

"Yes, sir," Tanner replied.

"Anyone else?"

"Sir, as secretary of the Navy, respectfully, I can't agree with the CNO's proposal," Parris answered. "This is a vital program for our country's security. Almost all weapon systems have development problems. Just look at the C-5A—one of the most controversial aircraft ever built and yet it has been an excellent, reliable aircraft." Parris stopped to take the measure of the room. "My suggestion would be that we arrest him as soon as possible for being in unauthorized possession of classified documents, and we confiscate these files from him. He's a lawyer, for God's sake, and nobody's going to trust a lawyer, especially one in possession of stolen classified military documents."

"So we attack him and defend the aircraft?" the secretary of defense inquired.

"Yes, sir. That's the nut of it."

"OK. Anyone else?" Harrell asked, looking around the group.

"Yes sir. With respect, he's not just a lawyer, Mr. Secretary," began General Kimball, commandant of the Marine Corps. "We've checked him out and found he has a distinguished active-duty record and that he performed in a precarious special operations position in Afghanistan. He was the real deal then, and is currently a US Army Reserve aviator. My hunch is that Lieutenant Colonel Baird sees this as an act of patriotism, however misguided. If we start trying to make this guy look bad, it could backfire on us. I say we try to talk to him. And if I might add," he continued, "it's the Marines' aircraft, so arguably we have more at stake here than anyone. We desperately need a replacement for our CH-46s, but I need to make sure my Marines are getting a safe aircraft. In my mind, a time-out might be worthwhile."

"Thank you, General Kimball. Chairman Cohen, your thoughts, please," Harrell requested.

"Mr. Secretary," said the chairman of the Joint Chiefs, "I've also had his personnel file pulled and my quick glance tells me that he's no kook. I think General Kimball is right. I think we should see if we can start a dialogue."

"OK, is that the majority view?" Harrell asked.

"Sir, if I might . . ." Secretary Parris started.

"Go right ahead, Secretary Parris," the secretary of defense responded.

"If those papers get filed and reach the press, it will cause such harm that a dialogue will be useless. The press is already negative on the XV-11, and this suit will give them ammo they want. Congress will certainly notice, and funding could be jeopardized. I'll go along with trying to talk to him, but we can't let the papers get filed."

"Anyone else?" Secretary Harrell asked. The nods of the men around the table and a couple of "agreeds" told him that was the consensus. "OK. So we need to find a way to stop the filing of the documents, correct?"

"Yes, sir. I suggest we dispatch security teams to his office and to the federal courthouse in Raleigh, where we anticipate the documents will be filed," Parris suggested. "Shouldn't be much of a problem, since it looks like it's a one-lawyer firm—just him and a secretary," responded Secretary Parris.

"But, Mr. Secretary?" Chairman Cohen began. Secretary Harrell nodded for him to continue. "As per the contact part, I suggest a chain-of-command approach, and get someone to work it down to Lieutenant Colonel Baird's Reserve Commanding Officer."

"I agree," said Secretary Harrell. "Admiral Tanner, will you take care of it?"

"Yes, sir. Right away," Tanner responded.

"OK," said the secretary of defense as he started to gather his papers. "I need to talk to the contractors. Now that I have consensus among us, I'll make that call. I imagine they're circling their wagons this morning also. Thank you for coming. I'll get back to you."

· · ·

Philadelphia, Pennsylvania
Tuesday, August 11, 2009
12:00 noon

The video conferencing center at Apex Helicopters' corporate headquarters was empty except for CEO Ross, Steve Robinson, and Monica, Ross's secretary.

"Everybody ready?" Ross asked. There were nods all around. He pushed the "open conference" button, and, a couple of crackles and aligned images later, another conference room with Glenn Laker and one other person appeared.

"Hello, Donovan."

"Hello, Glenn. I know we are all still waiting on word from Afghanistan, and we'll talk about that in due time. Meanwhile, we have a mess here that we need to fix."

"Donovan, before we go further, I am just wondering if anyone's talked to someone at the Pentagon? After all, it's their file that got stolen," Laker asked.

"Not yet. I thought it would be best if we had our conversation first, and once we all agree on what needs to be done, then we can call the Pentagon."

"Good idea," Laker said. "I will tell you, in confidence, that today we got inquiries from the United Arab Emirates, of all people. That's in addition to the interest already shown by the Brits, the Japanese, and the Israelis. I don't have to tell you what that means for our workers. We have to find an effective way to deal with this do-gooder before he kills this important defense project, along with the thousands of jobs it's going to generate."

"Glenn, you're right. This lawsuit could pose great problems, especially in light of today's reports from Afghanistan," Ross responded. "Like you, we are standing by to provide technical support for the military, but the initial word on the cause of the crash is not encouraging. The public relations battle we've been waging for years is about to heat up."

"Agreed. What do you propose?" Laker asked.

"Maybe we or the military can figure out if someone can talk to Baird. If not, we must get the government to stop him from filing," Ross responded.

"And if they don't?" Laker asked.

Donovan Ross hesitated. "Then we have to find a way to do it."

"My thoughts exactly. Do you have a way to accomplish this?" Laker asked.

"I think we have some resources that can be utilized," Ross said.

"I'll leave that in your capable hands, then. Enough said."

Ross moved on. "Let me call Secretary Harrell and see what he's thinking. I'll get back to you right after that telephone call. Will you be in your office?" Ross asked.

"Yes. Not going anywhere," Laker responded.

"I'll be in touch shortly," Ross concluded.

"Monica, would you please get Secretary Harrell on the phone?"

. . .

"Secretary Harrell, Good afternoon, sir. Donovan Ross calling."

"Good afternoon, Donovan. How's the weather up in Philadelphia today?"

"Great, how about DC?"

"Well, it was fine until these tornadoes blew through this morning," Harrell replied.

"Yes, we had the same weather phenomenon here, Mr. Secretary. That's why I called."

"You beat me by about five minutes," Secretary Harrell responded.

"What are your thoughts, Mr. Secretary, if you don't mind my asking?"

"Don't mind at all. First, as to the downed XV-11, information is still sketchy. We'll advise as soon as we have verified information. As to this law-suit, we discussed it among ourselves and we have two major points. First, Baird has had a distinguished military career. He's an active reservist and we're hopeful we can reason with him and convince him not to file the lawsuit."

Ross was relieved. "Good. You have someone who can talk to him?"

"We're trying to identify that person now," Harrell responded. "Second, in light of the events in Afghanistan of this morning, we have discussed what we can do to stop the further dissemination of these classified documents, which means if we can't reason with him, we need to prevent the filing of this lawsuit."

"We are all in agreement," Ross responded. "How would that be accom-plished . . . again, if you don't mind my asking?"

"We're developing contingency plans now to intercept the filing," Secre-tary Harrell responded.

"There isn't much time, Mr. Secretary," Ross warned.

"You're right, and I assure you we're moving as fast as we can. You must understand, however, that we're a bit preoccupied by the current situation in Afghanistan."

"Mr. Secretary, we've all worked hard to get this unique and important weapons program to where it is. This aircraft will be of great benefit to the troops and to the workers in the fifty states where it is built."

"I understand your message, Donovan," Harrell replied. "We don't under-estimate its importance to our Marines."

"Of course. That's why we can't let whatever has happened in Afghani-stan be inflamed by this ridiculous lawsuit. Not to mention the fact that it is based, allegedly, on classified documents clearly stolen from the Pentagon." Ross wanted to remind the Secretary whose fault this was.

Secretary Harrell was not in the mood for the blame game. "Mr. Ross, I'm fully aware of the alleged source of this information. But if the docu-ments are legitimate, it seems to me *how* they were made public will not be nearly as important as *what* is in them. And that should concern us both, since it looks like we weren't tending to things as closely as we should have," Secretary Harrell growled.

The reproach was not missed. "Understood, Mr. Secretary."

"We'll keep you posted," Harrell said.

. . .

"Glenn, it's Donovan," Ross said. "I just spoke to Secretary Harrell. Looks like it's under control. They will find him and talk to him, but they are also initiating a plan to stop the filing in case reason fails."

"That's great news, but I'm not comfortable with leaving it all to the military. I think we should go ahead with our own contingency plan regarding security. Do you agree?" Laker asked.

"Sounds like a good idea. We'll take the lead on that," Ross responded, then ended the call.

Ross turned to Monica. "Get Frank Fritz for me." She left the room, and a few minutes later, his intercom sounded. "Mr. Fritz is on the line for you, Mr. Ross."

He picked up the phone. "Frank, how are you?"

"Fine, Mr. Ross. And you?"

"Doing well, thank you. Steve Robinson is going to be calling you with an assignment. We have some lawyer down in North Carolina who intends to file a lawsuit alleging all kinds of nonsense about us and the XV-11. The government is going to try to talk him into not filing and, if that doesn't work, they intend to stop it. I think we need our own team there observing, reporting back, and maybe offering assistance to the government, if you know what I mean," Ross said.

"Certainly, sir."

"Take your best people and one of our corporate aircraft and get down there ASAP," Ross instructed.

"Got it, sir."

. . .

Fritz walked out of his office into a larger office with two men at their desks. "You two come into my office, please." Maggetti and Sullivan followed him into his office. He shut the door after them.

"OK, we have to take a little trip down to North Carolina. We'll take a company aircraft. Can you guys make a departure in one hour?"

"Sure," Maggetti answered.

"Get your stuff and be back here in an hour. I'll brief you en route."

"Sidearms then, right?" Maggetti asked.

"Right."

27

Northern Virginia
Tuesday, August 11, 2009
2:15 p.m.

Jake was just outside of Quantico, traveling northbound in a rental car toward Alexandria, Virginia. He'd wanted to avoid using his own vehicle in case agents had already identified him. In a little under an hour, he would be in the safe house as instructed by Kemp.

Forty-five minutes later, he slowly approached the safe house and noticed uniformed security people at their stations in front of and across the street from the townhouse. One guard positioned herself in front of Jake's car, signaling him to stop, and another came to his window. He noticed their blue uniforms and the Naval Security insignia. Other officers appeared and took positions in the street, facing outward. The officer at his door signaled him to roll down the window.

"Colonel Baird?" the man inquired.

"Yes."

"May I see some ID, sir?" the officer requested.

Jake pulled out his military ID and showed it to the officer.

"Thank you, sir. Please follow the guide in front of you and reposition your car down the driveway and into the underground garage."

Jake pulled into the garage and the guide motioned for him to stop, then walked to Jake's window. "Thank you, sir. Please step out of the vehicle. Do you have anything besides the briefcase?"

"Yes, a suitcase in the trunk."

"Thank you, sir. We'll get your things. Officer Walsh will escort you to your quarters," the officer said, motioning to the man at the other side of the car.

"Good afternoon, Colonel Baird. If you will follow me, sir," Walsh politely suggested.

They took stairs up to the third floor and stopped in front of a wooden door with a brass *24* on it. Walsh pointed to a guard in a chair several feet away. "This is Officer Morales. He or someone else will be posted outside your door at all times. If you need anything, just ask him or whoever is out here. We'll get food, drink, writing materials: anything you need. Also, you can call us by dialing 99. We must ask, however, that you do not leave the room. It's for your own safety."

"Understood," Jake responded.

Opening the door, Walsh said, "This will be your quarters, sir. Walsh stepped aside and Jake entered the room, which held a four-poster bed and a wood-burning fireplace. As Jake was looking around, another officer arrived with his bags and briefcase. "Anything else, sir?"

"No, thanks," Jake responded. The man left the room, closing the door behind him. Jake looked at his watch. It was now 2:55 p.m. He turned on the television and tuned to CNN. The Afghanistan XV-11 crash was all over the news. The newscaster was seated at a desk with a huge image of an XV-11 behind him.

. . . Still no word on the occupants of the aircraft. The military has confirmed that there were survivors, but not the number. We understand that an intense battle raged between the downed US troops and the Taliban forces. We do not know if that battle is still going. We also understand that reinforcements and a rescue force—in conventional helicopters—were dispatched and may already be onsite. At this point, we do not know whether the Sea Eagle was brought down by hostile fire or by mechanical failure.

At a news conference this morning, a Pentagon spokesman gave limited information beyond acknowledging the crash. We should receive an update sometime this afternoon. Nothing was said about the potential impact this could have on the XV-11 program, though it seems clear that this incident will raise new doubts about its survival.

Jake turned down the volume and turned away from the TV. He needed to finish his presentation for the admiral. He began to write out the military-style briefing he had mentally created on the way to Alexandria. As he started typing, more news flashed on CNN. He picked up the remote and increased the volume.

The Pentagon has just confirmed that the lone XV-11 that crashed near a village in Afghanistan was conducting a surprise combat assault on a meeting of that region's top Taliban leaders. The plan was to come in from a long distance and surprise a lightly guarded camp with a highly trained elite force.

We understand that rescue forces and reinforcements have now arrived at the crash site and that they are heavily engaged with the Taliban. We also have been told that some of the wounded Marines from the crashed aircraft have been evacuated and are being treated at medical facilities. Still no word on the type or number of casualties.

Please stay tuned to CNN for live coverage of the upcoming Pentagon briefing scheduled for 3:30 p.m.

Jake had not showered for over twenty-four hours and needed to get cleaned up prior to meeting the admiral. He was barely dressed when there was a knock at the door. Jake opened it to find Officer Walsh with a tray. "The admiral thought you might like some coffee and snacks."

"Thank the admiral for me, please."

"Sir, he also wanted me to be sure to tell you to watch the Pentagon briefing at 1530 hours on C-SPAN, channel 364."

"OK. Thanks."

"One more thing, sir. Admiral Lawrence said he would be here at seven to meet with you for dinner," the guard said.

"Understood," Jake replied.

Jake closed the door and poured himself a cup of coffee. As he picked up a sandwich, the TV picture went to the Pentagon, and the newsman said, "We have just learned that the secretary of defense himself will be giving the briefing. We expect him momentarily."

Secretary of Defense Harrell walked into the room and onto the small stage behind the podium. "In the early morning hours today, we launched an attack against a Taliban meeting site in a village in northwest Afghanistan, using an XV-11 tilt-rotor aircraft from a squadron that was secretly deployed to a secure, classified location. The concept of the operation was to hit the Taliban with a small elite force, Special Forces and Marines, in a low-level, surprise attack, and to kill or capture the entire lot, then withdraw.

"During the descent into the LZ, something happened—we don't know exactly what at this point—and the aircraft crashed. We have recovered the aircraft's digital flight recorder and cockpit voice recorder, which are being flown to Washington for analysis. We are in the process of speaking with those who were on the aircraft who are able to speak to us.

"As you have been told, immediately following the crash, a fierce firefight ensued, with the Taliban attacking our downed and injured troops with a variety of small arms, medium and heavy automatic weapons, mortars, and rocket-propelled grenades. No mercy was shown, no rules of combat obeyed. Even though seriously outnumbered and outgunned, our brave men took care of their wounded and held off the Taliban forces until reinforcements arrived.

"I'm pleased to report that all personnel on the downed XV-11 have been extracted and the village has been secured. The XV-11 itself was deemed unsalvageable and blown up in place by air strikes—after ground personnel removed the aircraft's black boxes.

"It should also be reported that the opposing forces were routed by our ground reinforcements and air assets. During the attack, numerous Taliban leaders and soldiers were killed or captured. Unfortunately, this was not without losses on our side. I am sad to report that of the Marines and Special Forces on the aircraft, seven brave men lost their lives, and I do not know presently whether these losses were due to the crash or the firefight. Of course, we will not give out names until notification has been made to the next of kin. Now, I will take a few questions."

A reporter in the front got straight to the point: "When do you think you'll know if it was hostile fire or mechanical problems that caused the aircraft to crash?"

"We expect first reading of all devices within the next forty-eight hours. This should give us an initial insight into the cause. It will probably take two to three days to initially analyze the data, during which time we should be able to complete most of the personnel interviews. I am hopeful that we can provide a preliminary report within two weeks."

"What about the flight crew? Have they been identified?"

"Not yet. We will make other announcements when we know. That's it for now. Thank you for coming."

Harrell abruptly turned and left the stage with the secretary of the Navy and the chief of Naval Operations following at his heels. Jake also caught a glimpse of Admiral Lawrence.

Just after four p.m., Jake grabbed his secure phone and called Florence.

"Jake?"

"Heard anything from anyone?"

"Not a peep."

"OK. Check the office voice mail overnight and call me the second you hear anything. If there is nothing on the machine overnight, go ahead as planned."

"OK," Florence said.

Jake had heard nothing from Kemp since receiving his text this morning. Jake was concerned that Kemp might have been captured. But he couldn't do anything about that, at least not now, so he focused on the task at hand.

. . .

At 6:55 p.m., there was a knock on Jake's door. Opening it, he found himself face-to-face one of the sharpest naval officers he had ever seen. Chiseled face, starched fatigues, shoes like glass. He guessed a lieutenant commander.

"Good evening, Colonel. I'm Commander Jobe, Admiral Lawrence's aide. I see you are ready for dinner. If you would be so kind, I will escort you to the dining room. The admiral is already here."

"Sure. Just let me get my computer," Jake responded.

"Certainly, sir," the officer responded.

They went down the stairs to a parlor on the first floor, just off the large foyer. They both waited a moment and heard a voice from behind.

"Good evening, gentlemen." The men turned to see Admiral Lawrence standing in the hall parlor, resplendent in his white uniform. He walked to greet the men and stuck out his hand. "Mr. Baird—excuse me—Colonel Baird, nice to meet you."

Jake walked over and gripped the Admiral's hand. "Very nice to meet you, Admiral."

"Come, Colonel, have a seat," the admiral said as he motioned to one of the leather chairs in the room.

"Commander, please tell the kitchen we will be having dinner shortly. But first, Colonel Baird, may I offer you something to drink?"

"Sir, to tell you the truth, I would love a beer, if that's OK."

"That will be fine. Commander, make it two, please."

"Yes sir," Commander Jobe responded, and disappeared.

"How was your trip up, Colonel?" the Admiral asked, as he sat in a chair opposite Jake.

"Just fine, sir."

A sailor arrived with two beers. "Here you are, sirs." He offered the tray to the Admiral first, then to Jake.

"Thanks, Johnson. If you would be so kind as to close the doors behind you, I would appreciate it."

"Glad to do it, Admiral," Johnson said, closing the parlor doors.

"Jake, thanks for coming all this way to visit with me. Captain Kemp has kept me posted on all of your efforts to sort through the XV-11 puzzle, and I must say I am impressed. I hope that head injury is healing nicely."

"Doing fine, sir," Jake said.

"I am eager to hear your thoughts on the whole issue. But I think it will make the most efficient use of our time if we do that over dinner. Is that acceptable to you?"

"Certainly, sir."

"Before we head in for dinner, I imagine the crash in Afghanistan is something that is on your mind."

"Yes, sir. Very much so," Jake said.

"Well, we don't have all the facts yet, but I can tell you, in confidence, that initial reports indicate that it was an aircraft control problem—and not enemy fire—that brought the aircraft down."

"Very sorry to hear that, Admiral."

"You and me both, Jake. Now, I'll bet you're hungry. Let's go eat and you can tell me all about what you have learned. Shall we?"

"Certainly, sir." Jake hesitated for a moment. "Sir, I have prepared a formal briefing for you whenever you're ready." He reached for his computer.

The Admiral stood up. "Why don't we do that after dinner once we've talked awhile?"

"Yes, sir," Jake said, rising.

"OK, Johnson, we're ready," the admiral said, loud enough that it was certain to be heard outside the room. "Jake, bring your beer. We also have some wine if you prefer."

The doors swung open and several members of staff in white jackets awaited them in the dining room. Once the men were seated, service started quickly and soon the men were through their salads.

During dinner, Jake explained to the admiral what he had learned from the documents Kemp had given him and from his meeting with Dr. Kolinsky. Lawrence told Jake that he was unaware of many of the details Jake related to him and was particularly curious about the differences between the tilt-wing and the tilt-rotor. Lawrence made the point that he had been appointed to his post as chief of NAVAIR *after* the choice had been make to go with the tilt-rotor over the tilt-wing concept.

Eventually, the men got around to sharing stories of their military careers and backgrounds and had a good time getting to know each other. Jake kept waiting for the admiral to bring up the briefing. He didn't.

"Let's go back into the parlor, Jake," the Admiral suggested. As they entered the room, Admiral Lawrence closed the doors behind him.

"Do you want the briefing now, Admiral?"

"Sure, but without your notes." Jake hesitated. "Look, Jake, I know you are thinking 'Admiral' and the standard military briefing. I got news for you . . . those briefings are generally as boring for me as I'll bet they are for you."

"Invariably, sir," Jake smiled.

Admiral Lawrence got up and began to walk the room. "You just told me about what you've learned and what you've been through. And I'll bet that has acquainted you with some things that you would like for everyone associated with the XV-11 program to know."

"Correct, sir."

"Jake, I have given this a lot of thought, so let me get to the point. Given what you have seen and your discussions with Captain Kemp and Doctor Kolinsky, you know a lot more detail about the pros and cons of this whole thing than I do. Plus, I have someone on my staff who served with you in Afghanistan and that person told me how articulate and persuasive you are, especially in those times when you disagreed with command's decisions." He paused, then said, "So how would you feel about testifying tomorrow?"

Jake almost dropped his beer. He'd never in a million years pictured himself testifying in front of Congress.

The admiral prodded. "Would you be willing to do it?"

"Sir, I would be honored to do it."

"That's good news. Now what would you say?"

"Well, sir, I would begin with how I got involved with the XV-11 by my representation of Lisa Thorpe, how I researched the developmental history and met with Dr. Collins, and then discuss the conclusions I drew—and give the reasons for those conclusions. I would probably talk about how I came into possession of the documents, give them my thoughts on Captain Kemp's reasons for giving me the documents, and talk about the hazards this aircraft presents to Marines. That's it in a nutshell, sir."

"That's a great overview, Jake. Since you know this subject, you are able to speak about it not only from the head, but perhaps more importantly, from the heart. Isn't that what litigation is all about?"

"Yes, sir."

"Then that is what you will do tomorrow."

"Understood, sir. I am grateful to speak for the troops and for those who won't have this opportunity—like Hadley and Kolinsky."

"Correct. Work out the details overnight. I'm sure you will do a great job."

"I appreciate your confidence, sir."

Lawrence yawned. "You can get back upstairs and do a bit of organizing and then get some rest. We both have a big day tomorrow," Admiral Lawrence said.

"Yes we do, Admiral," Jake responded, joining the admiral, standing.

"Have a good rest, Jake." Admiral Lawrence said, extending his hand. "I look forward to your remarks tomorrow. And if you don't mind, email me a copy of your prepared briefing so I can look at it overnight."

"Certainly, sir."

The admiral turned to leave, but Jake stopped him. "There is one question, if I might, sir."

"Sure, Jake. I think you deserve at least one."

"Well, Admiral, if these aircraft weren't ready, why were they deployed?"

The Admiral shook his head. "Human nature, really. People who had devoted their time, efforts, and souls to this project couldn't believe that it was as bad as critics said. Others who knew better lacked the courage to stand up. And then there were those people who didn't care about safety but only about their own interests—and their own pockets. It is hard to believe how a few misguided people can sabotage the good and honorable work of so many others. Finally, there were those at the top—including me—who didn't have an understanding of what was going on in their own organizations."

"Very human, unfortunately," Jake responded.

"Correct. But I will address that tomorrow. Good night, Jake."

Once in his room, Jake got back to work. He worked for three more hours, then decided that it was time he hit the sack. Before he turned out the light, he checked his secure phone to see if there was anything from Kemp, but there was nothing. He dozed off with the realization that Kemp and the Admiral had orchestrated the whole thing.

. . .

Raleigh, North Carolina
Tuesday, August 11, 2009
9:00 p.m.

At a hotel in downtown Raleigh, five men and two women were meeting in a small conference room.

"OK, now that we've all been introduced, listen up," instructed NSA agent Steven Sears. "Here's a preview that has been forwarded by secure transmission directly from the Pentagon."

Sears opened a PowerPoint program on his laptop and started his briefing. "A Raleigh attorney, Jake Baird, has possession of classified documents regarding the XV-11 program, which were stolen from the Navy Aircraft Acquisition Office at the Pentagon. Mr. Baird has used these documents to draft legal papers, which allegedly contain excerpts from the classified documents, and he has attached alleged copies of several of the classified documents to the legal papers.

"In communications to the highest levels of the military and service secretaries, as well as to the heads of the manufacturers of the XV-11, Mr. Baird has boldly indicated his intent to file these legal papers tomorrow morning and thereby make public the classified documents.

"Mr. Baird has committed a major security breach by unauthorized possession of these classified documents. He has compounded his breach by attempting to distribute the information to the public and others who are not authorized to be in possession of the documents and/or the information contained in those documents. This conduct constitutes a security threat to the United States of America.

"Therefore, Mr. Baird is to be apprehended upon sight. Secondly, Mr. Baird, or anyone acting on his behalf, is to be prevented from filing or distributing any of the documents that contain, summarize, or refer to the classified materials. You are to stop, detain, and arrest anyone who has possession of or anyone who attempts to file or distribute any such documents. You are to notify this office as soon as you accomplish any of these tasks."

Agent Sears turned from his computer. "OK. First, we were not able to locate Baird. We have had surveillance on his office and at his house and there has been no sign of him. Second, this is Florence Hilliard," Sears said, flashing her picture on the computer screen. "She is Baird's assistant. In Baird's absence, we must assume that Mrs. Hilliard will be filing the papers tomorrow, unless, of course, we spot Mr. Baird. We have called her home and her office, but she hasn't answered our calls. Our surveillance on her has yielded nothing unusual. We have decided against an office visit since we think we can intercept the filing at the courthouse."

After giving each officer his or her assigned location, Sears continued. "Apprehend Baird the moment he is spotted. As for Ms. Hilliard, we do not want any embarrassing situations. We don't want to stop her if she is just going for coffee. Once we sight her, we will observe her all the way into the courthouse, assuming she will be filing. The court officers have also been alerted to let us know if they see her or Baird, but they will not try to stop either—they can't. This is our show.

"Ladies and gentlemen, national security is at stake. Do your best. Any questions?" Several of the agents shook their heads no; nobody spoke. "OK. Great. See you at 0600. Have a good evening," Sears added.

. . .

At another downtown hotel, three men sat at a table in the lobby bar.

"Word is that the Feds have it covered," Fritz said. "Sullivan, you monitor Baird's office. Tony and I will go to the courthouse. I'll go inside—to observe. Tony, you'll stay outside. We'll stay in touch, but basically we'll monitor. This is the Feds' show. Agreed?"

They all nodded. No use getting in the way or risking themselves if the Feds were going to handle it.

28

Florence awoke at her usual time and went to her exercise bicycle in the sunroom, did her standard thirty minutes, and headed to the shower. She wondered why she wasn't more nervous. She did have a pit in her stomach, but it wasn't out of fear; it was more the uncertainty of what the morning would bring. Florence told herself she had filed hundreds of papers before. This was just one more time.

She dressed in a navy suit with a white silk blouse and started her one-cup coffeemaker. After breakfast, she grabbed her keys and the envelope Jake had given her and headed to the office. It was seven thirty a.m.

. . .

At eight a.m., Madison arrived at the *Raleigh Observer*. She approached the receptionist. "Good morning. I'm here to see Jeff Noe."

"Your name?"

"Madison Wright."

"Just one moment, please," the woman requested.

Madison waited, but not for long. She saw a man hurrying down the corridor into the foyer.

"Madison? Hello, Jeff Noe," he said, somewhat winded, extending his hand.

Madison extended her hand to him and said, "Nice to meet you, Jeff. Heard a lot about you."

"Some of it good?" Jeff smiled.

"All of it good." She opened her briefcase and pulled out the envelope. "This is for you from Jake Baird."

"Thanks. I need to—"

"Wait until after 9:00 a.m. to open it is what I understood," Madison said.

"Correct," Jeff responded. "Thanks for bringing this over."

"You're quite welcome," Madison said.

. . .

Alexandria, Virginia
Wednesday, August 12, 2009
8:15 a.m.

Jake had been awake at the safe house since five a.m. He had received no messages from Florence during the night, but still held out hope that she would call with news that the contractors or the military had agreed to his demands, halting the filing of the lawsuit. But even now it might be too late to turn things around.

He looked over his notes on his computer, making a few last-minute changes. Jake's concentration was interrupted by a knock at the door.

"Sir, the car will be here at 0930 to pick you up. It will then pick up the admiral and head up to Capitol Hill. The admiral is scheduled to testify at 1100 hrs."

"Thank you," Jake said.

While pouring the milk on his cereal, Jake looked at his secure phone. "Ring, phone," he muttered, hoping for a call from Florence. "Come on!" he urged. "Somebody step up," he whispered.

And where is Kemp? He's bought enough time. He should be calling.

The hour had come. He picked up the phone in his room and called Irwin's direct line.

"Hi, it's me."

"Yes, sir. How are you?" Irwin greeted him.

"Great. Thanks for asking," Jake said. "Just head over now, please."

"Understood. I'll leave immediately."

"Thanks," Jake said, and hung up.

Jake had one more call to make.

"Lisa Thorpe speaking," the voice said.

"Lisa, it's Jake Baird. Hope I'm not disturbing you this early."

"No. Good to hear from you."

"Look, this is kind of sudden and I don't have time to explain, but we will be filing your lawsuit this morning," Jake said.

"Oh, I see. I wasn't expecting this now, but if that's what you think is best, please do it."

"I have to tell you that the press will probably be calling, but it's best not to talk to them at all. If they get to you, just tell them you can't discuss pending litigation, OK?"

"Certainly. I wouldn't know what to say to them anyway."

"OK, Lisa. I have to run."

"Thanks for calling, Jake."

. . .

Raleigh, North Carolina
Wednesday, August 12, 2009
8:30 a.m.

Back in Raleigh, Irwin reached beside his chair and pulled out the envelope containing the XV-11 papers, then moved the papers from their plain envelope into a file marked "Beason vs. Beskind Motors." He stuck that file into his worn leather briefcase where it could not be easily seen and pulled the strap across the opening, but it was just for looks. The latch had broken years ago, and Irwin had never found the time to get it fixed.

Irwin opened his office door and spoke to his secretary as he went past her, "Allison, I'm headed out to the federal courthouse. I'll have my cell phone. Be back by nine thirty, I suppose."

"OK. Thanks, Mr. Thompson," Allison acknowledged.

Irwin looked at his watch. It was 8:35. The walk to the courthouse would take fifteen minutes.

. . .

Over on Salisbury Street, Agent Purdue, staking out Jake's office, watched Florence exit the street-level door with a manila file folder, walk to the parking lot, get into her car, and head in the direction of the federal courthouse. "She's left the building, headed east on Hargett in a silver Subaru wagon, North Carolina plate number TBC-4021," Purdue reported into the microphone in her sleeve.

"Roger. All agents keep a sharp eye," came the response from Agent Sears, just outside the courthouse. Across the street, the Apex agent, Sullivan, was observing and reporting the same thing.

A minute later, Agent Brandon sent a message from the corner of Wilmington and Hargett: "Vehicle passed here five seconds ago." This location was halfway between Jake's office and the courthouse.

"Good work," Sears responded. "Keep alert."

In two minutes, Agent Lassiter, three blocks west of the courthouse, reported, "Vehicle passing my location." A few minutes later, Masters reported, "It looks as if she is parking on Bloodworth Street. She should be inside the courthouse within the next three minutes."

"Roger," came Sears's reply. "After she goes in, Masters, you move to the front door and stay there."

Florence parked, picked up her purse and the envelope, and began walking up the sidewalk toward the front door of the courthouse. She had seen the agents en route and was aware she was being observed. Her pulse was racing, but she maintained her calm countenance. She looked at her watch— nine a.m. She rounded the corner and walked the additional hundred feet to the courthouse doors.

"Good morning, Florence," the court security agent said as she approached the security station.

"Good morning, Todd," Florence said, as she put her belongings on the conveyor belt.

"How's Mr. Baird?" the security guard continued.

"Fine," Florence said as she passed through the metal detector.

"Doing a little filing this morning?" the guard commented, pointing to the envelope in her hand.

"Yes, a little."

"You know the way," he said, helping her collect her things.

"Yes, I do," Florence replied. "You gentlemen have a nice day," she said as she left the security area.

She passed through the glass doors into the clerk's office and walked toward the counter where the papers would be filed. As she approached the counter, a man dressed in a dull, dark suit and a woman in an equally plain business suit moved in front of her, blocking her path to the counter. The clerk's office employees stopped to look when they saw what was happening.

"Mrs. Hilliard?" the woman said to Florence while showing her badge.

"Yes?" Florence replied.

"Mrs. Hilliard, I am agent Rose Williams of the National Security Agency and this is agent Steven Sears." Sears flashed his badge at Florence. "We have a few questions to ask you, if you don't mind."

"Certainly. But could you tell me what this is all about?"

"We can explain in a few minutes. First, would you just move over here with us for a moment?" Before Florence could respond, Williams had taken her left arm and Sears her right arm, and they were gently but firmly moving her away from the counter. Seeing this, the clerk's office discreetly called courthouse security.

As Florence was being questioned, Irwin Thompson was clearing security, greeting the court security personnel. "Good morning, gentlemen. How are all of you this morning?"

"Greetings, Mr. Thompson. We're fine. How are you?"

"I'm fine, Todd, how is your family?"

"They're all fine, Mr. Thompson, thanks for asking."

"Terrific. You guys have a nice day," Irwin said as he headed toward the clerk's office.

Entering the clerk's office, Irwin saw the plainclothes officers with Florence at the side of the filing counter. He also noticed that the female agent was looking through a manila folder that presumably had been in Florence's hands seconds earlier.

Distracted, but continuing across the room toward the counter, Irwin didn't see the man coming from the opposite direction. Bam! They collided, and Irwin's briefcase flew out of his hand, spilling its contents onto the floor.

The agents with Florence turned to see what the commotion was.

"Terribly sorry," the man said, as he knelt down with Irwin to help pick up the contents of Irwin's briefcase.

"That's OK. I got it," Irwin said, quickly picking up the Thorpe lawsuit papers that had tumbled out of their folder but had fortunately had landed facedown. Irwin brushed himself off, stood up, and continued to the intake desk. The man repositioned himself and attempted to blend in, but it was obvious he was interested in what was going on. He was Apex's Agent Fritz.

Once at the filing desk, Irwin heard the female agent reading Florence her rights. *Jake was right,* Irwin thought. *Good thing he had me as a back-up.*

Irwin knew he could not come to Florence's aid. At least not now. He needed to get the papers filed first. He continued to watch the agents and Florence out of the corner of his eye.

"Hello, Mr. Thompson," the clerk said, as Irwin removed the papers from his briefcase and handed them to her.

"Hello, Dee. How are you?"

"Just fine. I'm just not used to all this excitement in here," she said, checking out the activities unfolding on the other side of her counter.

Irwin kept her on task. "Yes, but nothing that can stop the efficient operation of this fine clerk's office."

"Of course not." Dee smiled as she took his papers from him, but she was interrupted by three men in blue blazers with badges hanging from their jacket pockets racing into the room, pulling their jackets back, revealing sidearms.

"Let her go," one of the court officers shouted to the agents holding Florence.

Agent Sears responded, "Hold on, fellows. This is a matter of national security. May I get my badge?"

"Sure, but nothing funny," the court officer said as two more court officers appeared.

Sears pulled out his badge, shook his head, and explained. "This was all supposed to be coordinated with you guys."

"OK," the court officer said, "but we're going to stay to observe."

"Sure, be our guest," Sears responded, smirking.

Dee got back to Irwin's papers and date-stamped them *Received/Filed.*

She kept the originals for the court's files, set aside a file-stamped courtesy copy for the judge's chambers, and handed a file-stamped copy of the Complaint and Requests to Admit back to Irwin, both of which he quietly slipped into his briefcase. Fortunately, Dee was distracted by activity and didn't even look at the papers, so she didn't comment on the nature of the suit, as she usually did.

"Thanks, Dee. I'll see you later," Irwin said, turning to leave.

"You're welcome, Mr. Thompson."

Irwin wanted to help Florence but thought better of it. No reason to tip off the agents that someone else who might know Jake was in the courthouse. Irwin did, however, make a point to get Florence's eye as he was leaving, but she wisely did not acknowledge him. Irwin figured Florence realized he was the back-up and that the papers had been filed.

As soon as he was a safe distance from the courthouse, Irwin called Jake.

"It's done," Irwin said.

"Great," Jake responded.

"They nabbed Florence before she could take care of it. She's with them now."

Jake sighed. "I was afraid of that. This should come to a head shortly. Is she OK?"

"She looked fine to me. It's the agents we ought to worry about," Irwin joked. "She saw me leave the courthouse. She knows I did what needed to be done."

"Great. Got to go. We'll be in touch," Jake said. "Turn your TV to C-SPAN at 1100," Jake advised.

"OK." They hung up.

Jake immediately dialed Jeff Noe's cell number.

"Jeff Noe," he answered, almost halfway back to his office at the *Raleigh Observer*.

"Go with it. It's filed," Jake said.

"Jake, Florence got stopped before filing. I was there," Jeff said, stopping to talk. "This complicates the running of the story."

"It got filed," Jake said. "I had a back-up. Trust me. Gotta go."

"OK, I'll look into it," Jeff said.

When Jeff got to his office, he turned on his laptop and logged into the court's website to check the filings. Nothing. So he headed back to the clerk's office, just three blocks away. As Jeff entered the clerk's office, he noticed that Florence was no longer anywhere to be seen. He went to the court's computers to check filings. Again, no sign that it had been done. He decided to check with Dee.

Approaching the filing counter, he spotted her and said "Hello, Dee."

"Hello, Jeff. What can I do for you today?"

"I would like to take a peek at the day's filings—new lawsuits—if you don't mind."

Dee pointed to a wooden file box at the end of the counter. "Sure. Not many yet, but they're over there. We haven't logged them into the system yet. All the complaints are in the box marked 'New Actions.'"

Jeff reached over the counter, picked up the three separate groupings of papers in the new filings box, and began to sift through them. On the bottom, the first case file that day was "Lisa Thorpe, Plaintiff, Civil Action Number 04-CIV-6096 JDF 9:10 AM, August 12 . . ." He also observed the file-stamped copy of the Requests to Admit. This was it. Filed, case number and judge assigned. He compared his copies to the filed copies. They matched. He returned his papers to his briefcase and quietly put the filed papers back in the box. "Thanks, Dee."

"You're welcome, Jeff. Anytime."

Jeff left the courthouse and raced back to his office. En route, he called John Farris, news director at one of the local television stations.

"John, good morning. It's Jeff Noe. It's on file. I've seen it myself. I'm going with a story in tomorrow's paper and a short blurb will be up on our website in five minutes."

"My crew said it didn't get filed—that Baird's secretary was stopped. You've seen the actual papers? "

"Trust me, it's filed. 04-CIV-6096 JDF. It's there. Just not logged in yet."

"Great. We'll go with it on the station's website, we'll alert the wires, and do a crawler on the screen. When can we come to see you?"

"Make it around noon. I should be free by then," Jeff advised. "But John, you'll do this, right? Credit me and the paper, and reference our web page, right?"

"Of course, Jeff, just like always. See you at noon—with a crew. Thanks."

At nine thirty, the story was on the paper's website and sent through the paper's Facebook page and Twitter accounts. Ten minutes later, the local TV channel interrupted its local programming with a bulletin. Instantly, the national news services had the story. Noe's and Farris's phones were ringing off the hook.

29

Alexandria, Virginia

Wednesday, August 12, 2009

9:30 a.m.

Just as the lawsuit's filing was rapidly spreading across the internet, Jake received a knock on his door.

"Sir, the car is here for you."

"OK," Jake said, and headed to the door.

After a short drive to the NAVAIR office at Crystal City, the admiral got in. "Good morning, Jake."

"Good morning, sir," Jake responded.

"Your lawsuit is on the web. I am sure it will be on all the major channels shortly. Interesting timing," Lawrence commented.

"Hopefully not bad timing, sir," Jake responded.

"On the contrary, it's excellent timing," Lawrence responded. "Are you ready?"

"Yes, sir."

"Good. We'll take you to a room just off the hearing room. I've got to go speak with Senator Jackson briefly to finalize matters. He cleared your testifying last night."

"Yes, sir."

"After that, you and I will have about fifteen minutes."

The admiral briefed Jake on the bad news from Afghanistan. "I wanted to tell you that one of the pilots was killed and the other was seriously injured.

We still don't have any information to indicate operational error or hostile fire brought the aircraft down. It still looks like it was an aircraft problem."

"I was afraid that might be true," Jake said. "Is that something we mention at the hearing?"

"Knowing how these hearings go, it is bound to come up. Let me deal with it."

"Yes, sir."

"Now, don't be concerned about these senators. You will be able to speak without a judge telling you if what you did was OK. Remember—as is clear from your briefing paper—you have knowledge. They don't."

"Yes, sir." Jake said.

. . .

At 10:00 a.m. CNN reported:

More bad news for the Marines' controversial XV-11 aircraft. Today in Raleigh, North Carolina, a lawsuit was filed in federal court arising out of the crash of an XV-11 near Patuxent River Naval Air Station in Maryland, on April twenty-second of this year, that claimed the lives of two North Carolina–based Marine Corps aviators. The suit, brought on behalf of Lisa Thorpe, one of the pilot's widows, alleges a conspiracy between the Department of Defense and its main aircraft contractors, Apex Helicopters and Vertical Aerospace, which covered up the fatal flaws of the aircraft. It references and includes documents apparently from the government's own files that are alleged to show substantial unethical and perhaps illegal conduct by the Pentagon and its contractors. Samantha Swift is outside the federal courthouse in Raleigh . . .

As Jake's picture flashed on the screen, the reporter said, "We've been trying to contact Jake Baird, the attorney who filed the action, himself a decorated Army aviator and pilot in the Army Reserves. Calls to his office have not been returned.

"An intriguing parallel story is developing," she continued. "Mr. Baird's secretary was taken into custody by authorities as she attempted to file the court papers this morning. It is our understanding that she was apprehended by federal agents with the papers in her possession *before* they were filed.

Her whereabouts are currently unknown. If this story is true, we are at a loss to explain how the papers actually were filed, when, or by whom. We are following our leads in the area and will report as soon as we have any follow-ups to this breaking news."

. . .

United States Capitol Building, Washington,
District of Columbia
Wednesday, August 12, 2009
10:15 a.m.

Upon arriving at a secure entry point at the rear of the Capitol, Jake and the admiral were escorted into an anteroom. Jake could see through the room's closed-circuit television that the hearing room was filled with throngs of reporters, cameramen, staffers, and spectators. He made out a couple of the reporters practicing their intros regarding the crash and the lawsuit.

The door to the hall opened and a senator's aide entered. "Sir, I'm Greg Vaughn, aide to Senator Jackson. He can see you now." The young man turned to Jake and a look of surprise came across his face. Jake figured that he must have recognized him from the news reports. Regaining his composure, Vaughn said to Admiral Lawrence, "Sir, I had no idea you had a guest."

"Understood," the admiral said, as he headed out the door to follow the aide. As they walked down the hall to another room just across from the hearing room, Admiral Lawrence asked Vaughn to keep Baird's presence quiet, adding "This will be public soon enough. So you can tell your tale then."

"Yes sir," Greg said.

They arrived at the senator's office and found Senator Winnfield E. Jackson, D-NC, chairman of the Senate Armed Services Committee, alone. A stately, silver-haired man in his sixties, he'd devoted his entire life to government service—starting out in the military, then as a state representative, congressman, and now a US senator—he commanded great respect from both Republicans and Democrats. Classically educated, his party had asked him on two occasions to run for the presidency, but he'd given it no thought, saying and believing he could protect the Constitution better from the Senate than he could from the White House.

"Good morning, Senator Jackson," the admiral said.

"Good morning, Admiral Lawrence," Senator Jackson said, extending his hand. Turning to his aide, he said, "Greg, if you'll excuse us."

"Certainly, Senator."

As the aide exited, Senator Jackson motioned for Admiral Lawrence to join him on a leather sofa.

"Wilson, I don't envy your task this morning, but if there is anyone who can handle it, you can," the senator began.

"Thank you for your confidence, sir," Admiral Lawrence said.

"You have done very well over the many years we've known each other," Senator Jackson continued in his gracious yet efficient manner. "Tell me what you need to talk to me about."

"First, Senator, with your permission, and in light of our conversation last night, I wish to discard the written remarks I submitted."

"Do you have another text you wish to use?" Jackson asked.

"Yes sir, but it's not written. I've been pondering almost nothing else for days. What I have in my head has been filtered through my conscience. I ask your permission to speak from that perspective."

"Highly unusual, Wilson," the senator responded. "Just for my peace of mind and respecting due diligence, I trust there will be nothing that will be a problem for us, correct?"

"No sir. It would pass any security screening or protocol test," Admiral Lawrence said.

"OK, then I'll allow it," Jackson responded. "Now what about Mr. Baird? Let's go over it in a bit more detail."

"First of all, he is testifying at the request of Captain Stanford Kemp."

"Yes, I know Captain Kemp. A fine man."

"Secondly, I have spent time with Lieutenant Colonel Baird, and he is also a fine man. People on my staff observed him in combat and he performed bravely and honorably. He came into possession of the documents because Kemp gave them to him. There is much more to the story, and it needs to be told. But suffice it say both Kemp and Baird acted out of duty toward their fellow service members and this country. Baird has a detailed perspective that I don't have, and the committee and the country need to hear it."

"I've thought about it some more overnight," the senator responded. "It seems to me this whole approach, though highly unorthodox, might just help to bring this matter to a head. OK, Admiral Lawrence, it's your show. You may proceed as you suggest."

"Thank you, sir," the admiral responded. "Sir, I don't know if you have had a chance to review the papers Baird filed, but I have a set for you," Lawrence said, handing the senator an envelope.

"Thank you," Jackson said, taking the envelope. Then, "Good luck, Admiral." The men shook hands.

Immediately, the senator called for his aide. "Greg?"

"Yes, sir," Greg responded, opening the door.

"Take the admiral back to his room, please, and make some copies of these papers for us if you would."

Senator Jackson turned the knob of the door, and stepped into the chaos of the hearing room.

30

Staff members frantically moved around the paneled Senate hearing room working to make sure all was ready. Papers flowed among the staffers as they simultaneously worked their BlackBerries and iPhones.

Photographers carpeted virtually every inch of the floor between the dais and the witness table. Reporters filled the gallery, making very little room for spectators. Press passes were at a premium, but the big names were all there, including the primary Washington congressional and Pentagon reporters of all the major networks.

The crowd was to be expected given the news of the last several days. Until recently, the XV-11 had faded into just another expensive, flawed procurement program. Today it was on the front page news and was the lead story on all the TV and radio networks. The crash and the controversy over the lawsuit produced a rare two-story lead.

Just before eleven a.m., Admiral Lawrence entered through a door at the left front of the room, beside and below the dais, right beside the American flag. The klieg lights made his uniform look even whiter. He was alone—no aide, no lawyer, military or civilian. Even the senators noticed.

What was not noticed was the entrance of Lieutenant Colonel Raymond Beech in his Marine "Service B" uniform: olive trousers, khaki long-sleeved shirt, and tie. Since he did not know how this was going to go, he eschewed the uniform jacket and his ribbons. No reason to make oneself conspicuous, he thought—not with the news of the theft of classified documents from his program and the crash of his aircraft.

Finally, Chairman Winnfield E. Jackson moved into the room in a slow, deliberate gait, with his chief aide, Andrew Holmes, right behind him. As he moved to the chairman's seat, the room quieted down and the senators moved toward their seats. The *tap, tap, tap* of his gavel cut through the room, silencing the crowd.

"Ladies and gentlemen," Senator Jackson called out so all could hear. "The meeting of the Senate Armed Services Committee is hereby called to order. We call as our first witness Admiral Wilson Lawrence of the United States Navy. Will the clerk of the Senate kindly administer the oath to Admiral Lawrence?"

The admiral stood and moved directly to the witness table, put his left hand on the Bible, and raised his right hand.

"Do you solemnly swear that the testimony you provide here today will be the truth, the whole truth, and nothing but the truth, so help you God?"

"I do."

"Thank you and good morning, Admiral. You may be seated," Senator Jackson said.

"Good morning, Senator Jackson," Lawrence responded.

"Admiral Lawrence, we originally invited you to appear before this committee to talk about a number of items, primarily the XV-11 program. Since extending that invitation, our plans have been overtaken by recent events. I speak, of course, of the loss of a XV-11 in Afghanistan, just one day ago, with loss of life and personal injury and the daring rescue of the survivors of that crash, perhaps only moments before their capture or deaths at the hands of enemy forces. I understand that an investigation has begun into the cause of the crash. So, before we get to your testimony, and even though somewhat premature, I and the other members of the committee, if not the nation, would appreciate hearing whatever information you have on the cause of that crash. As you know, rumors are circulating that this was yet another mechanical or design-related accident, as opposed to the aircraft being brought down by hostile fire."

"Certainly, sir," the admiral responded.

The senator continued, "The other matter we would like to discuss is the report of a security breach in the Pentagon, more specifically, in the Navy's Aircraft Acquisitions Office, a part of NAVAIR—your command—regarding the XV-11. And if you could enlighten us about these two mysterious persons, Captain Stanford Kemp and Attorney Jake Baird, we would be in your debt."

"I'll be glad to assist in those requests as well, Senator."

"Thank you. Finally, Admiral, I believe you have a statement. But for those of us who've already received a copy of Admiral Lawrence's prepared statement, I should tell you that Admiral Lawrence's opening remarks will be different," Jackson said, casting his eyes toward the members of the committee to his right and then those to his left, looking to stare down any negative reaction. "He requested my permission this morning to instead speak without written remarks, and I agreed to let him do so for reasons which, I believe, he will make clear."

Jackson now turned to the buzzing gallery and continued. "The admiral has assured me in a face-to-face meeting that there are good reasons for this substitution, and knowing Admiral Lawrence to be a man of unparalleled honor and principle, I have permitted an exception to the rules and the protocol of this committee." He stopped, focusing the attention of all present, then said, "Admiral Lawrence, you may proceed."

"A point of order, Mr. Chairman," interrupted Senator John Korman of Texas before Lawrence could speak. "This committee has never permitted such a deviation from its rules and I protest that it not be allowed now."

"Thank you for your comment, Senator Korman," Chairman Jackson said, not looking at the Texas senator and instead looking straight at the gallery. "Now, Admiral Lawrence, would you kindly proceed?" Korman leaned back away from his microphone. He was now on notice that further objections to the proceedings would receive a similar rebuke.

"Thank you, Senator Jackson," Admiral Lawrence replied. "I appreciate the opportunity to testify today before this committee.

"First, Afghanistan. Every one of our brave men has been extracted. They are either safely back at their bases or are in medical facilities receiving necessary care. The more seriously injured are being stabilized for transport to higher-level facilities.

"It saddens me to report that some troops did not make it. Seven brave souls aboard the aircraft lost their lives. Their identity and service positions remain confidential, pending notification of next of kin. I can confirm that deaths and injuries had both hostile and non-hostile causes. I have no casualty figures for the rescue forces, but I was told they also suffered loss of life and severe injuries."

The admiral hesitated, gathering himself. "Those fine people," he continued, "will be missed," he said, his voice breaking.

Clearing his throat, he continued. "The mission was a qualified success in that we inflicted damage to some of the senior members of the Taliban and their command and control structure. Five of the targeted seven people are confirmed dead by the rapid reaction force that not only rescued our people, but continued, and concluded, the fight. It is possible the other two were also killed—that will take some time to determine." He paused. "It seems as though the crashed aircraft was too much of a temptation and the Taliban leaders stayed around to participate in what they expected to be the slaughter of defenseless crash victims. They didn't know they were SEALs and Marines." This produced laughter, cheers, and applause in the room and smiles on the committee members' faces. "They also didn't know what we had in the sky and over the hill. They got an in-person introduction to our Nighthawks, Warthogs, and Apaches, not to mention the fine men and women of the Army Rangers. They won't forget." This time even louder applause and a few hoots.

"Before we destroyed the XV-11 with air-delivered ordnance, we recovered the aircraft's cockpit voice recorder and flight data recorder, which are already on their way back to the States. We eagerly await analysis of those devices to help us better understand what happened.

"That concludes my comments on the crash, Senator Jackson." Admiral Lawrence moved slightly away from the microphone and awaited the chairman's instructions.

"Thank you, Admiral," Jackson said, with his hand around the microphone neck. "We appreciate that account and understand why at this time that is all we will get." Jackson once again looked around at the committee members and said, "It will be more efficient to save questions until you have finished. You may proceed to the next items if you would, sir."

With his hands clasped together on the table in front of him and his back flagpole straight, Lawrence began. "Senators, these are difficult times for the people involved in the XV-11 program. Despite the efforts of great men and women on both the civilian and military sides of this program, it continues to be a problematic aircraft. The concept behind it was commendable: a vehicle that could carry fully-armed combat troops from the relative safety of a ship and deploy them rapidly to a battle area with the speed of an airplane and the maneuverability of a helicopter. Importantly, this aircraft would have been a lifesaver in its medical evacuation role. Its functionality is unprecedented in a military aircraft.

"The crash in Afghanistan and the prior crashes that claimed the lives of honorable members of our armed forces, with great loss to their families, are reasons enough to evaluate the program. But now, in addition, we have the actions of highly decorated and loyal military officers jeopardizing their reputations, and indeed their freedom, by obtaining and distributing classified documents relating to the program—apparently to bring to the public's attention the problems with this aircraft which were covered up by a few misguided individuals who were in a position to conceal their actions. The confluence of these events mandate that we halt the program in order to thoroughly evaluate its efficacy, utility, and most of all, safety." Cameras clicked like popcorn, and reporters began whispering to one another while typing furiously on their phones and devices.

"I should have called for this step earlier as one change after another was made to the design requirements, simply because of difficulty in meeting the original requirements. Some of this happens in any program, but here, the number of requirements that were eliminated relating to safety should have caused me to act earlier.

"Now, as my next-to-last act as head of NAVAIR, I hereby order that all of the requirements related to safety be reinstated and the program be suspended until it can be proven that each of these requirements is met. Until that point, the operational XV-11 squadron will stand down and all XV-11's are hereby grounded."

Lawrence paused, reached for the glass of water, and took a drink. Chatter among the reporters was getting louder, causing Senator Jackson to pick up his gavel.

The commotion quieted down the minute Admiral Lawrence recommenced his remarks. "I am clear that I was the person in charge at NAVAIR and I will not offer reasons or excuses for my flawed oversight. I am responsible. But there is someone who knows more than I about the details of this program and who has reviewed much of the aircraft's historical technical data. Chairman Jackson alluded to him earlier. In my last act in uniform, before I tender my resignation, I present Lieutenant Colonel Jake Baird, who will share this forum with me so that the committee's work might be more fully accomplished."

The room erupted as Jake Baird came through the same door Admiral Lawrence had entered from moments earlier. Cameramen raced to that side of the room in order to get a good shot of Jake. Meanwhile, Admiral Lawrence stood up and repositioned himself in front of a chair to the rear of where Jake would testify. It was Lawrence's way of showing he had Jake's back.

"Order! Order!" Chairman Jackson exclaimed, rising to his feet and slamming his gavel. He picked up his microphone from its stand and barked, "If order is not restored immediately, I will clear the room of all guests and will conduct a closed hearing." The committee clerk picked up a phone and within moments uniformed US Capitol Police entered the room and took places throughout the room. Suddenly, there was silence.

Order now restored, the chairman once again addressed the crowd, "All right. If you can maintain decorum, you may stay. Officers, monitor the gallery, and please remove any noisy or unruly individuals from this hearing room."

The Senator continued as people resumed their prior places. "Mr. Baird, if you would be so kind as to be sworn in." The clerk rose and moved over to Jake, Bible in hand. Jake stated the oath slowly and deliberately.

"Now, Mr. Baird," Senator Jackson continued, "please be seated at the table in front of the admiral." Jake followed this invitation and took his place at the table—but did not sit down—before the Admiral sat.

"You both may be seated, please," Jackson said. The room became quiet and the senator continued. "Mr. Baird, thank you for coming to speak to us today. I suggest that you tell us what you think is important for us to hear, and we will follow up with questions. Does that seem reasonable to you?"

"Yes, sir, Senator."

"All right, then you may begin."

"Thank you, Senator."

Although he had been before many juries and judges, this was different. Jake fought through the tightness in this throat and began. "Chairman Jackson and Honorable Members of the Committee, I represent Lisa Thorpe, who is now a widow at age twenty-eight, and Samuel Wallace Thorpe, who is now fatherless at five. Their husband and father, Major Samuel Ward Thorpe, lost his life in the crash of a XV-11 Sea Eagle on April twenty-second of this year.

"Once I became the lawyer for Lisa and Samuel Thorpe, I was obligated to find out why this crash occurred. When I was given information that enabled me to see the reasons behind the crash, I followed that information to its logical, inevitable conclusion. That is what I will discuss today.

"Not only has this matter caused the death of Major Thorpe and his crew, it has also cost—in the past week alone—the life of a dedicated Marine who tried to reveal the truth about this program, Sergeant Major Ron Hadley, and a brilliant aircraft designer who left the program when those in control would not listen to him, Dr. Stanislas Kolinsky. There is unproven but nevertheless credible information that Hadley was killed by rogue agents of the government who sabotaged the steering on his jeep, and there is evidence that the drowning of Kolinsky was done by renegade government agents once they discovered his whereabouts. Additionally, Colonel Charles Hartman now lies in intensive care at Bethesda because of the stress this matter has placed on his already weak heart. It appears that the people responsible for these deaths will stop at nothing to protect this program—"

"Mr. Chairman, please may I be heard?" Senator Randal Herschal from Pennsylvania broke in.

Jackson shot back, "Senator, you know that it is improper to interrupt a witness when he or she is delivering their opening remarks! Therefore—"

"But Mr. Chairman," Herschal interrupted, "we have before us in this honored chamber a man who illegally obtained and distributed classified documents making unsupported and egregious allegations against the United States Government! This must not be allowed!" Herschal was close to shouting.

Glaring at Senator Herschal, Jackson said, "Your preconviction of this man is not proper either, Senator. Now, I respectfully suggest that you sit back and listen to what he has to say, and then you may question him at the appropriate time."

"Mr. Chairman, I agree with the honorable senator from Pennsylvania," interjected Texas Senator Korman. "We should not entertain such disloyal speech in this body. It is un-American and we should not be a forum for this scoundrel."

Anyone who knew Senator Jackson well would know that he was boiling, but to the gallery, he appeared calm and cool. "If you gentlemen will allow me," he began, casting a glance first right to Senator Herschal, then left to Senator Korman, "we will let this witness present his opening statement *without further interruption*. This is not the Supreme Court and this is not an opening argument. You may examine him as vigorously as you wish when the time comes, but until then, please let him speak without interruption."

"But Mr. Chairman," Senator Herschal began, "I—"

"Your comments are in the record, Senator," Jackson responded. One further look was enough to silence Senator Herschal. "Please continue, Mr. Baird," Jackson said.

Growing more confident hearing Senator Jackson's remarks, Jake continued. "Thank you, sir. Responding to the Senators' concerns," he said, glancing at Senator Herschal and then Senator Korman, "I will be happy to provide the information I have to the authorities on all matters after I am through here today, but there is an even better way to be certain of these matters. I last heard from the man who has detailed information on the agents who carried out these murders, Captain Stanford Kemp, twenty-four hours ago. He was leading the rogue agents away from me so that I might come here to be with the admiral and you. I have great concerns about what might be happening to him at this very moment."

This comment created a large commotion in the hearing room. Even the senators began to talk to one another and to their aides. Kemp was well known in Washington, especially on Capitol Hill.

"Order, ORDER!" Senator Jackson growled as he struck the gavel. The Senate police started moving toward those that were loudest. The crowd calmed down. In the back, Lieutenant Colonel Beech began to squirm in his seat.

"Mr. Chairman, there is one person who knows all about Captain Kemp's capture and location, and I submit that if you find him, he will be able to tell you where Captain Kemp is. That person is Alex Oliver of the Naval Aircraft Acquisition Office. Find him and you will find Captain Kemp."

"One moment, Mr. Baird, if you will . . ." Senator Jackson asked, putting his hand over the microphone and motioning to his aide, Andrew. Jackson spoke with his usual calm voice but the red blush coming to his face gave him away.

"Find Admiral Thomas Joseph, NSA administrator, and give him this information. Ask him to keep me updated on the progress of his efforts to find captain Kemp and, if at all possible, find him and bring him directly here so I can see for myself he is free. Call Russell Briggs, assistant secretary of the Navy, and tell him that I respectfully suggest that he find Mr. Oliver and hold him so that the proper authorities might speak with him. Is all of this clear, Andrew?"

Andrew responded with a quick, "Yes, sir," and flew out of the hearing room. Neither Senator Jackson nor Jake knew that Kemp's pre-established rescue plan was already underway.

"Thank you for waiting, Mr. Baird. Please continue," Senator Jackson requested.

"Certainly, sir. The issue is: Why? Why was this program thought to be so important that it could not be stopped, whatever the cost? The aircraft at the center of this effort was merely another tactical weapons system. It will not end the war on terror and will not bring world peace. It is simply a flawed first step in a worthwhile design concept. But is not operationally sound nor is it combat ready, and it is a killer when operated outside its narrow, limited capabilities.

"The answer is that the aircraft became the mission, instead of the aircraft supporting the mission. Early on, this aircraft became untouchable. Regardless of what the engineers were saying, regardless of what the flight tests showed, regardless of what safety experts said, and regardless of the crashes and loss of life, the aircraft *program* could not fail, although the *aircraft* already had.

"The details are in the documents, which I did not seek, but which were given to me. Once I had these documents, there was no turning back. My officer's commission and my attorney's oath mandated I find and tell the truth. I would have preferred a more orderly release of the facts through the Thorpe case, but the deaths of Sergeant Major Hadley and Professor Kolinsky made that course impossible."

Jake continued, "If this weapons system is halted, no doubt jobs will be lost. But I have faith that the good men and women who build this aircraft will want no part of a defective aircraft that will kill their fellow Americans, some of whom might come from their own neighborhoods. I am confident they would agree that no job is worth the life of an American soldier, sailor, airman, Marine or coast guardsman.

"Senator Jackson and members of this committee, I appreciate the opportunity to come here today to speak. I conclude my remarks and await your questions."

"Thank you, Mr. Baird," Jackson said, and leaned back from his microphone to speak again with Andrew, who had returned with a volume of rules that he was discussing with the senator. The room buzzed. Newspersons assembled at the door, waiting to see what the chairman would do. It was amazing how well they could move while typing away on their handheld devices.

Jackson moved to his microphone. "Members of the Committee and guests, I believe that all would agree that Mr. Baird has offered us an interesting and provocative opening statement. I think, under these circumstances, there is good reason to adjourn for a short while so that the members of the committee may use that time to consider how we might proceed. Thus, I am proposing a one-hour recess so that members may have a chance to reflect upon what they have heard. If there is no objection, then I will adjourn the committee for one hour, and at the end of that hour, we will gather back here to discuss how to proceed."

Senator Jackson surveyed his committee members, who all nodded their agreement, and he adjourned the meeting.

The admiral reached out to shake Jake's hand. "Fine job, Colonel," his tone and expression revealing his pride.

"Thank you, sir," Jake said, as reporters rushed up to him, thrusting microphones in his face. As the Senate police rushed to Jake's side, he addressed the reporters. "Ladies and Gentlemen, I am still under oath and a witness before this committee. It would be inappropriate for me to say anything at this point." He walked away, but reporters continued shouting questions until he was out of the room.

31

In his office, Oliver turned away from the live feeds on his computer and furiously jammed materials into his briefcase. He tried to clean out what he could on his computer but he was too nervous to do a good job. *Well, if they never find me it won't matter what they find on here*, he thought, and raced out of his office, briefcase in hand. He tore down the hall toward the nearest fire stairway. When he was almost there, he saw a team of uniformed guards headed his way. He slowed down and tried to look normal as he passed them.

A few steps past Oliver, one of the guards yelled, "That's him!" They turned and raced after Oliver as he ran away, throwing aside his briefcase. More guards rounded the corner and fanned out across the hall in front of him, blocking his way. Oliver stopped running and slouched against the wall, out of breath. It was over.

Poking his head out of an office to observe the commotion was none other than Wiggins, the "fixer." As Oliver was led down the hall, he looked at Wiggins, trying to connect. Wiggins just smiled, arms folded, and watched Oliver being led away.

Once back at his office desk, Wiggins reached into a side drawer and pulled out a picture frame. Two young Marines stood in Vietnam, arms around each other. *To Corporal Wiggins, the best RTO ever!* It was signed, *Ser-*

geant Hadley. He patted the image of his father and Sergeant Hadley and slid it back into the drawer.

• • •

Northern Virginia
Wednesday, August 12, 2009
12:15 p.m.

Kemp once again was brought before Chaney, who was already behind his desk, waiting.

"I have given you a good portion of the morning to think about your situation," Chaney said.

Once again, Kemp said nothing.

Chaney shouted in frustration. "I am not going to go over it again! You have exhausted my patience! Take him away!"

The guards jerked Kemp from his bunk and pushed him out of the room. As he was thrust into the elevator, Kemp considered two possibilities: either they were bluffing, or they were, in fact, over it. Chaney's comments and Kemp's own body clock told him it was approaching midday. He figured any time now the cavalry would show up, just as he and Lawrence had discussed.

Upstairs, Chaney intended to end this mess *now* and wanted to make sure he was covered. He called Oliver's cell to get his approval, but there was no answer, not even voice mail. He tried Oliver's office phone—against the rules—but no one answered. Frustrated, he threw his phone across the room. The decision was his.

Chaney's thinking was interrupted by a buzzing sound outside. That must be it, Chaney reasoned; Oliver was coming by helicopter. *A bit dramatic,* Chaney thought. The sound amplified—it was getting closer. He heard loud voices and noises—feet running through the house.

Then Gonzales burst into the room. "Get outta here! They found us! C'mon!" Gonzales tore out, leaving the door wide open.

Chaney quickly followed outside, only to see three sedans, doors open, positioned to block the driveway. His men were standing in the yard, hands in the air, surrounded by uniformed officers with weapons drawn and pointed.

A special operations Hughes 500 helicopter sat on the lawn, rotors still turning. Three heavily armed men in black assault uniforms and a man in a suit climbed out of the helicopter and headed toward him. As they got closer, one of the men raised his weapon and pointed it directly at Gonzales, about ten yards off the porch. Two others raced onto the porch and pinned Chaney to the floor. Chaney heard more footsteps and saw more black boots coming around from the rear of the house. Then he noticed a set of wingtips right in front of his face.

"Mr. Chaney," the man in the suit said as he squatted down and brought his face close to Chaney's, "You have the right to remain silent. If you give up that right, anything you say can and will be held against you. We can get you a lawyer if you want one—courtesy of your ex-employer. The jig is up for you and your friends."

He recognized the voice. It was retired Admiral Thomas Joseph, head of the National Security Agency. Chaney was pulled to his feet only to see a look of calm rage on Joseph's face. "You have five seconds to tell me where Kemp is. Four, three, two . . ."

"He's two floors down! Off the elevator and turn right. Second door on the left."

Joseph signaled with a nod of the head for two of his men to go. "He better be OK, Chaney."

The wait for Kemp seemed eternal. Chaney now prayed Kemp was safe. Suddenly, he heard footsteps behind him.

"Not looking too good there, Stanford," he heard Joseph say.

"I'll bet, sir. I kept getting a bath at this lousy hotel," Kemp replied. "Glad you got the word when you did."

"Well, it took a little longer than we had hoped, but it's over now. You're OK, I hope. Got anything you want to say to Chaney here before we leave?"

Kemp rubbed his wrists where the handcuffs had chafed his skin. He moved around to Chaney's front and Kemp stared at his former captor. Chaney relaxed, assuming that Kemp was playing by the rules and would not harm a prisoner. Kemp turned away, and then *wham!* He slugged Chaney with a massive right-hand roundhouse. Kemp's blow was so hard that the guard lost his grip and Chaney fell to the floor. The guard picked-him up, and Kemp saw Chaney bleeding profusely from his nose and mouth.

"That was for Hadley!" Kemp growled. Chaney was almost back to vertical when *wham!* Kemp delivered another hammer-like blow with his left hand to the other side of Chaney's face. This time, the guard held on, but Chaney didn't. His nose was way over on one side of his face, he was bleeding from his right eye, and he couldn't straighten up. He was at the edge of consciousness.

"That was for Kolinsky," Kemp said, rubbing his left hand. He took two paces away, and positioned himself to deliver a karate kick but Joseph stopped him.

"Stanford," Joseph said, grabbing Kemp's arm. "I would love for you two to continue this conversation, but there is somewhere you need to be."

Kemp stared right at Chaney as he responded, "Yes, sir." Kemp and Joseph headed toward the helicopter, spooling up for departure.

Chaney was secured in the back of an unmarked van, by himself, and the van drove away. He was left to wonder how it all went wrong. Chaney had no idea that it was doomed from the start. He should have known not to challenge a legend.

. . .

"Where to, sir?" Kemp asked, as the helicopter spooled up.

"I'll brief you en route. We'll clean you up a bit, but I have orders not to change your clothing."

The helicopter departed, dipping nose-low as it quickly gained forward speed. Kemp could see they were headed east, toward Washington. He also recognized the area they had left—he had picked this area for a few "special houses" years ago.

They were flying very fast and very low, obviously in a hurry.

"Mind if I asked the time, sir?"

Joseph pulled back his sleeve so he could see his watch. "It's about 12:40."

"Thanks." Kemp was surprised at how well he had estimated the time. He also realized the hearing might still be going on. *Holy cow,* he thought, *that can't be where they are taking me.*

32

After the Committee adjourned, Senator Jackson went back into his office with his aide and remarked, "Exciting day up here, huh, Andrew?"

"Yes, sir!" Andrew responded.

"OK. Tell me what you've found out," Jackson said.

"From what I can tell, in the lawsuit and in his testimony, Baird has accurately referenced the documents he attached. The documents appear to be authentic—if twenty years of looking at government documents has taught me anything. Of course, I don't know about his allegations about the rogue NSA agents and their possible involvement in Hadley's and Kolinsky's deaths."

"Anything else?" the senator asked.

"Yes, sir. Baird is the real deal. There is nothing they can come up with against him. Problem is, all of his heroic acts are classified."

Senator Jackson started to get up. "Let's go see the Admiral and Colonel Baird." The men headed toward the door to the hall, when they were just about flattened by Greg Vaughn bursting in.

"Sorry, sir!" Vaughn said, almost shouting. "Call for you on line one. It's Donovan Ross, CEO of Apex Helicopters, and he says it's urgent."

"OK. Take it easy, Mr. Vaughn. Andrew, please go tell the admiral and

Colonel Baird I will be with them shortly. I can't imagine this will take long." Andrew left the room and the senator motioned for the breathless Vaughn to sit down.

Senator Jackson went back to his desk and picked up the telephone handset. "Good afternoon. This is Winnfield Jackson."

"Good afternoon, Senator Jackson. This is Donovan Ross from Apex Helicopters calling, and I appreciate your taking my call this busy morning."

"Glad to do it. What can I do for you?"

"Well, Senator, first, I speak for my company as well as for Vertical Aerospace's CEO Glenn Laker. I just wanted you to know that I have just gotten off the phone with Secretary Harrell to express my and Mr. Laker's deepest regret at all of these events. We both promise our full cooperation in getting to the bottom of all of this."

"Thank you, Mr. Ross. That is welcome news. What about the aircraft itself?"

"Beg your pardon, Senator?"

Jackson's jaw tightened as he tried to restrain himself. "The XV-11, Mr. Ross. What are you going to do about it?"

"Well, sir, we are looking at that now. Our top engineers are—"

"Forgive me for interrupting you, Mr. Ross, but I have to get back to the hearing. Have you read the legal papers that were filed?"

"Yes, Senator, I have, and our lawyers—"

"Let's leave your lawyers out of it. Did you watch or hear Lieutenant Colonel Baird's opening remarks just now?"

"Yes, Senator, I did, but—"

"Then respectfully, Mr. Ross, you don't need for me to explain it to you. You know what needs to be done. This is not a negotiation. When you figure it out, call me back. I look forward to hearing from you." He placed the phone into the cradle.

"If anyone wants me, I will be in the anteroom for a few moments," the senator said to Greg as he headed into the hallway.

The admiral and Jake stopped their conversation and stood up as the senator entered the caucus room. "Mr. Baird, that was quite an opening statement," Jackson said, extending his hand and smiling.

"Thank you, sir . . . I think," Jake responded.

"Oh, I meant it positively. Now we must think about this afternoon. I am guessing that the sharp knives will be coming out. You must be prepared for harsh, punishing questioning. They will come after you for all their political lives—and donations—are worth. Can you handle that?"

"Yes, sir," Jake said.

"If you and Admiral Lawrence would wait here," Jackson said, looking at each man, "I will need a few moments to gather my thoughts before reconvening the meeting. Andrew will come for you when it's time."

Back in his office, Senator Jackson's legal aide, Alan Hill, was waiting. "Hello, Alan. What can we do to keep Jake Baird out of jail—anything?"

"Sir, there are a few items I am still exploring, but in the meantime I called my contact in the attorney general's office, who has spoken directly with the AG about this. I am told that the AG himself watched the hearing, then called Secretary Harrell's chief counsel who, as you might imagine, is not very happy about all of this. But the word is that DOD is willing to discuss Mr. Baird's—and, for that matter, Captain Kemp's—situations, and has indicated that there might be some room for compromise—especially if the investigation leads to proof of severe wrongdoing in the XV-11 program."

"Good. Make a record of that conversation."

The senator turned to Andrew. "Any word on Kemp?"

"Yes, sir," Andrew instantly replied. "Kemp was freed and is on his way here now. Agents from NSA somehow knew of his location and had repositioned nearby, then made the short trip to Kemp's exact location once given the go signal. SWAT teams from the Loudoun County Sheriff's department surrounded the building and did not allow anyone to leave. Apparently they were tipped off, too."

"Good news, Andrew . . . and good work," the senator concluded. "Alan, stay in touch with the AG's office. And Andrew, confirm that Kemp will be brought here as soon as he is freed."

"Yes, sir."

"More good news, sir," Greg Vaughn chimed in. "Alex Oliver was taken into custody about thirty minutes ago as he tried to leave the Pentagon. Word is that he spilled his guts immediately."

"A good day it appears—at least so far." Senator Jackson sat down at his desk and began to scribble some notes as he read the court papers. He was trying to get his mind around the legal papers and the morning's events so he could make some concrete, relevant proposals when the committee reconvened. "Senator Jackson, sorry to interrupt," Jackson's secretary said through the intercom.

"That's OK, Pauline, what is it?"

"Sir, it's Mr. Ross of Apex Helicopters again. He said you would want to take his call."

"Certainly, Pauline. Ring him through."

Senator Jackson picked up the receiver and again said, "This is Winnfield Jackson."

"Senator Jackson, Donovan Ross again. Glenn Laker and I have spoken and we have agreed to recommend to NAVAIR that we halt production."

"That's a positive development, Mr. Ross. Thank you and Mr. Laker."

"Thank you, Senator. We are glad this could be worked out."

"What about the investigation?" Jackson asked.

"Pardon me, Senator. What investigation?" Ross asked.

"Well, Mr. Ross, people up here in Washington are going to be all over this for all kinds of reasons. I am sure that one of those people will be me. Do I have your and Chairman Laker's word that you will cooperate fully?"

"Certainly, Senator, certainly."

"With all respect, that came a little quick. But I will remember it once the investigations are underway. That's clear to you, isn't it, Mr. Ross?"

"Yes, Senator, it is," Ross growled. He had been beaten and wasn't used to losing.

"Thank you, sir. Now I have to get back to the hearing. Have a good day, Mr. Ross, and thank you for the call."

Senator Jackson collected his papers, got up from his desk, and had just started toward the door when his internal senate phone rang. He picked up the handset, squinted at the caller ID, and answered, "Yes, Senator." He listened for a while and then said, simply, "I see. Thank you very much for the call."

In his outer office, he told Greg to bring the admiral and Colonel Baird into the hearing room in ten minutes. Jackson then entered the hearing room, walked up the steps to his chair, sat down, and struck the gavel. "The hearing of the Senate Services Committee is back in session. Please maintain decorum in the hearing room," he said, looking out over the gallery. As he waited for Lawrence and Baird, Greg came to him on the dais and whispered into his ear. Once the aide finished, the Senator nodded, and his countenance seemed to brighten.

. . .

Approaching the Capitol, Kemp saw through the helicopter's window that an area had been cleared for them to land. The pilot made a steep final approach directly to the ground as guards surrounded the aircraft.

"Good luck, Stanford. These men will take you where you need to go," Joseph said.

"Thanks for the lift, sir," Kemp responded as he took off his headset and undid his seat belt.

"No. Thank you!" Joseph said, extending his hand. Kemp gave him a firm grip and saluted.

"Right this way, sir," one of the Capitol officials said to Kemp as he stepped out of the helicopter. They raced away from the aircraft toward a small door on the ground level of the Capitol, pushing past the crowd that had gathered. Inside, Kemp was led through a series of back halls and staircases, then he was handed off to group of uniformed officers with the words "US Capitol Police" on a patch on their shoulders.

"We will need to wait here for a moment," one of the officers said, pressing his fingers against an earpiece.

. . .

"Colonel Baird, might I remind you that you are still under oath?" the senator said once Lawrence and Jake were seated.

"Yes, Mr. Chairman, I understand."

"Thank you, Colonel." He took a long pause, and then began. "Colonel, we agreed to take a recess so that we might contemplate where we go from here. It was a remarkably productive hour. We now have agreed to adjourn the hearing at this point so that we may all have some time to consider the recent events, including your testimony. A few days could allow for perspective on several fronts regarding the XV-11."

The gallery responded with a collective gasp. The chairman looked at all of the senators and got a nod from each one.

"Understanding that the committee is in agreement, I have something to say before we adjourn." Jackson then continued in his dignified southern tone, "Colonel Baird, we were all captivated by your opening remarks. You have reminded us why we are here. Although unorthodox, your actions, and those of others, have spoken truth to power.

"I have no doubt that you did this honestly. It is obvious that you took seriously the oaths you spoke when you became a lawyer and a military offi-cer—that you will never reject, from any consideration personal to yourself, the cause of the defenseless or oppressed, and that you would support and defend the Constitution of the United States against all enemies, foreign *and domestic*. It was a good and right thing that your government saw fit to place in you 'special trust and confidence in your patriotism, valor, fidelity, and abilities'—as recited in your officer's commission."

The senator paused as the rear doors opened in the hearing room. Two uniformed guards led a disheveled, dirty, older man into the room. The whis-pers began to circulate as Greg leaned down and said in Jackson's ear, "That's Kemp." Jackson nodded as he looked over the crowd at Kemp.

Jake turned around toward the rear of the room. He smiled when he recognized Kemp and gave Kemp a nod. He was brought back around by the senator's striking of the gavel, followed by, "Ladies and gentlemen, please, if I may proceed."

The gallery quieted and the senator continued. "Colonel Baird, we might need to speak with you at a later time. If so, could you accommodate us?" the senator asked.

"Certainly, sir," Jake responded.

"With that said, this meeting is adjourned, and Colonel Baird, you are free to go," Jackson proclaimed, slamming the gavel down.

Jake sat stunned, not knowing what to do or think. He was jerked back to reality by slaps on the back and the press pushing to get to him. The senate guards formed a phalanx around him, protecting him, but he was still jostled as he was escorted out of the room.

In the back of the gallery, Lieutenant Colonel Raymond Beech was stopped by Capitol police as he tried to exit the hearing room.

When Jake got back to the senator's office, Andrew called him over to the phone. "Lieutenant Colonel Baird, a Ms. Wright wants to speak to you."

Jake took the phone and heard Madison say, "Jake Baird, you are just full of surprises! I am so proud of you!"

"Thanks," Jake burst into a huge grin.

"How are you feeling?" she asked.

"A bit overwhelmed, but OK. Look, I'll call you right back."

"OK, Jake. I love you."

"I love you, too, Maddy." Jake was surprised at how easily the words came out.

Jake then heard a familiar gravelly voice comment, "All that for her and nothing for the guy who got you on this roller coaster?"

Jake wheeled around to see Kemp standing right behind him. "Sorry I didn't get cleaned up—my hosts didn't give me time to take a proper shower—they used all their water for something else."

"Glad you're here . . . and safe!" Jake said, giving Kemp a firm handshake. "Where have you been? I was getting worried."

"Oh, I decided to let them catch me so I could have a little fun."

"How did that happen? You were supposed to outrun them and stay safe," Jake said.

"I know, but once your plan became operational it gave us an opportunity to not only catch the guys in the XV-11 program, but also their friends who were doing all the dirty work. We've suspected them for years, but you helped us to connect the two and cast a wider net."

Admiral Lawrence walked over and waited for the appropriate time to speak to Kemp. "Great job, Colonel Baird," he said, extending his hand. "You holding up all right, Stanford?"

"Doing great, sir. Just great."

"Jake, Stanford is right. By sending the papers to major players and then filing the lawsuit and getting immediate press coverage, you put pressure on all the right people and forced a quick response," Admiral Lawrence said. "Stanford had already figured out that if he got captured, he could frustrate his captors enough that they would get careless and start confirming what we already knew—that they killed Hadley and Kolinsky and that they were tied to Oliver and his folks. Your Senate testimony then brought attention to the entire affair and explained it so Congress and the public would understand.

Without your courage and decisiveness under pressure, none of this would have come together. The nation owes you a great deal."

"Thank you, sir. I was honored to be asked, but I also had some help," Jake said, nodding toward Kemp.

· · ·

After talking with Kemp and the Admiral for a few more moments, Jake caught Andrew's eye and motioned that he needed to speak to him.

"Yes, Colonel Baird?" the aide asked.

"There are a couple of important matters I have to take care of. Is there an office or room I can use for a short while?"

"Certainly. Colonel, if you would follow me," Andrew said as he led Jake through into a short hallway and opened the door to a very cluttered, cramped office.

"Sorry for the mess, but at least you'll have privacy. Let me know if you need anything else," Andrew offered as Jake passed him and squeezed into the office.

Jake nodded. "This is fine. Thanks," he said, pulling his phone from his pocket.

Now alone, Jake quickly pushed Florence's number into his phone. No answer. He tried again, and still no answer. He tried another number, still no answer.

He called Irwin's cell and found Irwin in his office. "Is this the famous Colonel Baird? My God, man, what a performance! You're all over the media! How is the star of Washington?"

"Just fine, Irwin," Jake interrupted. "Right now I am concerned that I can't get hold of Florence. Do you know where she is and how she is?"

"She's fine," Irwin said. "I talked to her moments ago and she'll be home shortly. They took her away for some questioning but apparently it was all done by the book. No rough stuff. "

"OK. Thanks. That's a relief," Jake said, feeling the anxiety leave his body. "Please ask her to call me when she can, and tell her I asked about her, OK?"

"Sure thing, Jake. Take care."

· · ·

Beaufort, North Carolina
Wednesday, August 12, 2009
3:45 p.m.

In Beaufort, North Carolina, the phone rang at Lisa Thorpe's house. Samuel was sitting on Lisa's lap, his eyes glued to the television.

"Lisa Thorpe speaking."

"Lisa, it's Jake Baird. I wanted to see how you were doing and if you managed to catch the news—"

"Yes. Samuel and I saw everything. We're so proud of you!"

"Thanks very much. I'm not yet exactly sure what all of this means for your case, but I am sure it helps."

"I knew you would be thinking about us, Jake. But more important than my case, I am so grateful that the truth will finally come out, and the aircraft will be made safe. That's most important now," Lisa said, then she continued. "You know, earlier today Samuel looked up at me and said, 'Mr. Baird is our hero, isn't he, Mommy?' I said, 'He certainly is.'"

"Well, thank him for me," Jake barely got the words out. "Take care, Lisa. I've got to get back."

"Good-bye, Jake—and thank you."

Jake closed his eyes, put his face in his hands, and for the first time since it all began, let all the emotions through. The strain was too much. His eyes welled up as he exhaled and leaned back in the chair, totally spent.

33

For the first few minutes after passing through the welcome center at Arlington National Cemetery, Jake was quiet. He held Madison's hand as they walked up the hill on the asphalt walkway.

"Since this is your first visit to Arlington, I should probably take you to the changing of the guard at the Tomb of the Unknowns," Jake said.

"Sounds good. I've always wanted to see that," Madison responded.

"As many times as you've been to DC, I'm surprised you never came over here."

"Well, maybe it's because we never had anyone in my family serve in the military."

"Maybe so," Jake said, looking straight ahead.

After passing John F. Kennedy's gravesite and the eternal flame, they headed to the Tomb of the Unknowns. Along with a hundred others, they stood silently as instructed by the relief commander and watched the precise movements of the impeccably uniformed soldiers of the 3rd US Infantry Regiment skillfully handle white-glove inspections of their M-14 rifles as one guard relieved the previous one.

"Very impressive," Madison said, after they left the viewers' area.

"They're out there twenty-four hours a day, seven days a week, three hundred sixty-five days a year, whether it's sunny, raining, snowing, hot, or freezing. They're out there, walking their post," Jake said.

"An incredible tradition," Madison said.

"Just one more stop," Jake replied. He led Madison down the hill a different way from the way they had come. Again, Jake was quiet. Madison followed his lead.

After about a fifteen-minute walk, they entered a flatter section of the grounds and moved toward the cemetery boundary. He led her down though the rows of white grave markers, each containing a name, rank, branch of service, and dates of birth and death, and any military awards.

Finally, Jake stopped in front of one marker and knelt down in front of it.

"Oh!" Madison gasped as she read the words chiseled into the headstone. "Major Samuel Ward Thorpe, United States Marine Corps, Purple Heart." Madison knelt down beside Jake and put her arm around him.

Jake reached out and placed his hand on top of the marker and bowed his head. After a few moments, he stood up, saluted, took three steps backward, did an about face, and waited for Madison to join him. They moved away, arm in arm.

"The sacrifices these people made for their country—it all becomes real here," Madison said.

"Yes, but it's more personal for them than that. It's for you and me and their buddies beside them, and because they want to make the world safer for their families. They're the ones who pay the price—no more saying prayers together at night, no more playing catch with Dad, no more Mom nursing a skinned knee. It's not just what they did. It's who they were—fathers, mothers, brothers, sisters, sons, and daughters."

Jake walked a few steps farther and looked around. "We can never forget, Maddy. We can never forget."

ACKNOWLEDGEMENTS

The attempt to give credit and thanks to all of those who have contributed to this work is destined to be incomplete, but is nevertheless necessary. The trail of gratitude is long, but not to start at the beginning would be wrong.

First credit and thanks must go to my Mom and Dad who started my love for language and ideas, and for principle, and the relatives and townsfolk of my small Southern town who influenced me.

Appreciation also goes to the educators and college professors who inspired me--Mr. Ewing, my English instructor at Randolph-Macon Academy, who honed my love of the written word, and Professor Bill Jackson of Davidson College, who guided me through the turbulent sixties and stoked my interest in great issues and politics, and who has become a dear friend.

There are also the members of my own profession who taught me what was really important in the representation of others. Stuart Speiser, a gifted and talented lawyer and the best legal writer I ever read, whom I miss dearly. Chuck Krause, a mentor, and one of the smartest and most capable attorneys I ever met. To Frank H. Granito, Jr., a wise mentor who set the example for what an aviation lawyer should be, and to Tony Jobe, a great friend who recommended me for my first job as an aviation lawyer.

I must sing the praises of my family who stayed with me and helped me get through the "first novel" challenge. My dear wife Edna, who somehow managed, through the logistical tornados associated with rearing three minor children, to find flaws in the story that needed correction and thereby made the work better. There are also the three children that heard way too many times, "Daddy is working," and nevertheless still like and love me.

Technical advice on portions of the book was freely and expertly given by William S. Lawrence, Colonel, USMC (Ret'd). Where I got right, it is to Bill's credit; where I got it wrong, I followed my own inclinations.

Then there are the readers who helped get this into shape. Steve Cohen, my first Army Reserve commander in New York, who has become the dearest and most special of friends. Bill Jackson, who gave me encouragement and the will to move along. Karen Shook, editor at the *Times of London*

Higher Education Magazine, who gave me the opportunity to write publicly, and whose constant praise of my book reviews for her magazine bolstered my courage and confidence. Joe Neff, an in-depth reporter for the local newspaper whose reporting always meets the highest standards of journalism and makes the world a better place. Keith Sipe, who published my first work, the co-authored *Aviation Accident Law*, an acclaimed aviation law case book, who has become an important supportive friend. Arnie Reiner, a fellow Army Reserve aviator and former USMC aviator and safety expert at Pan Am Airways, who gave me invaluable comments. And the other readers: Jack Veth, Gary Little, Ben Coleman, Sara Just, Colin Summer, Gary Allen, Tom McHale, Steve Cohen, and Omar Malik.

Also thanks to my primary editor, Betsy Thorpe, who also became a terrific advisor and friend, to my delightful second editor, Lisa Kline, and to my copy editor, Maya Packard. There are no better editors anywhere. Praise goes also to Brett Miller who did a great job on the cover and the layout. Bob Diforio, my agent, worked tirelessly and gave great advice, and who has my deepest gratitude. Credit and thanks also to author Randy Russell, who guided me and befriended me when I needed it most. Finally, appreciation to fellow Davidsonian and author John Hart, who encouraged me at the start and has given ongoing support.

Special recognition goes to Shelley Magee Arizmendi, who worked with me on corrections and typing of the manuscript. We have known each other for twenty years and along the way she became a dear friend. Without her help, this novel would not have been possible.

ABOUT THE AUTHOR

James T. Crouse was born in Asheville, North Carolina and grew up in the small town of Lexington, N.C. He was graduated from Randolph-Macon Academy in Front Royal, Virginia, a military preparatory school, after which, as an Army ROTC Scholarship student, earned his B.A. in Political Science at Davidson College.

Upon graduation from Davidson, Mr. Crouse was commissioned in the U.S. Army as an Infantry officer, and attended helicopter flight school and Aviation Maintenance Officer Course and Test Pilot School as a Transportation Corps officer. During his initial six-year active duty career, he flew research and development flights for the Army's Night Vision Laboratory. He retired as a Lieutenant Colonel after having flown over 1500 hours in his 26-year active and reserve career, performing medical evacuation, attack, and maintenance test flight duties.

Since graduating from Duke Law School in 1980, Mr. Crouse has practiced aviation and product liability law in which time he has represented several high-profile clients and was lead liability counsel in the world's largest civilian helicopter disaster (North Sea Boeing 234LR, 1986). Other notable experience includes major airline accident cases and general aviation, helicopter, and military crashes, as well as non-aviation mass disaster litigation. Over his career he has investigated over three hundred aviation crashes.

Mr. Crouse has co-authored a case law book, *Aviation Law: Cases and Materials,* which is critically acclaimed by scholars and practitioners. He is the editor-in-chief of Aviation Safety Blog, http://aviationsafetyblog.com/, which is devoted to reducing aviation accidents, and is a published aviation and Civil War book reviewer for *The Times of London Higher Education* magazine.

Mr. Crouse has taught Aviation Law at Duke Law School, The George Washington University School of Law, and at St. Mary's University School of Law in San Antonio, Texas. He is a frequent speaker at aviation and legal symposia and has had numerous articles published in legal periodicals.

He lives in Raleigh, North Carolina with his wife and three children.

www.jamestcrouseauthor.com

CPSIA information can be obtained
at www.ICGtesting.com
Printed in the USA
LVOW11s1008151216
517390LV00002B/210/P